Caught Up in
RAINE

To Joe -
Get Caught Up...

LG O'CONNOR

LG O'Connor
XOXO

COLLINS-YOUNG PUBLISHING

For permission requests, please address Collins-Young Publishing, LLC.

Published 2016
Printed in the United States of America
ISBN: 978-0-9907381-2-1 (Trade Paperback)
ISBN: 978-0-9907381-5-2 (eBook)
Library of Congress Control Number: 2015910738

For information, address:
Collins-Young Publishing, LLC
1 Sentry Lane #6
Chester, NJ 07930

This is a work of fiction. Names, characters, places, and incidents portrayed in this novel are either products of the author's imagination or are used fictitiously, and any resemblance to actual persons, living or dead, business establishments, events, or locales is entirely coincidental.

Cover Design: Derek Murphy, Creativindie

Dedication

y husband Leo, for all of his support, and to every
woman who has loved a younger man.

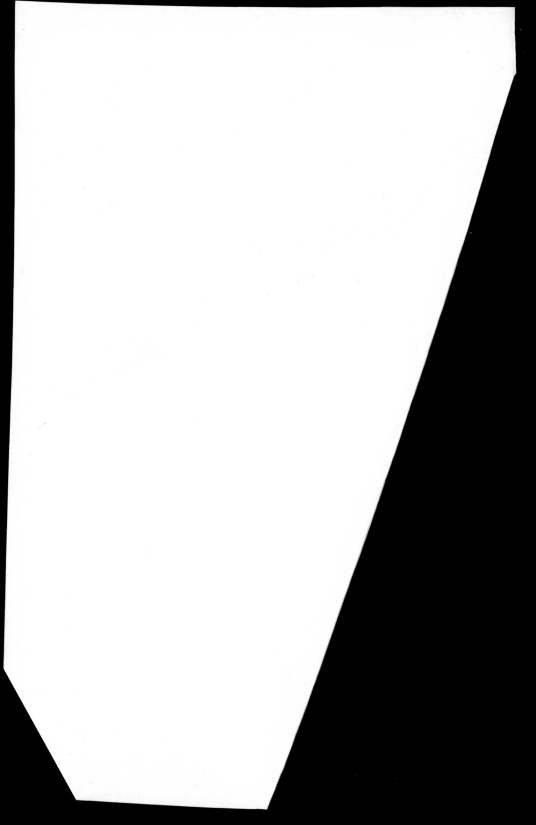

Dedication

To my husband Leo, for all of his support, and to every woman who has loved a younger man.

Acknowledgments

I want to say thank you to my tremendous team for all your love and support. Thank you to my critique partner, Joan Sorensen, for her critical feedback throughout the whole birthing of this book; the "cross-stitch" beta reading crew (Marilyn Keyes, Pat Campbell, Lesley Aman, and Eileen Higgins); my first editor, Zetta Brown, for the initial, superfast edit after NaNoWriMo 2013 in order to get the manuscript submitted into the RWA's 2014 Golden Heart Contest® (1 point short of making the Finalist list); developmental muse, young adult author, Trisha Leaver.

A very special "thank you" goes to paranormal romance author, Carla Susan Smith, who dropped everything over Labor Day weekend 2015 to jump to my aid and read my manuscript during last-minute rewrites before production. I'm eternally grateful! To April Eberhardt, Alice Orr, and Kristen Harnisch, for offering their honest opinions, and to Joanie for the two-hour brainstorming session to help me hold it all together.

You are all my rocks, and without you this book wouldn't have been nearly as good.

Chapter 1

Jillian

BEEP . . . BEEP . . . BEEP . . .

Unable to keep my hands still, I entwine my ringless fingers so tightly the bones grind together and almost cut off my circulation. The steady rhythm of the heart monitor should be reassuring. But it's not. To me, it's a harbinger of death. Counterintuitive, I know, but then again, all I've ever experienced here is death.

I lost my husband Robert two years ago, Dad two before that, Mom thirty years ago, and Drew, my first love, in between. Granted, a lot of time has passed since Mom and Drew died, but those four times were my only experiences in a hospital before today.

The antiseptic smell only intensifies my despair. It might seem strange, but I'd rather be hit by a bus and die instantly than end up in this place.

"Jillian?"

My eyes shift away from my mom's twin sister who two weeks ago sat at my dining room table laughing and talking about my latest book release, and toward the familiar voice behind me.

My lips warp into a weak smile and I brighten. "Hey, Kitty."

Kitty shuffles into the room wearing sensible shoes, a pair

1

of shapeless slacks to hide her way-too-generous hips, and a blouse that went out of style over a decade ago. The purse slung over her shoulder gives her an off-balance appearance. Devoid of makeup, and with her graying hair overdue for a dye job, Kitty looks older than fifty-three. But what my older sister lacks in style, she makes up for in heart.

I stand to greet her, and she clutches my shoulders, giving me a kiss on the cheek. I catch a whiff of her distinctive cherry-flavored lip balm. Her refusal to wear lipstick still baffles me.

"How's Aunt Vera? And how're you holding up, sweetie?" Kitty asks.

"The nurse said she had dialysis right before I arrived, so she'll probably be asleep for the next couple of hours."

I glance back at the hospital bed, and my heart clenches as I stare at my aunt. Long, gray wisps of hair cling to her skull; ashen, paper-thin skin along with a respirator tube taped between her parted lips gives her that "near death" look I know so well. Relief floods through me whenever her leg twitches underneath the thin sheet, giving me hope that there may be some fight left in her.

The sunny August afternoon beckons through the window just beyond the bed.

God, I want out.

When I look back, Kitty gives me a pointed look. "You didn't answer my question. How are *you*?"

I blow out a breath, feeling helpless. "As well as I'll ever be in this place."

But that wasn't it. Every time I look at Vera, I feel as if I'm staring at a broken shell that used to be a woman who, even at eighty-two, was still vibrant, funny, and full of life. There's an emptiness there that resonates with me. A feeling I've lived with for most of my adult life, tempered now and filled with things I create through my writing. Things that aren't real. Characters. Stories. Other people's lives that aren't mine.

Unhealthy? Maybe. But at least my characters can't die

without my permission.

Kitty touches my arm and squeezes gently. "Why don't you go and pick up Jenny in Summit? You go, I'll stay."

Guilt accompanies my relief at Kitty's offer. Picking up my niece from the train station sounds like a fine idea. "Are you sure?"

Kitty nods and looks at me with kind eyes, a much darker shade than my golden-brown. "Honestly, I'm surprised you were able to come here at all."

Vera and Kitty essentially raised me after my mom died when I was fourteen. It was the three of us, and my dad, against the world. They were my pillars when Dad passed, and then again when Robert died.

I glance back at Vera, feeling the heaviness reenter my heart, and whisper, "How could I not? I can't believe she's even here."

"I know. A bypass at her age is a miserable thing to deal with, but she should make it."

I hold back a snort, wishing I had inherited Kitty's optimism. "I hope so." But I can't convince myself to believe it. No one I've ever loved has made it out of this place alive.

I give Kitty a quick peck on the cheek. "Thanks. I'll drop Jenny off at the house."

"You want to stay for dinner?" she asks. She's obsessed with making sure I eat properly, knowing I have a hate-hate relationship with my kitchen.

"Can't. Not tonight."

Her eyebrow lifts. "Oh? Do you have another date?"

I wrinkle my nose. "No . . . that's Saturday night."

I hate dating almost as much as I hate cooking and hospitals. But it seems a shame to pack it in at forty-two. Two years of widowhood, and I'm just starting to dip my toe back in the proverbial dating pond. My first impression: it sucks.

I rattle the car keys against my palm and head to the door. "Later."

"You sure you don't want to stay for dinner?"

3

"I'm on deadline. If I don't get Brigitte a synopsis for this book, she's going to skewer me. I'll pick up something on the way home."

Kitty rolls her eyes. "Fine, but you're going to fade away to nothing one of these days."

Hardly. I would do anything to get rid of the muffin top hanging over my jeans. Mistakenly, I believed never giving birth would spare me from midlife belly fat. *Uh, wrong.*

Maybe that's why I write about young heroines who don't have to deal with the disappointment of a slowing metabolism. That, and I give each one of them something I've never had: a "happily ever after" in the arms of their hero.

My heart lifts and my shoulders relax the moment I step outside and the sun hits the crown of my head. The click-clack of my high-heeled sandals across the parking lot marks the distance between me and this godforsaken place. After a silent prayer for Vera, I switch mental gears and find my escape.

Drew, the male lead in my novel who's loosely based on my real-life Drew, slips into my head the moment I sit behind the wheel. He's particularly loud today, begging me to write some hot scenes with Becca. Ah, to be young and brimming with hormones.

I smile and flip on the air-conditioning. "Down, boy. You'll need to wait until I get home." I picture him scowling at me with his muscled arms crossed.

One glance in the rearview mirror tells me I need some major construction on my face. Thank God for waterproof mascara. Kitty missed my mini-breakdown before she arrived. No wonder she kept checking to see if I was okay. I look like total crap.

I pull out my compact and smooth my face with mineral powder, dab on some lipstick, and feather on a subtle layer of blush. Makeup always cures what ails me to some degree. "Look good, feel good," Aunt Vera always says.

Rather than heading out the front entrance, I turn onto the long, winding drive toward the east-side exit. A chunky dump truck emblazoned with "Petrillo's Landscape Design" blocks my way. Saplings with puffy treetops are visible over the side.

Seriously? Swearing under my breath, I calculate my chances of squeezing my SUV past the truck and arrive at an unwanted answer. So I shove the car in neutral, set the brake, and get out. I stalk around the oversized Tonka toy to where four guys are digging various parts of a new landscape bed.

My eye gravitates to one in particular. *Oh. My. God.* Above a pair of dirt-encrusted jeans, his broad, sun-kissed shoulders glimmer in the sunlight. A landscape of ripples contract along his back and arms as he works. His tawny-blond hair is drawn back in a ponytail at the nape of his neck.

I force my slack jaw back into place. "Excuse me."

Four heads turn at once, and when the blond turns, my breath sucks in fast.

Drew. He looks like Drew—at least in my head and from what I remember. Narrow waist, hard, and lean. Unlike the rest of guys with shovels, he hasn't used his body as a living canvas for self-expression. He has no ink. But I only wonder why for about half a second. My brain is too busy superimposing Drew as I fight not to gape.

"Um, can someone pull up the truck? I'm trying to get out," I say, doing my best to be polite. I look away to hide my blush.

An older, dark-haired guy tosses a set of keys to the blond. "Yo. Catch." By process of elimination, he has to be the "Petrillo" named on the side of the truck. The other two men are smaller Hispanic guys, and the blond doesn't particularly strike me as a "Petrillo."

My heart races as the blond trots over with the keys. He

scoops up a white T-shirt lying in a mound on the grass on his way over, and wipes his face. Giving me a crooked smile, he heads to the driver's side. "Hey, sorry about that. You're the first person to head down this way all day."

"This exit points me closer to where I need to go. Sorry to be a pain."

"No problem," he says, and climbs up into the cab. The timbre of his voice sends chills down my spine. It's Drew's voice . . . or maybe just my overactive imagination.

He stares down at me quizzically. "You good?"

I realize he's waiting for me. "Uh, yeah," I say, waking up from my daydream haze and forcing myself back into the SUV to back up.

Acrid black smoke rises skyward from the truck's vertical exhaust accompanied by the dull roar of the engine as he drives past me, his profile catching my peripheral vision.

My brain short-circuits as my sandal hits the gas pedal. How can I just leave?

The idea hits me like a sledgehammer, and I jam on the brakes. The blond guy is on his way back to where the other guys are planting trees when my mouth develops a mind of its own.

"Excuse me," I yell impulsively through the open window.

He alters his direction and comes over. Stooping down, he leans his hands on my open window. "What's up?"

His sudden proximity heightens my heart rate. For a split second, I almost lose my nerve until I look into his stunning blue eyes—*Drew's eyes.* For a second, I'm back in the summer of 1990, sitting behind the wheel of my dad's Chrysler.

Drew drops his backpack of schoolbooks onto his driveway, and leans into the open car window. His eyes, blue like the summer sky, connect with mine. Tawny blond hair falls down around his face. "I'll pick you up at six-thirty for the concert," he says and presses his lips to mine. Then he steps back, juts out his hips, and breaks into an air guitar riff. "Wanted . . . dead or alive!"

6

Giggling, I shift into reverse. "Later, Bon Jovi. Love ya."

"Love ya, too," he shouts back, scooping his books off the blacktop.

If I'd only known how little time we had left, I would've done so many things differently, kissed him a little longer . . . held onto him a little tighter.

I take a second to compose myself and clear my throat. "Um, this may sound strange, but how would you like to be on a book cover?"

His head jerks back slightly, and his eyebrows fly up. "*What?*"

Undeterred, I give him a sweet smile and repeat slowly, "Would you. Like to be. On a book cover?"

He chuckles. "I'm not mentally deficient. I heard the question. I'm just not sure what you mean."

I can't help but stare at his delicious full lips, wishing I were half my age. I take a deep breath and prepare for his refusal. "You happen to resemble the male lead in a novel I'm writing, and I haven't had a book cover designed yet. I'm wondering if you'd like to be on it."

The corner of his mouth tips up. "I think I'm flattered."

I can't suppress my smile, secretly glad I fixed my face earlier.

"What would this entail, exactly?" he asks.

"A two- to three-hour photo shoot." As if I haven't been impulsive enough, I add, "Sometime this week."

He gives me a pointed look. "Clothed, right?"

I tilt my head, a spark of hope flaring inside me. "Pretty much the way you're dressed right now, except with cleaner clothes."

He looks down at his pants and grins. Then his mouth turns into a frown. "Hmm. This week might be tight."

"Is that a yes?" My heart picks up tempo.

Petrillo yells over, "Yo! Stop flirting with the nice lady and get back to work, man."

"Hey, I gotta go."

"Wait." I fumble in my purse and pull out a business card. Without thinking, I thrust the card at him and blurt, "I'll pay you $300 in cash."

His eyes light up. "Really?" Then he glances at my card. "You're on, Jillian Grant. By the way, I would've done it for free." Wearing a lopsided smile, he shoves the card in his pocket and taps the side of the SUV with his hand. "I'll text you."

A thrill shoots through me as he heads off, and then I remember. "Wait! What's your name?"

He turns and calls, "Raine. With an *e*."

I smile. *Raine with an e.* It suits him, almost better than Drew.

For the first time all day, I feel alive.

Chapter 2

Raine

"HEY, MAC. Grab a tree on the way over," Mikey yells as I saunter back to where the guys have made some decent progress digging holes.

Changing direction, I head to the truck. The sun feels good, but I pull my T-shirt on over my head anyway. Last thing I need is a sunburn. I'm fighting enough crap for one day. I hop up into the truck bed and take out my phone. At least three texts came in over the last hour. Raking a hand across my forehead—less because of the heat, more because I anticipate my blood pressure rising from what I'll find—I ready myself and hit the Messages icon.

I'm right. My face fills with fire.

Fuck, fuck, and fuck. Or maybe, *bitch, bitch, and bitch* would be more accurate. Actually, the c-word would be even more appropriate, but I've always disliked using it, even when it fit. Before she died, Mom taught me to have respect for women. But Vanessa has made that almost impossible.

Raine, you piece of shit! When are you coming for your boxes? You said you'd be here at lunch! It's 3 o'clock, can't you tell time?

I hold back a snarl.

If you're not here by 4, I'm burning your crap!

It's 3:55. I release my snarl.

Just for fun, I might burn it anyway. Better yet, I'll dump it in the middle of Route 287.

I snap, and almost scream *that word* instead of my split-second substitution. "Fucking bitch!"

How the hell did I put up with her for two years? No, how the hell did I *live* with her for two years? I slam my fist into the side of the truck before I can stop myself.

"Mac, I'm growing old over here. Bring me a goddamn tree!"

I huff and grab one of the saplings by the trunk and lower it until the root ball touches the ground before I crouch and jump down from the truck to join it. I trudge back with the tree, trying to figure out how fast I can get the hell out of here and retrieve my shit.

Pedro grabs the tree from my hand and plops it in the nearest hole while José shovels dirt around it. We don't talk much since my Spanish sucks. Too bad they don't speak Latin . . . or Swedish.

"What'd that lady want?" Mikey asks, raising an eyebrow and sporting a wolfish grin. "She wanna piece of ya?" Five years older than me, Mikey and I grew up on the same block. He's taken my leftovers since high school. Too bad he's married now; otherwise, I'd try to pawn Vanessa off on him. On second thought, scratch that. I wouldn't do that to my worst enemy.

A small smile creeps onto my lips when I think about the woman in the SUV. She was pretty hot. Nice ass. Unlike Vanessa, the woman was a lady—to use Mikey's term—someone worthy of respect. I could tell she was nervous—it was kind of a crazy request, I got that—but she definitely wasn't hitting on me. I picture her face. Her eyes were huge, really light brown, more like gold. Pretty. And a great smile.

I give Mikey a smart-ass smirk and shrug. "None of your business, dude." I glance to where her BMW SUV had been and pull the card back out of my pocket.

Jillian Grant
Author / Photographer
(973) 555-6837

Mikey leans on his shovel. "Come on, man. All that's left for me is living vicariously through you."

I spot a tiny spark of jealousy in his eye and snort. "I won't tell Maria that." At nearly thirty, he already has three kids, all under the age of four. I gaze back at the card. "She's a writer." That's all I'm willing to say.

He wiggles his brows and pumps his fist salaciously. "Married? Wants a little *Mac-a-Tastic* love on the side?" Over the years, Mikey has created a whole *Mac-abulary* based on my nickname, short for my last name, MacDonald.

"Don't make me sound like a gigolo," I say, giving him a good-natured shove. "And I have no idea if she's married. It didn't come up."

"If the shoe fits . . ." He chuckles, making another obscene hand gesture.

"Fuck off, and stop using me for wish fulfillment. Besides, I have enough problems with the Loch Ness Monster. She threatened to throw my shit all over Route 287. Is there any way I can jet out of here to go pick it up?"

He frowns and waves his hand. "Go. We're almost finished here anyway."

Tension releases from my shoulders and I head to my old Ford pickup.

I smile again. Jillian Grant, author-slash-photographer, has put me three hundred bucks closer to freedom from my soon-to-be temporary living arrangement. I didn't lie to her. I would've done it for free. Vanessa may have kicked me to the curb, but Jillian sees something worth putting on a book cover.

My smile fades. I hope the character isn't an asshole.

Either way, at least now I'll have money to pay for my books when school starts this week.

Chapter 3

Raine

I TEXT VANESSA before I pull out of the lot at the hospital. Of course, I receive another classic Nessie reply:

Too late . . .

I grind my teeth for the entire fifteen-minute drive across Morristown wondering what Vanessa has done with the stuff that I didn't take with me, until the tension in my neck gives me a stress headache. All my most important possessions — wallet, laptop, phone, a couple of pictures of me and my mom, some of her precious keepsakes, and my gaming console — are already in a duffel on the passenger floor of my truck. And that's where I'll keep them while I stay with my dick of a father for the first time in more than three years. I hate to think that he'd steal from me but it's a real possibility given our history. Growing up, my favorite things would randomly disappear or show up broken. Toys when I was young. Electronics, video games, and other things as I got older. I couldn't pin it on him until I turned sixteen when I found my Swiss Army knife and a bunch of other missing stuff hidden inside his desk.

The thought of living with him curdles my stomach, but I'm out of options. Mikey's wife won't let me sleep on the couch, and none of my other friends are in a position to put me up for more than a night or two. Most of my cash went to my fall tuition bill, so I'm too tapped to pay for someplace new to live right now. Not to mention, I already paid Vanessa my share of the rent, and it's not even the end of the month. I can't ask her for money back without making things worse.

Bitch.

As my truck rounds the corner onto the block that has been my home until this morning, I see my entire drawer of Calvin Klein underwear dotting the green lawn of Vanessa's townhouse. I slam the wheel with the heel of my hand and my jaw locks tight. I've never hit a woman before, and I never would, but I wonder if I could classify her as "sea demon" and be done with it.

Jamming on the brakes, I make a full stop at the end of the driveway, which is strewn with the rest of my stuff: CDs, books, clothes, my soccer ball. . . . A jolt of nausea hits me from the violation of having my possessions scattered recklessly on the hot asphalt.

My hands shake as I stalk up to the front door. The key no longer opens the lock. No surprise there, but I curse anyway and pound on the front door, ready to rip it off its hinges.

"Vanessa!"

The window opens above me. "I'm on a conference call. You know — *a real job*? Shut up before I call the police!"

I step back and stare up into her green eyes. Long, black hair drapes down around her evil, beautiful face. My hands twitch at my sides ready to reach up to the second floor window and wring her neck. "What the fuck, Vanessa?" I scream. "Just because I don't yammer on the phone all day doesn't mean I don't have a real job — which I had to leave to get over here. You couldn't wait for an hour? It's not like you've got anywhere to go!"

"This conversation isn't worth the wasted air-conditioning." She flips me the bird and slams the window shut.

A growl rises in my throat. How did our relationship turn into this shit show? The truth? I guess it's my fault for opening my big mouth. But I never thought telling Vanessa that I had no intention of getting married until after I graduated from college would be the death knell of our relationship. Granted, at this rate, I won't finish school for almost another two years, when I'm twenty-six. But since we already lived together, what the hell was the rush? Big mistake. That conversation was two months ago, and our relationship unraveled from there. Still, I have a hard time reconciling my admission with her batshit-crazy behavior since then, not that she was a picnic before that. Who knew wedding bells would be the price for keeping some stability in my screwed up life? Then again, two years isn't such a bad run, I guess.

My face burns as I dip down and scoop up my briefs, one pair at a time.

"Where the hell are my boxes?" I yell up at the closed window.

No answer. I drop my underwear back on the lawn in a pile, then storm over to the garage and punch in the code. It opens.

Ha! There they are. The boxes are still intact. I haul them out and carefully collect my things, giving them the respect I want for myself. When I get to my clothes, I refold and place them neatly back inside the cardboard containers. Some things need to be washed. I separate as I go. It only takes ten minutes to get everything organized and packed beneath my pickup's flatbed cover.

Between anger at Vanessa and dread at returning to my father's house, my head is throbbing. I check my phone. 4:43 p.m. Plenty of time to catch a bite to eat over a beer at The Grasshopper and a trip to the Laundromat. What I need is a shower, but that would mean showing up across town early. I can't motivate myself to go there yet. I'd rather chance offending people with body odor than spending one minute longer than I have to with my father.

I'm still fuming as I find a parking spot behind the bar. I grab my toothbrush, deodorant, and a clean shirt I managed to salvage from the driveway, and head straight for the men's room. I need to feel human again. I click the lock shut behind me, place my stuff on the toilet tank, and brace myself against the sink. Drawing in a deep breath, I glance up. Whenever I miss my mom, like now, I look in the mirror to see the shades of her inside of me.

You'd think after six years I'd be over her death. But I'm not. The day she died is still burned into my memory along with a gaping hole in my chest over losing her. Maybe I'm idealizing our relationship now that she's gone, but there's no denying we were close. She was my mentor, my biggest supporter, and the one person in the world who always believed in me . . . the exact opposite of my dad.

If I concentrate, I can see her image in my reflection. I squint into the mirror, looking past the angry lines etched across my forehead. They make my eyes a piercing bright blue, one shade darker than hers. I have my mom's nose, straight and nicely shaped. She always considered it her best feature. As an artist, she used to say our eyes and nose shared the same symmetry and perfect proportions. I didn't understand what she meant until she showed me one afternoon in her studio when I was seventeen. Taking a compass, she measured all the angles on our faces and sketched our portraits side-by-side in pencil. Then she pointed out all the similarities. After that, whenever I wanted to picture her, all I had to do was look for her in the mirror.

The only thing that ruins it is my mouth. Set right now in a hard line, it's all Dad. His full lips, she said, were her favorite part of his face. Funny, I hate my mouth because it reminds me of him.

Speaking of . . . there's one precious thing I hope to retrieve at my father's — a painting of my mom and me. She finished it

15

before she died. It should be there, as long as my father still has the boxes from the move out of our big house to the dump he lives in now. I left too quickly the last time to find it and take it with me.

I turn on the faucet, splash water on my face, and do a quick wash. A large wad of paper towels later, I'm dry and looking cleaner. Freshly brushed teeth and a shot of deodorant make me feel absolutely alive. A clean, casual button-down shirt goes on next. On a whim I throw my dirty T-shirt in the garbage. One less thing to wash. I let my hair down and comb through it with my fingers. It brushes the tops of my shoulders. I'll cut it when I get a job after college. Right now it's a chick magnet. Not that I'm ready for anyone new yet.

I dump my toiletries in the truck and head back inside.

"Hey, Declan," I greet the bartender and slip onto a barstool.

"Hey, Mac, Celtic got hammered," he says in a Dublin brogue and snickers.

"Yeah, well, Liverpool didn't do so well, either," I say as he hands me a perfectly drawn pint of Guinness. My Scottish heritage drives my choice in European football teams. Lucky the Irish and Scots have a better relationship than either has with the English.

"How's the wee lassie?" he asks, toweling down the bar in front of me. It's early and still empty since it's only Tuesday.

The creamy top touches my lip as I take a long pull on my glass. "We broke up," I say, unwilling to go further.

Declan gives me an assessing look. "You want some hours on Saturday night? I'm down a couple of bartenders."

My eyes widen. "Really? Timing couldn't be better. I could use the cash." Vanessa made me quit working here after I moved in. She didn't want to give up Saturday nights, plus she couldn't handle women hitting on me. Trust was an issue with her even though I'd never given her a reason to doubt me.

"Are ya jokin' me? The tip jars have been desperate since you've been gone. We have a good band playing on Saturday night, so I'd say you'd make a fine wage."

I smile and lift my glass. "You're on. Six p.m.?"

"Aye, Mac." He winks and leaves to serve another patron at the end of the bar.

While I'm thinking about cash . . . I take the card out of my front pocket. Here goes nothing.

I text: *Are you available tomorrow afternoon for that photo session? Raine*

Tossing the phone back onto the mahogany surface, my eyes fix on the small screen as I wait for a reply.

Chapter 4

Jillian

"HEY, BRIGITTE." I clasp the wheel, and speak into the cell phone magic of Bluetooth.

"Please tell me you're sending over your synopsis," she says without preamble.

I cringe. "Um, not exactly. But it's my top priority. I even turned down a dinner invitation at Kitty's this evening to finish it. You'll have it tomorrow. I promise." I cross my fingers as I speak and hope I'm not lying. "Can I tell you why I called?"

Brigitte sighs. "I'm all ears."

Not only is Brigitte my agent, but she's one of my oldest and dearest friends. We met in college at Villanova.

My shoulders clench in preparation for Brigitte to push back hard, and then I spew my words so fast they blend together in a jumble. "I-found-the-cover-model-for-*Twisted Up in Drew*. I'll have the photos next week."

"I *think* you just said something about finding a cover model." Her voice is impatient. "Jillian, the publisher hasn't even seen the synopsis yet. Not to mention, you're behind on your deadline. Aren't you getting a little ahead of yourself?"

"Maybe, but who cares? He's perfect."

"It doesn't matter. The publisher still controls the cover," she says, resigned.

My blood pressure rises, and I snap. "I don't care, B. Make it happen. All their covers look like crap. The last one was the worst I'd ever seen. Otherwise, you can sell the goddamn thing to another publisher. I owe them a book, but I don't owe them this book. To your point, they haven't seen the synopsis yet. I can hand you anything tomorrow, and they'll never know."

My book deal specifies four romantic suspense novels. There's nothing in my contract that gives them options to my future work outside of my current obligations. Not to say they wouldn't be furious.

Brigitte snaps back, "What's got you so bent out of shape? Wait, it's the Drew thing, isn't it? Jillian . . . I still don't think you should base your male lead on Drew. You have too many unresolved emotions tied to him that are better suited for a therapist's couch than a romance novel."

My hands tighten around the wheel. "Thanks, B. So now you think I'm crazy?"

"Not crazy. Obsessed." She releases a loud breath, and then says more calmly, "Listen. I promise to shut up about him after I say this, and then you can do whatever you want. But I was there, Jillian. I was the first person you met after Drew died, and I've been watching you carry the specter of him like an albatross around your neck since our freshman year in college. It's gotten worse now that Robert's gone. You're one of my best friends. I love you, and want what's best for you. But it's time to deal with this, once and for all."

She's right. I know she's right. But that doesn't change my position on using Drew one bit. "I'm a big girl, B. This is how I'm dealing with it. It's why I want to use him. I'm ready." I'm ready to release the grief-stricken, eighteen-year-old girl locked inside of me, so that I can move on. It's what Brigitte has said, just done my way.

It's only been over the last three years, beginning not long before Robert died, that I discovered myself through writing. I found it cathartic to create characters based on the people I loved who had died, both to pay tribute to them and to provide an outlet for my grief. Mom, Dad, even a character based on Robert, have all been woven into my books. And now that Robert's gone, it's finally Drew's turn. It's time for his book.

Brigitte grunts. "Fine, but I don't believe you. I've said my piece. So where the hell did you find a cover model anyway?"

I pull into the Summit, New Jersey, train station and park where I texted Jenny earlier to look for me.

"Memorial Hospital. Sorry to be so grumpy, but I sat vigil at Aunt Vera's bedside all afternoon. You know how I feel about that place." A wave of despair hits me as I think of my aunt, and I wonder when I'll be attending another funeral.

"Geez, I'm sorry about that. How is she?"

"It's not looking good. Her organs are shutting down. If they can't turn it around in the next couple of days, I'm not sure . . ." My heart squeezes. I can't finish.

Her voice is softer, less irritated. "Hey, it's okay. I'll keep her in my prayers." Then her voice changes and she purrs, "And . . . you stumbled across a handsome young doctor who looks like Drew while you were there?"

Brigitte has been a big impetus behind the current "get Jillian back into the dating pool" campaign. She didn't even trust me to write my own Matchup.com profile. She did it for me one Saturday night last month over a bottle of wine. Being a divorcée with a solid track record when it comes to dating, at least Brigitte has a clue about this sort of thing. Me? After eighteen years of marriage, I don't even remember what it's like to date.

"Not quite. He was working outside with a group of landscapers planting trees."

"Oh, God. What I have I told you about fishing below your economic pond?"

I frown in disgust. "B, I'm not going to date him! I just

want to take a few pictures. He's way too young for me."

"Why? How old is he? If he's at least eighteen, you're golden."

"Are you crazy? I'm old enough to be his mother for crissake!" Still, a group of butterflies perk up in my stomach. He's traffic-stopping for sure, but I'm not delusional enough to think someone that young and hot would ever be interested in me. *Seriously?* I snort.

"I didn't say you had to marry him. At least at that age, all his equipment is still in working order."

Boy, was that a sore topic. Robert suffered from erectile dysfunction the last couple years of his life. Little did we realize trying to cure it would trigger the heart attack that ultimately killed him.

I release a breath at the same time a horn blows in the distance, signaling the train's approach. "Even if I was willing to stoop to that level, which I'm not, I can't imagine something like that ending well." What would he have to offer me except a broken heart when he found someone else younger and more attractive? The way I see it, it's a lose-lose. Correction—it's not even a possibility.

People stream out the doors of the station. My niece Jenny is among the flow. She smiles as she heads over to the SUV. I click the locks open for her.

"Hey, B. See what you can do for me about the cover. In the meantime, Jenny's train just pulled in and she's here. Gotta go."

"Okay, I'll see what I can do, but don't hold your breath. Send me your synopsis tomorrow by noon. I mean it, Jillian."

"Yeah, yeah." I disconnect.

The passenger door swings open, and Jenny drops her briefcase on the floor.

I smile at my niece. "How was your job interview?"

Buttoned-up and conservative, with much better taste than her mother, Jenny looks polished and professional in a pinstriped suit with her light-brown hair coiled in a tight bun.

She has her father's bright-blue eyes. Tall and thin with shapely hips, she's a knockout.

She claps her hands together, brimming with enthusiasm. "I think it went well. They're making their final decision in the next two weeks."

"That's fantastic, sweetie! Tell me all about it," I say as I edge out into the flow of cars leaving the station.

She beams and then turns on her serious face. "Well. This job would report to the digital advertising director and would manage client accounts behind the scenes to maximize the return on their digital investment. The salary is decent."

"That sounds very exciting." If you like that kind of thing. Sounds kind of dull, but hey, as long as Jenny maximizes Kitty's return on investment for her $250,000 education at NYU, I'm all for it.

Jenny looks at me with wide eyes. "Aunt Jill, I've been in a near panic all summer thinking I would be working as a waitress for the rest of my life. I really want this job."

I smile. Jenny tends to be melodramatic. "Sweetie, even if this one doesn't pan out, you'll get something. It's been only a few months since graduation. I guarantee you won't be working in food service for the rest of your life."

Kitty had hoped Jenny would be a CPA like her, or go into finance like her father. Instead, Jenny chose digital communications. I applaud her for making her own choice. At least it wasn't ancient basket weaving techniques, or something equally as useless.

She sighs. "Sometimes it feels that way."

I reach over and squeeze her hand. "I know. But it'll work out, I promise."

Turning in her seat to face me, I glimpse her expression shifting to worry. "How's Great-Aunt Vee?"

I sigh. "Not good, sweetheart. Your mom can fill you in more when she gets home."

Up ahead is her street. I flick on my blinker. "How's

Russ?"

Silence.

I glance over, and she's staring out the window. "Trouble in paradise?"

"He accepted a job in California," she whispers.

My eyes widen. We all expected that Russ would be a part of our family someday. They've been dating since their junior year in high school. "Did he ask you to go with him?"

Crossing her arms over her chest, she wipes away a tear. "No. He didn't. It's over."

"I'm so sorry, Jen," I say softly, my heart breaking for her. "When did this happen?"

"Two days ago. That's why I have to get this job. I need to show him he's not the only one who's important."

I frown at her. "Don't ever let anyone else determine your self-worth—especially some guy. We love Russ, but we love you more. You need to stand on your own two feet, always." But as I say the words, I can't help but wonder how much I ignored my own advice with Robert when he was alive. My photography career was more lucrative at the beginning of our marriage, until I let it slide. I hit a lull in my thirties when my life shifted to entertaining Robert's clients, supporting his career, and trying to start a family. I went from living my own life to letting myself get swept up in Robert's wake. More my fault than his.

Jenny wipes away more tears. "He said nothing has to change, that we can visit each other and see how the long-distance relationship works out. But if he really loves me, he would've asked me to go."

I shake my head. "I know you're not going to want to hear this, but you're young. This isn't such a bad thing. Almost everyone I went to college with who got married or lived together out of school broke up or got divorced before they turned thirty. You need to experience more of the world to really know what you want."

She turns to me. "But you married Uncle Robert when you

were only a year older than me."

My brows furrow. "I have to admit sometimes I think I should've waited."

"Really?"

I press my lips together and nod. God help me. It's true. Marrying Robert seemed right at the time. I loved him, just in a different way. He was my best friend, my savior—rescuing me from myself and my all-consuming grief. Honestly, he was the perfect distraction... the safe choice. I was happy with Robert—I really was—but the passion I felt with Drew... that just wasn't there. Right or wrong, after what happened to Drew, I convinced myself I probably didn't deserve it. Looking back, I should have waited and worked out my guilt another way. Maybe then I wouldn't be wrestling with even more guilt... that my sadness over Robert's death is tinged with relief. But I could never admit that to anyone, much less my niece.

"Tell me how you feel about Russ," I ask.

"Huh?"

"What does it feel like when you think of being without him?"

She sniffles. "What do you mean?"

"Can you go on? Can you breathe?" Part of me isn't sure if I want to open this can of worms, but another part of me wants someone else to learn from my mistakes.

"Remember, senior year of high school, that day you saw Russ and that girl at Starbucks?"

"Amber?" Jenny interjects.

"Yes, Amber." I smirk. "You saw them through the window with their heads bent down together, whispering. You came home crying, convinced Russ had found someone else. You wouldn't come out of your room, skipped school for two days, wouldn't take Russ's phone calls... you drove your mother crazy. Remember that?"

"Yes, I remember," she whispers.

"Turns out he was failing calculus and Amber was only

helping him study," I remind her. "That's what it feels like not to breathe, to need somebody so much your soul aches with the mere thought of him being gone. Does it feel like that this time?"

She shrugs. "It hurts, and I'm so mad. But I can breathe . . ."

"Then, I promise, you'll be fine. If Russ was still *the one*, you would feel like you did that day."

She gives me a weak smile. "Is that the way you felt about Uncle Robert?"

I pull into her driveway. "When I was a little younger than you, I felt like that, but with someone else. I married Uncle Robert later." At eighteen, Drew and I had our lives mapped out—same college, marriage after graduation, career then kids . . . a boy and a girl. Hannah and Alex. A Boston terrier named Spike. In one breath, one summer day it was all taken away by a hunk of twisted metal, and I buried my first love two weeks before my freshman year of college. Jenny knows nothing of Drew. For eighteen years, my marriage was the perfect place to hide . . . and forget that I was the one driving the car.

I lean over and give Jenny a kiss on the cheek. "I want you to have the best in life. Don't ever sell yourself short, okay?"

She reaches for the door handle. "Thanks for the ride, Aunt Jill, and the advice."

"Tell your mom I'll call her later tonight."

"Okay." She closes the door to the SUV, and I release a sigh and hope I haven't scared her. I want better for her than I've had for myself. For years I've believed that the absence of emotional pain equaled happiness. I'd never let one of my heroines settle for that.

The second I turn into my driveway in Chatham, my phone *plings* with a new text. I pull into the garage and park before taking it out. It's from Raine. I only half believed he would contact me.

Are you available tomorrow afternoon for that photo session? Raine

My palms are suddenly moist, and with shaky fingers, I reply.

3 p.m.?

With surprising speed, I receive a response.

I can make that work.

Chapter 5

Raine

I CAN'T DELAY the inevitable any longer. After two hours in the Laundromat, clothes that were dirty are now clean, folded, and repacked inside the bed of my truck. Dread coils in my stomach as I navigate my pickup toward the other side of Morristown. My father expects me by ten o'clock. Less than fifteen minutes from now.

I promise myself I can be out of there in a month. That should be long enough to scrape together a small security deposit and the first month's rent for a shared living situation. The thought of being here doesn't thrill me, but before I know it, tuition for spring semester will be due.

My skin crawls when I spot his house, probably a sign my body is remembering past injuries at a cellular level. Dad is like Dr. Jekyll and Mr. Hyde. For the most part, when he's sober he's manageable. When he's loaded—coke, alcohol, whatever—all bets are off. I wish I had a weapon.

His random attacks started when I hit puberty and got worse after his sobriety ended the day of my mother's funeral. Openhanded slaps and "the belt" turned into punches by my mid-teens—all done outside my mother's line of sight. My father was nothing if not calculating. He always found leverage, something I couldn't or wouldn't tell my mom, to keep me quiet and force me to lie and pass off my black eyes and bruises as sports injuries. Once I bulked up and learned to fight, I shut that shit down with a couple of rare exceptions that happened while he was loaded. At least he never lifted a hand to my mom; he worshipped her. Had he touched her, I might've had to kill him.

I pull into the driveway, cut the engine, and fill a small overnight bag from the boxes in the back of my truck. Everything of value stays locked in the truck—only toiletries, something to sleep in, and tomorrow's clothes come in with me.

I ring the bell to his unit and shift awkwardly on my feet. My lungs contract a little, like I'm preparing to step into a small enclosed space without an exit.

An air conditioner hums in the upstairs window. My gaze sweeps across the covered, dilapidated porch of the multifamily Victorian while I wait. It's a dump, but it comes with a detached garage, giving my father a place to store everything he kept from the Mendham house. The dim glow cast by an outside light reveals the peeling paint on his door. A tricycle sits in the corner along with some dirty plastic lawn furniture and dead potted plants.

The seal on the door cracks open and I face my father. I've only seen him once since I moved in with Vanessa. We met for breakfast. It went well enough until he asked me to loan him some money for a debt he had to pay off.

His hair and thick eyebrows are mostly gray, and he looks worn. But I've learned never to underestimate him. A couple of inches shorter than me, there's still power behind his wiry frame. His forearms are roped with veins over muscle. If nothing else, he's never lost his vanity when it comes to keeping in shape.

"Come in, son," he says. "Your phone call surprised me." His voice is amiable, without its usual condescending and resentful tone. True to his word, he's sober.

I size him up. "Thanks for letting me crash here. It should

only take me a few weeks to find a new place."

He opens the door wider, and I step inside.

The apartment is sparse, but neat enough. The living room is a strange blend between some of the small pieces of nice furniture that were once in our Mendham house and some practical IKEA necessities. My father sold all the best furniture over time. I have no clue what he did with the money, and I don't want to venture a guess. Despite what he's told me, even if he's sober, I suspect his gambling has slowed but not fully stopped.

I reach into my pocket and pull out five twenties. "Here. For the first week," I say, handing him the amount we agreed upon. It gets me a room and a place to shower, but I'm on my own for food.

He lights up and takes the money without hesitation. The look in his eyes reminds me of a junkie the moment before he sinks a needle into his vein. Even after six years, I still have trouble reconciling the man standing before me with the polished Wall Street investment banker I idolized as a child.

"How's school?" he asks.

Bile rises in my throat. "Good," I say trying not to grit my teeth. No thanks to him. I'd be living a whole different life if he hadn't stolen it from me.

He glances at my hair — drawn back in an elastic — like he's thinking of making a comment but decides against it. I shift my bag in my hand and tip my head toward the back bedroom where I stayed for a couple weeks three years ago. "I'm going to take a shower, then settle in."

He nods and gives me one last look. "Make yourself at home."

"Thanks." I think about the irony of his words. *Home* is not a place where he and I would ever coexist. This is merely a pit stop on my way to somewhere else.

I stop halfway down the hall. "Do you still have Mom's paintings from her studio in the garage?"

"Some of them. Why?" he says from the living room.

"No reason, just asking." The last thing I need is to have him blackmail me over the piece I want.

I take my stuff into the bathroom and lock the door behind me. Thankfully, the shower looks like it's been cleaned recently. I sigh, feeling better with a locked door between us.

Fifteen minutes later, clean and dressed in sweats, I take all my things into the bedroom. It looks the same as it did the last time I stayed here and holds the musty smell that comes with lack of use. The queen-size bed takes up most of the space. A dresser, chair, and a TV are the only other things in the room.

"Shit." The bedroom door doesn't lock properly, so I wedge the wooden Windsor chair underneath the door knob.

Drained, I collapse on the bed and stare at the ceiling.

A knock sounds at my door and I tense.

"Yeah?"

"I thought you might want a key. I'll slip it under the door." My father's voice is muffled through the heavy wood.

I make no move to get up. "Thanks."

As his footsteps recede down the hallway, tension eases out of my shoulders. Sweeping a hand over my face, I click on the TV as my cell phone chimes from inside my bag with a new text. I rummage around until I find it.

Welcome back. Declan says you're back in the saddle on Saturday night. I'm savoring the tips already. Let me know if you want to go for a ride to heal your broken heart. Fi

Fuck. Fiona. I snort and shake my head. If I had any intention of returning to our pre-Vanessa "friends with benefits" arrangement, I'd be sleeping in her bed tonight rather than lying here. I like Fi, but there's no mistaking that she's a bit psycho, and I have enough problems right now. Plus, I have a general policy against having to fuck someone in order to keep a roof over my head—hence my issue with Vanessa. We stopped having sex about a month ago when my anger far outpaced my desire. My fingers fly over the touch screen.

Appreciate the offer, but not ready for anything. See you Sat nite.

My eye catches Jillian Grant's phone number in my list of text messages, and I smile. The thought of being on the cover of a book gives me a little thrill. Then I remember her ass, and smile wider. Now that's something I could get excited over.

Chapter 6

Jillian

MY STOMACH LURCHES at the sound of the doorbell. I see a slice of him through the slim fan light flanking the large entrance door.

After another hospital visit to see Aunt Vera this morning, I came home to set up my studio. Her improvement since yesterday lifted my spirits and propelled me into motion. The last two hours flew by in a blur.

It's been a long time since I've held a photo shoot, so setting up the lighting and preparing the backgrounds were no small tasks. All of it made worse by the nervous anticipation taunting my midsection as I worked. I chided myself more than once. *He may look like Drew, but he isn't.* There's no denying he's attractive in his own right . . .

Finding something to wear had proven more difficult. Nothing looked right. I settled on one of my more flattering pairs of jeans and a white, summery blouse that hid my sins. Then there was the makeup. Subtle, yet enough to hide even more flaws.

I will my face to relax and open the door.

Raine fills the entrance, a heavy backpack slung over his shoulder. I hadn't realized how tall he was yesterday. Standing in my flat sandals, I tip five-six, but I have to look up to meet his eyes. I smile, and he smiles back. It softens the lines of concentration on his forehead. He stands at probably six-two. His tawny-colored hair is pulled back tight at his neck. He's wearing a casual button-down in a flowing fabric, open low enough to get a peek at the top of his pecs, the sleeves unbuttoned. It's paired with nice-fitting jeans and . . . flip-flops.

"Hi. Come in," I say and step aside. I take him in from behind. *Gah!* The woman inside me purrs at his deliciousness. There it is. What I glimpsed yesterday . . . the most perfect posterior I've ever seen in a pair of jeans. Holding my breath for the true test, my eyes drop down to the floor. The flip-flops are Tommy Bahama, and his feet are well manicured and nicely shaped — sexy. My fantasy is safe for now. Relieved, I release a silent breath. Nothing kills my passion faster than ugly feet. I give myself a mental slap and remind myself again that he's not Drew, in addition to being way too young for me.

He turns back to face me. "I brought some extra stuff. I wasn't sure how you wanted me to dress . . . or undress." He blushes, then smiles shyly. His discomfort is endearing.

I eye his backpack and tease, "Looks like you brought a lot of stuff."

His brow knits for a moment in confusion, and then he cracks a smile. "Oh, it's not all clothes. I have my laptop and some books for class." He shifts it off his shoulder and into his hand.

Brigitte's words from yesterday — *as long as he's over eighteen* — come back to me. "Where do you go to school?" If he names a high school, I might faint.

"Rutgers."

Pheww! He's in college. I walk ahead and motion for him to follow me. "What are you studying?" I ask, leading him to the stairs down to the lower level. His backpack rustles as we take the stairs.

"Right now, I'm focusing on digital art and computer-aided design," he says.

"Really? Sounds interesting. When do you graduate?" I ask, liking his artistic bent. Drew could sing but he didn't share my passion for art of any kind.

"I'm going part-time, so at this pace, it may take another two years." His voice carries an edge of frustration.

We reach the open door to my studio and enter. "Why? How long have you been going?" By the tone of his previous answer and some quick math, I suspect he's easily over twenty-one.

His jaw twitches and instead of answering, he places the backpack on the floor and glances around. "This is an amazing space. I meant to say something upstairs. You have a beautiful home."

Clever. I wonder why he sidestepped my question and what's causing his angst. "Thanks. But it's a little big for just me."

His expression changes to surprise. "Just you? You're not married?"

My smile wavers and suddenly feels pasted on. "Not anymore. My husband died two years ago. And before you ask, we didn't have any kids." I prefer to blurt it all out at once to shut down any remaining questions. It's not so much that it upsets me to speak of Robert, but rather it upsets other people when I don't react as if it does.

Pain shoots through his eyes and he lays his hand on my shoulder. "I'm sorry for your loss. That must've been difficult." His empathy surrounds me, and right then, I know he's lost someone, too.

I start to ask him who it was, but stop. I don't know him well enough to pry. So I clear my throat. "Thank you, but it's okay, really."

"So I don't put my foot in my mouth again, what now?" He steps back and looks over at where the lights are set up. The room is large and divided into three areas: a photo studio, my old office, and a work area with a long table and floor-to-ceiling shelving along the back wall. I let go of my dark room, now a storage area, with the advent of high-tech digital cameras.

"Why don't we talk through the shoot before we start?" I point toward a small modern table and two chairs set up next to the desk in my office area.

We amble over and he takes the seat next to me. The release form he needs to sign is in a colorful folder on the table in front of us.

"What time do you need to leave?" I ask, getting down to business.

"If I leave by five, I'll make it in time for class at six-thirty."

Glancing at the clock on the wall, I chew my lip. "Would you be able to come back tomorrow if we don't finish today? I'm thinking this is going to take closer to three hours."

His eyebrows fly up. "That long?"

I chuckle. "Don't look so surprised. Professional models have it much worse. I'll try not to make it too painful. Sometimes it takes hundreds of shots to get just a few."

He crosses his arms in front him, amused. "Who knew? And I thought sitting for a portrait was bad."

My interest piques. "Who did you sit for?"

He loses his smile and looks away. I'm left to gaze at his chiseled profile.

"I'm sorry. I didn't mean to pry." I suppress the urge to touch him. Whoever it was is tied to his loss. I sense his pain cuts through him deeply; the clarity leaves me breathless, because I recognize his reactions as my own. I can only hope that his number of losses doesn't equal mine.

He sweeps a hand over his face and looks back at me. "No," he says softly. "You didn't pry. Don't be sorry. It's all me." He touches my hand and my heart rate rises. His palm is callused but warm. There is no mistaking he uses his hands for work. His blue eyes pull at me, daring me to drown inside them.

He slides his hand away slowly and folds it with his other

in front of him. "Tell me about your book. Who am I supposed to be?"

I take a breath and move on to somewhat safer ground. "I'm writing a contemporary romantic suspense about two twenty-something adults, Becca and Drew. They were high school sweethearts. Becca thinks Drew is dead until she runs into him five years later . . . and the intrigue begins from there."

"So I'm the dead boyfriend Drew, who's really alive?" he asks, smirking. The moment I hear his words I get a strong sense of déjà vu. That's exactly who he is . . . in more ways than one.

"Um . . . Yes."

He shrugs. "Okay. But please tell me this guy doesn't turn out to be a total jerk. I'm not sure I want to lend my likeness to an asshole."

I laugh. "No, he's not an asshole. I loved him." I don't realize what I've said until the words pass through my lips and it's too late to take them back.

Raine's eyebrows lift. "Loved? Is he a real person?"

My smile disappears. God, what a pair we make. "He's just a character," I lie.

His eyes bore into me and he leans forward, his mouth twisting up into a very sexy smile. "You're lying."

I'll be damned. He just called me out. Instead of being angry, I'm amused. I lean toward him. "I'll make you a deal. If we become friends, we'll trade secrets over a bottle of wine one night because I'm not the only one at this table who has them."

Tension sits between us for a moment then he leans back. "Look at you. Observant. It's a deal." He brings his fist up and offers it to me. I laugh and fist-bump him. Just like that, the tension leaves the room.

"Okay, let's get this going." I pull the folder toward me and open it. "These are a bunch of covers I printed off to give you an idea of what I'm trying to create."

He flips through them with interest, his brows knitting in concentration with the same look he wore when I opened the door and found him on my porch. "I like these. I can help you make the book cover when you have the picture you want. When I'm not landscaping, I freelance doing websites and graphic design."

Now it's my turn to be surprised. "I might take you up on that." I glance at the clock and slap the table. "Let's take some pictures."

"You got it." He rises and so do I.

We decide to start with him dressed as he is. I show him where I want him to stand. I've already marked the spot with an X of masking tape. After I position the lights, I walk up to him. I realize I could have just asked him to do what I'm about to do, but I hunger for contact.

"One more thing." I reach around to the back of his neck. "May I?"

My breaths get shallow a moment before his Adam's apple rises quickly and falls. Does he feel it, too?

Our eyes meet. "Whatever turns you on . . . *Jillian.*" He adds my name like he's taking it out for a test drive.

More than you know. I tug the elastic and free his hair so that it cascades down around his shoulders. The resemblance floors me, and I suck in a breath.

I turn my back to hide my blush, and grab my camera. "Let me know if you want some music on."

"I'm good for now."

When I turn around to face him, the camera provides a protective layer between us. Through the lens, I study him unguardedly, and allow myself to create a slightly altered vision of reality. One that still includes Drew. In a way, photography is not so different from writing a novel. "When you look at the camera think about . . . ." *The obvious.* "Your girlfriend."

He gives the lens a seductive stare. "Don't have one right now."

My heart flutters. "Then pretend the camera is your lover."

And he does, because if he wasn't pretending, he could've fooled me. Thirty minutes in, I'm longing to drown in his kiss. His packaging is one thing, but his expressions are riveting.

He takes off his shirt for the next set of pictures, and I turn on the fan for a wind effect. I have to do everything in my power not to drool. Gazing through the lens, I help it caress every muscled peak and valley that covers his naked torso. His chest is smooth and hairless, with the barest hint of blond hair under his arms. I wonder if that's his natural state or if he does something to maintain it. We take another fifteen minutes' worth of shots.

"Have you ever thought about doing this for a living?" I ask, through the continuous snapping of the camera shutter.

He flips his hair and smiles for the camera. "Nope. I've got bigger fish to fry."

"The camera loves you."

His smile falters. "Thanks."

My cell phone rings on the table. I stop shooting. "I have to take that."

I dash over to answer it.

"Hi, Aunt Jill, I'm upstairs. Can you let me in?"

Disappointment rolls through me. "Be right there, Pumpkin." I run over and snap off the fan.

"Pumpkin?" Raine grins.

I give him a tight smile and head for the door. "My niece. She's upstairs. I hope you don't mind, but I asked her to come and help us. I need a few shots with her back to the camera in case I go with both Becca and Drew."

As I pass over the threshold, I add, "Oh, and you can put your shirt on." I'm not sure if I want him covered because I don't want Jenny to get an eyeful or because I don't want to share him. On the page, the idea of Drew is something I can deal with. But the living, breathing facsimile—Raine with an *e*—makes me wish for more than I deserve. Another chance.

As I head upstairs, reality hits the center of my chest,

awakening a thread of grief buried deep inside me. My foot almost misses the top stair. I couldn't see it through the haze of tears threatening to break free.

Chapter 7

Raine

JILLIAN DISAPPEARS through the doorway, and I put my shirt back on.

I like her . . . a lot. As sorry as I am for her loss, I almost fist-pumped the air when I found out she was single. There's something about her. I don't know, but whatever it is, I feel a connection. A spark. Different than when I first met Vanessa. Better. Maybe it's because Jillian lost someone she loves, or maybe it's because she's older.

I'll admit it. I get a charge from seeing the interest in her eyes when I speak. And when she throws admiring glances my way, a fire lights in my gut, because I don't think she realizes she's doing it. My only question is: Is it me she's seeing or this guy Drew?

I rake a hand through my hair, and frown. For all I know, it could be my imagination on overdrive. This thing with Vanessa is still too raw for me to be a good judge. It's left behind a big dent in my ego and more self-doubt than usual. That said, I stop short of thinking she's out of my league.

While she's gone, I wander around her studio, studying all her photography work mounted on the walls. It's good. Really good. I sit down at the table and gaze over at her desk. A cluster of photos in nice frames are the only personal touch.

Her home is palatial. Classy. It reminds me of the house I grew up in a lifetime ago. A yearning for my old life hits me for only a moment before I shut it down. I drum my fingers on the table. No sense in going there, it will only ruin my good mood.

Instead, I think back to what Jillian said to me earlier. *"If we become friends, we'll trade secrets over a bottle of wine one night because I'm not the only one at this table who has them."*

Staying friends isn't a problem ... it's the trading secrets part that worries me. Will she run away screaming if I share them? If it were me, I might. It's not like she's the kind of woman who needs to be friends with a guy who has a major chip on his shoulder about his past, $263 in his bank account outside of what he's saving for school, a maxed-out credit card, and an unstable junkie gambler for a father.

Chattering approaches from down the hall, and Jillian walks in with a pretty girl. Tall with curvy hips but still toothpick thin, she has long brown hair and big blue eyes. My guess is she's around my age.

"Raine, this is my niece, Jenny," Jillian says and averts her eyes. I wonder why as she fumbles with her camera.

"Hi," I say, extending my hand to Jenny.

She gives it a quick shake. "So, Aunt Jill said that she met you outside the hospital." I hear an appraisal beneath her words.

My gaze drifts to Jillian. "Yeah. Something like that."

"Jenny, sweetie, since Raine is running out of time, can I ask you to have him show you the camera mark?" Jillian says, and catches my eye. "Would you mind taking Jenny?" The chemistry in the room has changed, and Jillian is suddenly on her guard.

Uh-oh. No way. A twinge echoes in my gut. Was her intention to set me up with her niece all along? I hope I'm wrong.

"Sure," I mumble and lead Jenny back underneath the lights.

41

"Jen, I'll need Raine to face the camera and take you into his arms." Jillian shifts her focus to me. "First set, look at Jenny like she's your long lost love, and then for the second set, I'll have you look at the camera."

I nod and wrap my arms around Jillian's niece. She feels too much like Vanessa. I resist the urge to push her away. Instead she pushes closer, her small breasts touch my chest, and she stares up at me with a smile. "You look like you're in pain. What's the matter?"

I chuckle. "Sorry, it's not you. Memories of girlfriends past." The camera snaps rapidly before I realize Jillian has restarted the shoot.

"That's good," Jillian says from the background.

I can't get my body to relax, despite Jenny's warmth next to me. I don't realize she's noticed until she pinches the top of my butt cheek through my jeans away from Jillian's view. "Will you relax? You look constipated," she hisses next to my ear.

I burst out laughing. "I'm sorry. I'm nervous, I guess."

Snap. Snap. Snap.

"You've never modeled before, have you?" she whispers.

"No," I whisper back.

"Raine?" Jillian says my name and my head snaps to attention.

She smiles but it's missing her earlier warmth. "Can you look at the camera now? Pretend you're looking at a lover."

I look at the camera, and I imagine . . . Jillian. My body relaxes. I imagine staring into her huge golden-brown eyes, and gliding my fingertip across the curve of her bottom lip. Yeah, that's something I could get into. In contrast, when I think of her niece in my arms, I stiffen, and not in a good way.

Snap. Snap. Snap.

"Hey, Raine."

"Huh?" My concentration breaks, and I glance down to see a mischievous glint in Jenny's eye. She twists in my arms. "Aunt Jill. I have an idea."

"What's that?"

"Trade places with me."

Jillian lowers the camera and freezes like a deer in headlights. "Why?"

Jenny looks up at me with a sly grin. "Indulge me," she says, wiggling out of my motionless arms.

Catching my eye, Jillian gives me a helpless look.

Jenny trots over to take the camera as Jillian tentatively approaches. My mouth breaks into a smile. I sweep her into my arms with the intent of winning her over, and having her drop any stupid ideas about fixing me up with her niece. She tenses next to me.

"Relax." Funny, it sounds different to me when I say it. Jillian's body is softer and curvier than Jenny's; it feels like Heaven against me. She fits into my contours perfectly, softening my hard edges. Electricity snaps over my skin where her body meets mine, and I suppress the instinctive urge to press her closer.

"Aunt Jill, put your arms around his waist. Raine, look at her like you want to eat her for breakfast." Jenny follows her comment with a wicked chuckle.

"Jenny!" Jillian protests.

I laugh, and Jillian closes her arms around me. Her hands clasp behind me and rest at the base of my spine. I dip my head down into her hair. The smell of vanilla fills my nostrils. "Come on, relax. It can't be that bad," I whisper into her hair.

She looks up. Her eyes meet mine, and she smiles. The tension leaves her as she melts into me. I wink and take it as permission to pull her closer.

Snap. Snap. Snap.

"You're enjoying this, aren't you?" she says accusingly.

I look down into her wide, golden eyes, aware of the camera in the background, and give her one of the panty-melting grins I used to be known for pre-Vanessa. "Yup."

My grip tightens around her ever so slightly. *That's what I'm talkin' 'bout.*

"Good one!" Jenny says.

The trill of my cell phone sounds from inside my backpack and shatters the moment. I glance at the clock. 5:35. *Crap!*

Jenny stops shooting.

I tense. "Hey, I'm supposed to pick up a friend on the way to class. That's probably him. Can we finish tomorrow?"

Jillian's arms drop from around me, and she moves back. Her face has a flush to it. "No problem. Go. I don't want you to be late."

I give her an apologetic look, sorry that I had to be the one to kill the best part of the photo shoot. "I'd stay longer if I could."

Across the room, I retrieve my phone from my backpack. My hunch is right. It was Dave. His car is in the shop today and his fiancée is working late, so I promised to swing by and pick him up for class. It starts tonight.

I send him a text. *Sorry, dude. Got caught up. Be there in 15.*

"Aunt Jill, I have to run, too. My shift starts at six," Jenny says from behind me. "Do you need me tomorrow?" I hear her whisper.

"No, we'll be fine."

"You *sure*?" This time her voice carries an edge of worry.

I chuckle silently, wondering what she's so afraid of, and then pull my hair back in an elastic and sling my backpack over my shoulder. "I'll text you later."

"I'll walk you both out," Jillian says, again looking anywhere but at me. I'll have to take care of that tomorrow. We follow her up the stairs to the front door.

Jenny dips in and gives her a kiss on the cheek. "See ya, Aunt Jill."

Jillian brightens. "Thanks for helping us out, sweetie."

I give a quick wave then head to my truck. It's parked next to a shiny new Toyota that must be Jenny's.

Catching up to me, she grabs my forearm. "Wait."

Her tone puts me on the defensive. "What is it?"

"What do you want with my Aunt Jill?"

"What are you talking about? I barely know her."

"But you want to," she says, narrowing her eyes. "The camera doesn't lie."

My gaze hardens on her. "So what if I do?"

"How old are you anyway? You're a little young for her, don't you think?" she snaps.

I shake my arm lose. "What are you saying?"

After a quick glance at the door, she lowers her voice. "What I'm saying is if you decide to pursue her, make sure it's her you want and not her money."

My head jerks back like I've been slapped.

Jenny locks her arms across her chest and glares at me. "She deserves someone who's going to be there for her for the long haul. Not that I'm judging you, but she deserves more than some eye candy young enough to be her son with not much to offer other than some hot sex."

My hands clench, and heat blazes in my cheeks. "That sounds pretty fucking judgmental to me. You don't know a thing about me. How would you know what I have to offer? That's not who I am at all. So back the fuck off."

She's struck a tender nerve with pinpoint accuracy, drilling straight into my self-esteem issues—the ones created by my asshole father—with her insinuations. The memory I hate comes rushing back.

I'm fifteen again. My father has come home early from a business trip while my mother's at a gallery opening, and catches me having sex with Angie Doyle in my bedroom. He's got me pinned by the neck, lying naked on the floor, his knee grinding into my groin as he chokes me. Red hot pain shoots straight from my balls through my body, ripping the breath from my lungs. "Your mother said you got a C in English. Maybe you'll be good for something after all, you worthless little prick."

On top of being my most humiliating moment, it was the first time he ever hit me with a closed fist.

Shame and feelings of unworthiness rage in my gut as I remember.

Her face softens, and she looks me up and down. "Let's hope not. I love my aunt, so don't hurt her. That's all I'm saying." She walks to the driver's side of her car and gets in.

I yank my door open, toss my backpack onto the floor next to my duffel, and start the engine. Is that how people really see me? As some loser with nothing to offer? An attractive guy only good for a quick lay? Jenny's words sting. She's as wrong as my father was, and that pisses me off.

Maybe I shouldn't come back tomorrow. Maybe it would be better to run. Never see Jillian again.

I'm not some man-whore. But I can't deny that I need the money . . . or that I enjoyed the feel of Jillian in my arms.

Chapter 8

Jillian

"SO WHAT DO YOU THINK?" I ask, rubbing my hands together, unable to hide my smile.

Raine and I sit at my work table, hovering over the pictures from yesterday's shoot. His jaw hangs slightly open next to me. I know the feeling. It's exactly the same reaction I had after I laid them out earlier. They blew me away.

That is . . . after I got up the courage to actually look at them. Two full glasses of Cabernet were required to calm my nerves after Raine and Jenny left yesterday afternoon. Determined to push Raine away after I left him in the studio to get Jenny, my plans were undone the moment I landed in his arms at the photo shoot. The sensation of his body against mine was . . . intoxicating. But it's more than that. If only I could separate the ghost of Drew from my attraction to Raine.

He glances at me with a look of disbelief. "I can't believe these are all me."

I touch his arm. "Believe it. The camera loves you. I think you missed your calling." In the early years when I did fashion photography, I rarely had this much of a yield with a short photo shoot. So much so that I think we're

47

done.

I plant my elbows on the table and lean forward, trying to take them all in again. I already have too many pictures to choose from: Raine seducing the camera with and without his shirt; side shots that give him an ethereal look; and many that catch a subtle look or feeling.

"This one is fun." I point to a picture of him laughing with Jenny in his arms.

He chuckles, and gives me a sideways glance. "She told me I looked constipated."

"She didn't! Did she?"

"Yeah." His smile fades momentarily, looking like he's tasted something unpleasant before he points to another shot, one with me. "If you're looking for a picture of both your characters, I like this one."

I blink. Some of the best shots are the few Jenny took of Raine with me. Though she's done me proud—I put a camera in her hands at ten years old—it's slightly ego bruising to know her pictures are better than mine. She caught me at my best, and the expressions she's captured on Raine's face are breathtaking. They cover the range from tender and loving to downright sensual and hungry. I'm almost afraid to speak. "That's my favorite," I say softly.

His gaze finds mine and holds it. "Then you should use that one."

I shuffle the photos into a stack, and shake my head. "I don't look anything like Becca."

He shrugs. "Does it matter? It's your profile. You could be anyone there."

He has a point. I glance back at the photo. The way he's looking at me in the photograph, not to mention the memory of his arms around me and the feel of his body against mine, makes my pulse race. He felt so good, too good—dangerously addictive.

And I'm aware of him now, sitting next to me. I keep reminding myself he's someone I couldn't and shouldn't have, but it doesn't stop the hunger growing inside of me. Being in the same room as him stirs something within me and makes me feel alive. I notice he's wearing a scent today that he wasn't wearing yesterday — fresh and citrusy with a hint of spice. It fits his undeniable masculine presence while providing a hint of vulnerability. I catch his chiseled profile from the corner of my eye. I'd bet he has Nordic roots somewhere in his family tree.

"Do you have the photo files? I can get my laptop and we can have some fun," he says with sudden eagerness as we hunch over the work table. Then, as if struck by a thought, he turns to me. "Unless you need more pictures."

"Get your laptop. You gave me plenty to choose from."

Wearing a pleased smile, he slips off the stool and crosses the room.

"Meet me at the table by my desk. It'll be more comfortable." I go retrieve my laptop and sit down.

He settles in next to me and fires up his Apple.

"Just choose my Wi-Fi network: Writergirl," I tell him.

His fingers fly over the keyboard, and his lip curls up. "Cute," he says, his eyes glued to the screen. "Pick three of your favorites and email them to me. We'll create some covers."

"What's your address?" I ask with my fingers poised over the keys.

"Hot-guy-with-a-brain at Gmail dot com."

I arch a brow and look at him. "You're kidding, right?"

He laughs; it warms his features. "Yeah, of course I'm kidding. What *tool* would actually use that as an email address? No, it's RMac at Gmail dot com."

I type it in. "What does that stand for?" I sort through the files, already knowing which pictures I like best. The only problem is there are many more than three. I reluctantly limit my choices and include the one we both like of us.

His fingers stay in motion. "It's my name. *R* for Raine,

and my nickname, Mac. Short for MacDonald."

"Scottish? I would've guessed you had some Nordic blood in you."

His lips turn up in a smile. "I'm Swedish on my mother's side." He squints and his eyebrows lift. "I see you're just as creative, *JGrant152*."

Sheepishly, I shrug. "I'm creative in other ways."

"Other than writing, any others that I should know about?"

"Not at this point," I say, and realize I sound like I'm flirting.

"We'll see about that," he murmurs, and continues to stare at his screen. He stops typing and looks at me. "What concepts do you want for the cover beyond the photo?"

I slip into business mode and decide to work this like a session I'd do with a real cover designer. "Here's what I'm thinking. The images we've taken provide the romantic element, so capturing how Drew feels — or how we think he feels — about Becca is important. Since this is a suspense novel and there's a dark theme underlying the book, I'd like to reflect the mystery through the color scheme. I'm also thinking since it takes place in an urban setting, maybe use a cityscape in the background."

Raine nods and his face pinches in concentration. "That's good. I have some ideas." He pulls out his phone and sets the alarm. "Give me thirty minutes to work something up. What's the name of your book?"

"I'm going with *Twisted Up in Drew* right now. What time do you need to leave for class?" When he texted me earlier to arrange today's time, he mentioned he had class again tonight.

He presses his lips together and glances at the time on his phone. "In a little over an hour."

I move to get up. "Would you like something to drink?"

"Sure, as long as it's not a bottle of wine. I'd like to save that for when we have more time," he says. Despite the cocky grin, I see his shoulders stiffen like he's bracing himself.

A tingle dances down my spine when I hear my offer from yesterday. I get the feeling he's testing me. "Um . . . that wasn't exactly what I had in mind. How's soda, bottled water, or a cup of coffee?"

"Bottled water," he says and I head for the door.

"Jillian?"

I turn and his face is solemn. "Were you serious yesterday? You know . . . about the wine?"

I wonder how much it cost him to ask. I sense he's reaching out, hoping I'll meet him halfway. I see it in his eyes. Indulging in my private fantasies is easier than thinking about stepping across the line into actual reality. For better or for worse, I want to know him better. I don't want him to walk out my front door an hour from now, never to return.

"Yes." I duck out to hide my spreading blush.

When I come back, I set the water next to him as he works and peer over his shoulder. He shuts the lid on the laptop. "No peeking until I'm done," he teases.

I throw my hands up, and blurt a Jenny-ism. "My bad." Walking over to my desk, I spot the colorful folder.

Crap! I remove the release form and sit down next to him while he continues to tap away.

"I need you to sign this before you go, and I have cash for you."

He nods but doesn't look up. "No problem and thanks. I need to buy some books tonight."

The alarm on his phone chimes. "I'm almost done," he says and resets it. "Come on. Move your chair over."

I scoot it around so that I'm sitting right next to him. His thigh brushes mine, sending a warm ripple through me. The subtle scent of his cologne wafts over to greet me.

His screen fills with images—book covers—and I draw in a quick breath. They are stunning. He hits a button, and they queue up so that I can examine them one at a time. The first one has the two of us against a dark-blue color palette and a ghosted image of a city behind us. My name is in big lettering on the bottom, and a caption including my *#1 New York Times Best-Selling Author* status at the top.

I point at it. "How did you know about this?"

He looks at me like I'm less than smart.

"What?" I ask.

"There's this little company called Google."

I smile and give him a gentle elbow in the side.

"Hey, don't abuse the talent." He chuckles and flinches away.

My eyes gravitate to his lips. The thought of abusing him would never enter my mind. Kissing him . . . now that was a problem.

He spins me through the rest of the covers he's designed.

"So, do you like any of them?" he asks. His eyes search mine, wide and blue. Again he gives me the impression he's preparing for rejection of some kind.

Without thinking, I take his hand and squeeze it. "These are unbelievably good," I say sincerely. "I love them all. I'd be honored it you'd let me use one of them."

He shakes his head and smiles. It lights up his face. "Yeah. I'd like that."

His cell phone chimes again. He lets it ring for a second before he removes his hand from mine and shuts it off. "I gotta go."

"Okay," I lean back and reach for the envelope on my desk and hand it to him. "Thanks. You did an amazing job. But I need you to sign the release form." I feel like a broken record, asking again.

"Let me pack up first." He takes the envelope and powers down his laptop. "Just a sec." He heads over to get his backpack, and puts his stuff away including the envelope. He stares at the blank form.

"Do you have a pen?"

I grab one off my desk, and my heart trips in my chest. I'm serious about the bottle of wine, but I don't feel right taking it further. The thought of not seeing him again guts me. But having this flirtation is silly. I need to move on to real life. Where I can find a man my own age to date and possibly marry.

He fills out the form, except his signature, and stands.

I frown. "You need to sign it."

He slings his backpack over his shoulder, snatches the release form off the table, and gives me a crooked smile. "I realize that."

My eyes widen as I imagine him slipping out the door without giving me the right to use his photographs, and my blood pressure rises. "Then why aren't you signing it?"

His meets my gaze. "Because if I take it with me, I know I'll see you again. Say you'll have dinner with me, Jillian."

My heart nearly stops and my mouth drops open. I'm not sure I know why I'm so shocked other than I never really believed he'd be interested beyond a friendly chat. The look in his eyes tells me there's desire behind his request, and frankly, I'm stunned.

He tilts his head. "Say something."

I blink twice and my lips move but no sound comes out. "Yes," I finally manage to whisper.

A smile spreads across his face. He signs it and tucks the paper into his bag. "I promise to give it to you when I see you for dinner."

I plant my hands on my hips. "That's blackmail."

He winks. "Yes it is. But, I assure you my intentions are good. Besides, you said you were serious about that discussion over a bottle of wine, and from my perspective, I have more to lose."

"How's that?" I ask.

"You'll just have to find out for yourself. In the meantime, I'll send you all the book covers as an act of good faith." He heads toward the door. "Hey, I can't do dinner until early next week, but do you have plans on Saturday night?"

"Actually I do. Why?" He doesn't need to know it's a blind date from Matchup.com.

"I'm bartending at The Grasshopper in Morristown, and there's a good band playing. If you wanted to stop by and say hi, I could leave your name at the door to get you in and buy you a drink." He shrugs. "If you're interested. Otherwise, I'll be in touch."

Suddenly the gap in our ages feels as wide as the Atlantic Ocean.

My smile feels strained. "If anything changes, I'll let you know."

But I'd be lying if I said I wasn't tempted.

Chapter 9

Jillian

I SHIMMY INTO A flattering black dress and sit down in front of the mirror. Pushing back my hair, I take my earring and thread the gold wire through my earlobe, then repeat the process on the other side. The diamonds sparkle next to my cheeks.

After artfully applying a layer of makeup, I smile, pleased with what I see. My smile wavers when I think about my Matchup.com date. We're supposed to meet for dinner in Summit at seven-thirty. I pick up the scrap of paper I've written a few notes on. Gerald, forty-seven, six feet tall, lawyer, lives in Westfield, likes traveling and mountain biking. On paper he looks fine, but I'm suddenly wishing he was in his twenties with long blond hair.

I can't stop thinking about Raine. If I'm being honest with myself, I haven't stopped thinking about Raine since he left on Thursday. True to his word, he sent all the book covers to me on Thursday night at almost midnight. A blush spreads across my cheeks when I think about my visit to the spa for a bikini wax earlier today. At the last minute, I went for a full Brazilian, and I can't say it was for Gerald.

I toy with the idea of ending the date early so that I can drop by The Grasshopper. Then I remind myself: although unconfirmed, Raine's probably half my age.

Picking up the slip of paper again, I do my best to generate some enthusiasm.

My cell phone rings and I glance at the number. It's Brigitte. I managed to send her my synopsis on Wednesday morning which should satisfy her professionally for a while. I hope this is just a social call, or better yet, about the book cover.

"Hey, B."

"Good luck tonight! I can't wait to hear all the details tomorrow," she gushes. "What are you wearing?"

I gaze into the mirror at the sleeveless, scoop-neck black dress. Enough but not too much of my cleavage is displayed. A nice diamond necklace that matches my earrings lies subtly at my throat.

"The standard uniform."

"You don't sound very excited. What's the matter?"

I release a breath. "Nothing. He sounds nice over the phone, but you know how these things go. The chemistry could be crap when I get there."

"True, but try to be positive," She lowers her voice. "Don't forget to bring condoms in case you decide to go back to his place."

"B! Come on, really? No. I may write romance novels, but I don't believe everything I write."

"Yeah, but you haven't had real sex since Robert died, either," she counters.

I roll my eyes. "Define 'real.' It wasn't like Robert and I had a blazing sex life before that anyway. I'm used to my state of deprivation."

Brigitte clucks at me. "'Real' as defined by a man actually being attached to the penis."

"That's highly overrated in my opinion. I'd much rather stick to mechanical means if my last two dates are any indication of my alternative." I think of Raine and flush. He's the only temptation I've run across since I got married.

"Speaking of romance, I got the covers you sent."

I sit up straighter. Enthusiasm returns to my voice. "What did you think?"

"They're very good. There's no denying the guy has talent, Jillian. And he's hot with a capital *H*, but I still don't think we'll have much luck getting the publisher to approve them."

"Don't give up, B. I really want to use him," I say with conviction. Now that I've seen the covers, I can't imagine there being anything better suited.

She sighs. "Don't worry. I haven't. Call me tomorrow." Then she quickly adds, "And have fun on your date!"

"Will do." I hang up and eye the clock. Time to get moving.

***

After a deep breath, I walk into the bar at Huntley Tavern, an upscale restaurant known for its wine bar and Arts and Crafts theme. High tables are scattered in front of a line of booths in the two-story room which also boasts an open kitchen, a long bar covering one wall, and a fireplace at one end. The low-lit room is warm and welcoming.

I smile at the hostess and walk past her to find a seat at the bar. My eyes dart around looking for Gerald. Not seeing anyone who fits his description, I pull out my phone to make sure he hasn't canceled at the last minute.

My stomach tightens as I wonder if I can make it through a whole dinner. This makes my third blind date since I ventured into this online dating adventure. The first two were okay, but clearly not a match, no pun intended.

Someone taps me on the shoulder, and I turn.

"Jillian?" he asks. I recognize him from his picture, only I wonder how long ago it was taken. At forty-seven, Gerald looks much older than Robert did when he died at forty-eight.

I force a smile. "Gerald?"

"That's me." He points back to the hostess. "Our table is ready."

"Lead the way," I say and slip off the bar stool. In my high heels, I'm his height. Why did I think he would be taller? Rather than waiting for me, he walks ahead . . . way ahead. He's already lost points and we haven't even sat down yet.

I count to five and say a silent prayer asking for patience and fortitude.

They seat us in my favorite area on the covered porch. Removable window panels insulate us from the chill of the outside air.

"Are you a wine drinker?" he asks, picking up the menu.

I unfold the napkin onto my lap. "Yes, but I prefer red."

"Let me guess: Merlot?" he says with a snide undertone.

My jaw tightens and I will myself to relax. He seemed much nicer on the phone. "That depends if I'm drinking it with or without dinner. Usually, I prefer a nice Australian Shiraz or an Argentinian Malbec unless I'm having beef, and then I prefer something heavier like a Cabernet or a Cote de Rhone."

"I'm sorry. I didn't mean to offend you," he says, giving me a tight smile.

I return his smile with an equal degree of tightness. "You didn't."

"Why don't we order by the glass then," he says.

"Great idea." I clench my hands under the table and wonder if I'll make it to the appetizer. Beyond his comment rubbing me the wrong way, I already know he's not for me. His sports jacket doesn't hide the fact that his mountain biking isn't having the desired effect on his waistline—which I can overlook. It's the pinched look of unhappiness on his face that I can't. I've had enough misery touch my life, and I'm not in the market for any more.

The waitress takes our drink order and leaves.

"What kind of law do you practice?" I ask to kick it off.

He folds his hand in front of him and seems to relax. He would actually be handsome for an older man if he focused on something positive. "Intellectual property, mainly. There seems to be no shortage of work these days. Especially when it comes to piracy over the Internet. So, you're a writer?"

I smile and this time it's genuine. "Yes, I'm actually in the middle of writing a novel right now."

"Oh? What kind of novels do you write?"

My glass of Shiraz appears in front of me, as does a glass of scotch for him. I wonder why he's starting with hard liquor after he grilled me about the wine.

"Romance, mostly." I take a sip from my glass.

His eyebrows rise. "My ex-wife was a big romance reader. She was especially intrigued by that Fifty Shades of something trash."

My hackles rise and I take a breath. "I don't write erotica, but if I did, I wouldn't mind having that author's success or her following."

He takes a sip of his scotch. "But I'm sure your novels contain sex just the same?"

I narrow my eyes at him. "Generally, to sell a romance, it needs to contain sex to satisfy the reader, yes. And your point would be what?"

"Well, no point really. So you like sex then?" he asks and his stare slithers over my skin. How the hell do I answer a question like that?

"What are you asking? Are you wondering whether I like writing about it or having it?"

"Both." He gives me salacious look before taking another sip of his scotch.

"I think it's a little too soon to ask something so personal. Don't you?" My hand chokes my napkin under the table.

His lips purse and I wonder if he's trying to be sexy. "Just sizing up my chances for later." Then he winks at me.

My stomach turns. *As if!* "I take it you've never actually *read* a romance novel, have you?"

He sniffs in disgust. "No disrespect, but no, and I don't think I ever would. I prefer nonfiction."

Irritation swirls inside me, and I decide to switch topics.

"Your profile says you like to travel. Have you been anywhere interesting lately?"

"Not lately with the divorce and all. But I'm thinking my next trip will be to the Far East. I'd like to see China since its economic rise."

Finally, something that seems like a safe topic. I sit up in my seat. "That sounds interesting. I think I'd like to see Europe before I expand my horizons into the Far East."

"You haven't already been there? I'd think by your age you would have ventured into Europe several times."

By my *age*? I bristle at his assumption. "My husband wasn't much of an international traveler. Since I married young, that leaves a lot left for me to see." I have no reason to add that Robert had a morbid fear of flying.

"I suppose," he says. "What did your husband do?"

"He was a real estate developer in New York City and northern New Jersey."

He perks up with interest. "Oh. That must have left you sitting pretty. I can't imagine writing romance pays very well."

My anger flares at the audacity of this guy. "That would be none of your business, and as a *New York Times* best-selling author, I do quite well on my own." I drain my wine glass as the waitress approaches the table. "You know, I'm wondering if maybe we should skip dinner. I think we might have a compatibility issue."

A look of shock washes over his face. "Why would you say that? I thought we were getting along quite well."

"I don't understand how you could say that. You've insulted me from the moment I sat down."

"How have I done that? Was it my comment about romance novels?"

Seriously? I try to keep my jaw hinged shut. "If you don't know, that's a problem."

I place my napkin on the table, and push my seat back ready to leave.

"I find it appalling that you would end a perfectly good date. I can't imagine you're getting a lot of offers."

I freeze and stare at him, incredulous. "Excuse me?"

His eyes travel over me, and I cringe. "For one, I wouldn't be wearing such a formfitting dress when you could stand to lose ten pounds. Not to mention, I expected you to look . . . younger. I thought I was being generous offering to have sex with you."

My face flames red and fury rises inside me with the intensity of a force five hurricane. "Are you serious? I think you have it wrong. The situation is actually reversed. I'd be the one doing *you* a mercy, *grandpa!*"

I throw a twenty dollar bill on the table and storm out as my eyes fill with tears. As much as I don't want to believe his cruel words, they still cut me to the quick. He's obviously a bitter, miserable jerk. I'm surprised his wife didn't divorce him sooner for his pompous attitude.

Rounding the corner, I thrust the valet ticket and a five dollar bill at the boy standing there and dab my eyes with a tissue. With incredible speed, my SUV is waiting with the driver's side door open. I slide in and close the door. My hands grasp the wheel and I sit paralyzed. To think that I could've taken Raine up on his offer tonight instead. But as the thought enters my mind, Gerald's words come back. I look down at my midsection under my coat. Is this dress really too tight? My shoulders slump. The bulge is small but it's there. I glance into the mirror and stare at the crow's feet around my eyes and the fine lines around my mouth. A subtle honk comes from behind me. I step on the gas and pull away.

Tears blur my vision. I don't think I look that bad. I hunger for someone to take me into his arms and tell me it's okay. No, not just anyone. I hunger for the feel of Raine's arms, strong and sure. I think about the playful look in his eye as he gathered me up and held me close at the photo shoot, and I want that . . . right now.

I hate that I let those ugly words affect me and remind

myself that even though words have power, it's up to me to take that power away.

My car takes me through Summit and into Chatham, but it doesn't stop. It snakes its way all the way to Morristown. It's only eight forty-five when I park across the street from The Grasshopper. My hand trembles as I turn off the engine, and I check my makeup in the rearview mirror. I'm not thrilled with what I see, as if I'm looking at my face through creepy Gerald's eyes.

Glancing across the street, I see a group of young people, the same age as Raine, hanging outside the door next to the bouncer. Lights pulse on the other side of the darkened, steamy windows. The band must be on stage. The girls are all twig thin, dressed in short skirts with long flowing hair. They look like Jenny, and I look like I could be their mom.

I keep my seat belt on until tears once again cloud my vision. I feel foolish. I said I'd go to dinner with Raine next week. I must be crazy. What the hell am I doing here now? My discomfort grows as I think of walking in there with puffy eyes feeling like some old cougar on the prowl for young flesh. How desperate is that?

I sit immobile behind the wheel. If I go in, what good will come of it? I can only imagine how dark and noisy it will be, having to scream to be heard. Raine is bartending, so he won't have time for me anyway. I can't put him in the position of having to make up for my bad night. Worse yet, what if he rejects me, too?

After brushing away my tears, I start the engine. I tell the weaker part of me that wants to rush across the street into the bar to shut up and let the stronger part drive me home.

I haven't felt this lonely since Robert died.

Chapter 10

Raine

I POUR FOUR TEQUILA shots and almost miss the fifth glass. I swat Fiona's hand away from my ass as she passes behind me.

My first impulse is to yell at her, but we're reduced to using nonverbal communication. With the band playing, it's impossible to hear anyone not close enough to scream in your ear over the thump of the bass.

So I give her the evil eye.

She winks and grabs a bottle of Shiraz.

The bar vibrates underneath the shot glasses. I could use an aspirin to counteract the headache I'm getting from the pulsing lights. The two guys take their tequila and step away.

Two busty blondes belly up to take their place. One of them gives me a come hither look and leans over the bar. Her tits almost spill out of her shirt.

I squelch my urge to laugh and give her a sexy but compulsory smile. "What can I get for you?"

She wraps her hand around my neck and pulls me closer until her lips touch my ear. "Sex on the beach and a Merlot."

Smirking, I pull away and grab the vodka and peach schnapps. Bottles hit the bin under the bar next to me as I mix the cocktail. A quick pour of Merlot, and I hand them over.

"Fourteen dollars."

The girl smiles pretty at me and hands me a twenty with a slip of paper. "Keep the change." She and her friend melt back into the dense crowd.

I ring the sale, throw the extra six bucks into the tip jar, and open the paper.

Brandy 973-555-3568

Figures. I take the pen next to the register, write "Mac" on the back, and throw it into the jar next to the tips. At the end of the night, we'll count the number of come-ons. The bartender or server with the highest number gets an extra twenty bucks.

After serving up another couple of beers, I look down the length of the bar. Declan's brother, Liam, and Fiona are covering it with me. I know it's silly, but I'm jonesing to check in with my friend Sean who's working the door to see if Jillian has made an appearance. I wonder what her plans were for tonight and hope it wasn't a date. But if she was seriously involved with someone, I'm almost positive she would've said something. She strikes me as pretty honest.

I've been racking my brain since Thursday trying to decide where to take her to dinner. Someplace nice, but I can't lose sight of the fact that I need to gather a deposit for someplace to live. Of the three hundred bucks she paid me, I have a little over one hundred left after buying books. And tonight I should do really well.

I don't notice Fiona's fiery red hair until she's standing on her tiptoes next to me. She pulls my head down to get her mouth close enough to my ear. Her heavy brogue pierces through the pounding music. "Mac! Will ya stop yer woolgathering, and pay attention? I've been trying to signal ye for five feckin' minutes. Ye have comp'ny at the other end of the bar."

My heart leaps. I leave Fiona behind to cover for me as I stride down to the other end and stop dead. It's not Jillian.

My eyes narrow and I scream across the bar to be heard

since I refuse to get anywhere near her. "What are you doing here, Nessie?" I size up her sexy fashion model get-up. Glossy and beautiful, she's like a tainted chocolate — something that's pleasing to the palate, but makes you sick as hell after you eat it.

Vanessa glares at me. "Don't call me that."

"It's better than 'bitch,'" I say, feeling less than charitable.

She takes a FedEx envelope out of her purse and shoves it at me. "I was trying to be nice."

"How did you even know I'd be here?" I ask, and snatch it away from her. There's only one thing this could be — the paperwork for my internship in New York City over the Christmas break. All my regular mail goes to a post office box in town. It makes it easier when you move as much as I have. But FedEx won't deliver to post office boxes.

"I called Mikey to find out where you were staying, and he told me you'd be here tonight," she says and glances around with her lips puckered in a sour look. "It didn't take you long to come back here. Are you sleeping with Fiona again, too?"

I grit my teeth. "It's no longer any of your business who I sleep with. Got that?"

A good-looking guy with dark hair emerges from the crowd behind Vanessa, and drapes his arms possessively around her. He's glossy, just like her. Fucker probably drives a Mercedes. Leaning in, he whispers something in her ear, and she smiles.

My blood pressure shoots up. _That bitch!_ "So, maybe I should be asking who _you're_ screwing. How long were you cheating on me, Loch Ness?"

The guy's head snaps up. "Hey, man. Back down."

I put the FedEx envelope under the bar, ball my hands at my sides, and try to swallow down my humiliation. "You don't have the right to speak to me, so fuck off!"

Her green eyes blaze. "Does it really matter? It's been over with us for a long time."

I lean across the bar and feel my brow pinch in anger. I

keep my voice as low as I can for her to still hear me. "Oh, really? I thought things were going pretty well until you turned into a total fucking bitch about two months ago."

She leans into me. The vein in her neck that pulses when she's pissed is jumping wildly under her skin. "You know what, Raine? It took me that long to figure out what a loser you really are, and that you're only good for one thing. When that stopped, there wasn't anything left."

My nostrils flare, and my nails bite into my palms. "Get out before I have you thrown out," I say through gritted teeth. My cheeks burn as I stalk away. I leave Liam and Fiona behind the bar and press my way through the crowd into the employee locker room. I need to cool down before I hit something or someone. Too late. I slam my fist into one of the metal lockers and leave a dent, welcoming the sting on my knuckles.

I swallow past the lump in my throat. Her words resonate with what Jenny said to me on the driveway, and it hurts. A lot. Is that what Jillian sees when she looks at me, too? A hot, young guy that she'd like to fuck? Only good for one thing? Someone not to be seen with in public? Did she really have something else to do tonight? Maybe she only said yes to the date next week because of the release form. What do I really have to offer her anyway? I hoped good conversation and companionship would also mean something. Jillian certainly doesn't need me for my money, and if everything goes well, I'll have a white collar job at some point and make a decent living anyway. Isn't that enough? Isn't that good enough?

I don't understand it. I'm not a bad person, a slob, or painfully boring. I'm going to school, trying to better myself as fast as I can and be productive. So why is it that people always try to make me feel worthless?

I check the clock. It's already midnight. If Jillian planned to stop by, she would've been here by now. I hate to admit it, but I could've used the boost.

My mind shifts to the slips of paper in the come-on jar, but going there would only make me feel worse and give credence to what Vanessa said.

A tear slides down my cheek. I wipe it away and feel like an idiot.

Chapter 11

Raine

AFTER MY ENCOUNTER with Vanessa and a couple of shots to calm my nerves, the rest of the evening flies by in a cloudy haze. I breathe a sigh of relief when the clock strikes two and we shuffle the last of the patrons out the front door.

I'm alone in the employee locker room counting my tips, including the twenty for the come-on pool, when Fiona walks in. I won by a wide margin. Financially, it's a good night.

She sidles up to me as I stuff my take into my pocket. "Mac, ya look like ya lost yer best friend tonight. Let Fi make it better," she says, rubbing up against me with a wicked glint in her blue eyes. After the night I had, I'm tempted to take her up on her offer to soothe my insecurities—but only for about a second and a half. There are a whole host of reasons why that wouldn't be a good idea. Not least of which is because I have my sights set on Jillian. I've already decided I'm going to follow it through as far as I can take it. The worst she can do is turn me down.

I shake my head. "I can't, Fi. I'm sorry."

She moves back and crosses her arms over her chest. "Why the hell not?"

I'm in no mood. "Because I'm interested in someone else."

Her eyes flash and she purses her lips. "Sean mentioned you'd left a woman's name at the door. But I don't think she came, did she?"

"None of your goddamn business, Fi. If you want to keep me as a friend, respect that it's over between us," I snap at her, officially reaching my limit of taking other people's shit for the night. Pushing past her, I head for the exit. I need out.

The drinks I had two hours ago have worn off, and the cool night sobers me even more as I head to my truck.

Halfway across Morristown, I realize I left my wallet in my locker at work.

"Fuck!" I bang the heel of my hand against the steering wheel in frustration. I never do that sort of thing. Between Vanessa's visit and my run-in with Fiona, my brain is scrambled. As long as I can get home without being pulled over by the cops I should be fine. I can pick it tomorrow morning.

When I pull in the driveway, the house is dark but my father's car is missing. I lock my cash in the glove compartment before I go inside and thank the Lord for small favors. I'm happy I'll make it to sleep without needing to cross anymore proverbial land mines.

I brush my teeth, but I'm too tired to shower. I shed my jeans and drop into bed. I swear I pass out the moment my head hits the pillow.

My door bursts open and I spring upright; my heart hammers as I try to make sense out of what's happening. The light from the hall blinds me a moment before I'm caught in a chokehold. I'd forgotten to put the chair in front of the door. I claw at my father's arm.

"Where is it?" he hisses in my ear, and a cloud of whiskey assaults my senses. My father's arm tightens around my throat.

I squeeze out one word at a time as I struggle against him. "What ... are ... you ... talking ... about?" I try to find some leverage, but my position on the bed makes it impossible. No doubt that was his intention. Even in the darkness, stars dot my vision and I struggle to breathe, trying not to panic. I tear at his forearm to get him to release me.

"Your mother's engagement ring," he grinds out. He loosens his grip.

"Don't ... have ... it," I choke. With unbelievable strength, he shoves me off the bed and I land on my hands and knees, gasping for air.

"I don't believe you." A swift blow to the back of my head sends me sprawling. My teeth slam together with such force I hear something crack before I collapse in a heap on the floor. My one and only filling lands on my tongue and I spit it out. Excruciating pain travels over my skull and shoots down my back. Panic grips me. I have to get out of here before I pass out or he kills me.

"Do you know how much I hate you?" he snarls. I crawl away and stagger to my feet. I move into a defensive position and turn around, but I can't steady myself. The club he's using lands with force against my ribs, and I hear another crack as the wind is knocked from my lungs. I stumble in a slow circle and groan.

"I never wanted you! I begged Selka to get an abortion. But she wouldn't listen," he says, more to himself than to me, but the words slam straight into my core nonetheless and I wince. Of all the horrible things he's said to me since my mom died, this was the worst. Unable to hold my guard up, I fall backward when his fist lands on my right eye.

"She promised she wouldn't love you more than me, and she lied!" he says. "Now, give me that ring!"

I drag myself back onto my feet, and something snaps inside of me. My anger rises up in a tidal wave and adrenaline floods through me in one colossal burst. I refuse to let him take another thing from me ... or allow him to ever hit me

70

again. Our hate is mutual. My hand finds the wooden chair, and I grasp the leg firmly in my palm. I ignore the white-hot agony in my side and swing it at his head with all my strength. My vision swims as I make contact. The wood shatters and the chair bursts into pieces.

Time moves in fits and starts.

I vaguely remember pushing past his collapsed body, grabbing my pants with the keys still in the pocket and running for the door. I can't see right, but I'm aware enough to know I want to be in the emergency room.

A vast field of swaying poppies lies ahead of me. I want to run through them, but I'm afraid to end up like Dorothy and her crew in *The Wizard of Oz* asleep in the field of flowers. All the images are juxtaposed on top of the dark road ahead of me in a continuous movie as I drive. My head feels like it might split open to liberate my throbbing brain. It hurts to breathe, but the sun feels so good on my face.

I think I park. I'm not sure as I stand looking at the keys in my palm. The lights are so bright here, but I can't really see. My knees go weak, and they fold under me as my world goes upside down.

"Someone get a gurney!" I hear through a thick, white fog and then everything goes black.

Chapter 12

Jillian

"UHH." A groan of sleep-filled frustration passes through my lips as my hand fumbles across my nightstand looking for my offending cell phone.

"Is this Jillian Grant?" An unfamiliar female voice asks.

"Yes," I mumble into the pillow.

"Um, I'm sorry to bother you, but I'm hoping you can help me."

I catch a glimpse of the red numerals on my alarm clock. "At 3:30 a.m.?" It feels like I just went to bed—because I did. After a bottle of wine, a pint of rum raisin, and a *Downton Abbey* marathon to ease the memory of my date, my head didn't hit the pillow until 2 a.m.

The woman releases a breath on the other end of the phone, and I snap awake. "Wait a second, who is this?" *Holy Shit, please don't tell me someone died.*

"This is Nurse Swenson at Memorial Hospital—"

"Oh, my God." I sit up thinking the worst as my mind flashes to Vera. "Please don't tell me—"

"No. Oh, no! I'm so sorry, it's nothing life threatening," she says, suddenly backpedaling to calm me. "We have a young man, a John Doe, here at the hospital. Your business card was the only thing on him. He has no I.D. and we're hoping you can help us identify him."

My heart lurches. *It can't be, can it?* "Blond hair? Mid-20s?"

"Yes."

Raine.

"Is he okay?"

"He has a concussion and is a little confused. He doesn't seem to remember his name. It looks like he was in a fight. No broken bones, just some severe contusions. You know him?"

My heartbeat picks up steam, and I carry the phone to the closet and pull out a pair of jeans. "Yes, his name is Raine MacDonald. I'm coming."

"Are you family?"

Before I can stop myself, I lie. "Yes."

"How are you related?"

I don't even hesitate. "I'm his aunt." I thought about saying his mother, but that would've been way too weird. At least "aunt" leaves the possibility that he isn't as young as I'm afraid he might be. Not to mention, the thought of being anyone's mother scares the crap out of me.

"Oh, thank God we called you. We need to keep him until his test results are back. Do you know if he has insurance? We have some paperwork."

Shit. I have no idea.

"We'll figure it out when I get there." I hang up.

I cast a glance at the jeans in my hand. They aren't "Mom" jeans, thank God, but they aren't super sexy, either. I pull out my favorite pair of high-heeled sandals. Yup. At least as his aunt, I don't have to dress dowdy like my sister Kitty. Fuck it. I grab the clingy top — the one that hides my baby muffin top. I do the best I can to fix my face so I don't look like I just rolled out of bed. My feet carry me down the stairs and into my car.

Without breaking land speed records, I hyperventilate all the way to Memorial Hospital. How the heck am I returning to this place for another person in the same week? Concern for Raine consumes me. I can barely consider him a friend at this point, yet I can't deny I care . . . too much.

The night nurse on Raine's floor looks up as I scoot in, putting on my best "concerned aunt" face.

"Hi, Nurse Swenson called about my nephew Raine. Concussion?"

She glances at her roster and hands me a pass. "Room 512."

It hits me as I round the corner, and I screech to a stop outside of Raine's door. Does he even expect to see me?

Too late now. I swallow and peer inside.

My hand flies up to cover my mouth, but not before I gasp. His blond hair lies matted around his head on the pillow. Shades of purple and blue bloom around one of his closed eyes, and his bottom lip is cut and swollen. His skin looks pale and sickly under the fluorescent lights. I step inside, and he opens his eyes . . . rather, he opens one of them.

"Jillian?" he whispers hoarsely.

I smile reflexively hearing my name, and gather the courage to go to him.

"Hey." My voice is soothing even to my own ears. I reach down and clasp his hand in one of mine and sweep back a strand of his hair with the other. "What happened?"

He winces and tries to swallow. "My father . . . drunk . . . cold-cocked me." He stops and licks his split lip. "Was sleeping . . . fight . . . ended up here . . . no phone . . . no wallet . . . they didn't know who else to call. Sorry to wake you."

His *father* did this to him? Dumbfounded, my hand squeezes his harder, but my mouth won't form words. I just open and close it a couple of times before I clamp it fully shut. I want to kill his father. Yes, for the first time in my life, I want to physically harm someone.

His eyes dart to mine, and fill, glassy and pleading. "I'm sorry." His fear is palpable, and I realize he needs me to say something . . . right this second.

I lean in and kiss his forehead. "Shh. It's okay. You have

nothing to be sorry for. You didn't do anything wrong," I whisper and rest my cheek against his hair, his hand still in mine. "Don't worry about anything. Okay?"

His head nods underneath my cheek. "Okay," he whispers.

"Do you have anywhere to go?" I ask, and continue to stroke his hair to soothe him with my free hand. My fingers are almost numb as he crushes my other hand in his.

He shakes his head. *He has nowhere to go.* The thought unexpectedly guts me. I clasp my hand over my mouth to stifle a sob that threatens to rip from my lungs. I don't trust myself to speak. Loosening my grip, I release my hand from my mouth and draw in a deep breath, letting it out slowly. "You'll come home with me then. Can you do that?"

Very slowly he nods his head. I wipe my fingers over my eyes before I take in another deep breath. I don't want him to see the tears.

I look down into his half-shut eyes. "I said I was your aunt to get in here. Don't blow my cover, all right?"

He squeezes my hand harder, and his one eye opens the rest of the way. It flashes a not-so-happy sentiment at me, shattering his moment of naked vulnerability.

"What the hell?" he says in a raspy whisper. It didn't occur to me that my lie would piss him off. Would it be so bad to have me as an aunt? It's not like I said I was his mother.

I cringe and give him a guilty shrug. "Sorry, it was the best I could do in my semi-comatose state when they called."

He snorts and shakes his head.

"Hi. You must be Jillian." I turn toward the voice behind me. The nurse comes at me with an outstretched hand. "Nurse Swenson. I just wanted to check in to see if we need to file a police report for your nephew's altercation."

An aggravated huff comes from the bed.

"He still doesn't seem to remember what happened," I lie. "When can I take him home?" I'm dying to get us both away from the antiseptic smell I hate so much.

She looks over my shoulder. "That depends. We stitched up his scalp, and the X-rays showed no fractures to his skull. But he really should stay the rest of the night for observation."

A hoarse growl comes from behind me. "I wanna leave."

The nurse purses her lips, and turns her gaze back to me. "If you take him home and he falls asleep, you'll need to wake him periodically for the rest of the night and then bring him back tomorrow morning for a follow-up with the doctor."

I nod vigorously. "Got it."

"I'll need insurance information in order to process his release."

"No problem. I'll meet you out at the desk. Can he get dressed?"

"Yes, he's free to dress," she says unhappily.

I turn to Raine after the door latches shut. "You wouldn't happen to have insurance, would you?"

He scowls at me and shakes his head. *Just great.*

I grasp the sides of my head. "Fine. I'll be back."

I arrange to pay Raine's hospital bill personally, since we can't produce insurance for him. We figure out that he drove to the hospital—I'm still wondering how—and decide to leave his truck there until he's able to drive tomorrow. But not before he retrieves a duffel bag he has on the floor by the front seat and an extra change of clothes from boxes in the back.

Raine sits silently on the passenger side of my car, staring out the window. He hasn't said much since we left the hospital.

"Are you okay?" I ask quietly.

"I'll live. Just tired."

His hair and clothes are still bloody. I bite my lip not wanting to press him for details.

"Why did you say you were my aunt?" His voice echoes in the dark next to me. It holds an edge of anger I don't understand, putting me on the defensive.

Seriously? "Because I know the drill in that place all too well. Family members get full access to the patients. Why are you so upset about it anyway?"

He doesn't answer, just stares out the window.

"You're not that old," he says softly.

For some reason, instead of being flattered by his response, I'm mad. "Yes. I am that *old*. You realize I was probably like eighteen when you were born, right? In case you haven't done the math, that's old enough for me to be your mother, much less your aunt. So, yes, goddamn it, I am that old." A flush rises in my face, and I realize my diatribe is more for myself than for him. God, I hope I wasn't any more than eighteen when he was born. Stubbornly, I refuse to think the gap in our ages could be any wider. That's already enough to make me flinch.

"Is that the way you think of me? As a dumb kid? As your *son?*" Hurt is laced through his murmured words, and my heart softens. I want nothing more than to put my arms around his broad shoulders and soothe him, and not in an aunt-like way.

Exhaustion grips me, and I slump. "No. That's not how I think of you at all," I say softly, and touch his shoulder, giving it a gentle squeeze.

"Good. That's good," he whispers into the window, still twisted away from me.

"What happened tonight? You don't have to tell me. But I'd like to know."

He snorts. "Honestly, I'm not really sure. When I got home after my shift ended at the bar, he wasn't home. I was beat, so I collapsed into bed and fell asleep." He pauses and swallows, continuing on slowly. "The next thing I remember is the smell of whiskey in my face and getting nailed on the back of the head. He thought I had something and demanded it back." He hesitates. "If I'd been awake, he would've never gotten the jump on me or hit me with that bat."

"He hit you with a baseball bat?" I yell, tightening my grip on the steering wheel. My pulse jumps and I hunger for blood.

"More like a billy club, and it wasn't the first time," he whispers and touches the back of his head, flinching on contact.

"He could've killed you!" I shout, feeling helpless and homicidal.

"Please don't yell. It hurts."

"I'm sorry. I'm furious that your own father could do this to you," I hiss, trying to keep my voice low.

"It wasn't always like this . . . Can we save the rest for tomorrow?"

"Sure we can." Without thinking twice, I find his hand and take it. He twines his fingers in mine and squeezes.

"Thanks for everything, Jillian."

Suppressing a yawn, I smile weakly in the dark and try to wrap my head around the fact that I'm about to have a house guest.

Chapter 13

Jillian

DAWN IS DUE TO BREAK in less than an hour when I get him to the guest room. His injuries look worse in the light, marring his handsome face and obscuring any resemblance to Drew. I shove back another surge of anger toward his father. He sets the duffel on the bed and seems unsteady on his feet.

I point to the private bathroom. "Everything you'll need is in there. Shampoo and conditioner are in the shower, there's a new toothbrush and toothpaste in the drawer next to the sink, and extra towels are in the closet."

He turns his back to me and his shoulders droop as he fumbles with the zipper of his bag. "I need help." His voice is small and weary, catching me off guard.

"Um, sure. What do you need me to do?"

He sits on the bed, and wipes his eye—the one that's not swollen shut. "I want to take a shower, but I... I'm feeling dizzy. I'm afraid I'll pass out or something."

Alarm bells sound in my head. *Does he want... ? Is he asking... ?*

"Can you help me?"

Keeping my voice steady, I ask softly, "Are you asking me to come into the shower with you?"

79

He nods, and dips his head. "I'm sorry. I know that sounds weird. I'm not being weird. Please don't think that. I just want to feel clean." His voice breaks and his hand trembles as he raises it to cover his mouth. Nurse Swenson warned me the concussion could cause erratic emotional responses for a while. His brain had a bit of a jostling. Tomorrow they want to check for any additional swelling.

I walk over and sit down next to him. Without thinking, I rub his back in gentle circles over the soft cotton of his T-shirt. "Wait here for a moment, okay?"

He nods without looking up.

When I turn the corner out of the guest room, my pulse quickens. I have an idea. I rummage through my drawers and pull out my one-piece bathing suit — the one with the built-in tummy reducer. Then I pause and think: Robert's clothes. Still neatly packed in boxes, I never got around to donating or discarding them. Raine is a bit taller and more muscular, but he should fit in Robert's bathing trunks. I locate the box in the second guest room closet and pull them out. I've set a new speed record. The whole adventure takes me less than five minutes.

Raine is still on the bed where I left him. I kneel down in front of him and take his hand. "To make this more comfortable and keep our sense of modesty, I found you these." I hand him the swim trunks and hold up my bathing suit. "This one is for me. Good?"

He gives me a half smile and nods.

"How about I help you down to your underwear, and then you take it from there while I change and come back?"

"Okay." He stands, and moves to remove his shirt. Mid-movement he groans and winces.

"Here, sit. Let me."

He obeys, and I take the hem of his soft T-shirt in my hands and lift it slowly over his head to reveal the rippled contours of his torso. I try not to gasp at the angry purple welt on his ribs. After discarding the shirt on the bed, I tenderly pass my fingertips over his bruised ribs. His eyes lock on mine. I press, and he screams.

"Shit, Raine! Your ribs are *broken*." How the hell did the hospital miss that?

"I know."

Could this get any worse? I wonder.

"I'll tape you up after we shower," I say evenly. "Can you stand?"

He gets up, and I unbutton his jeans. I steady my fingers and carefully sneak them under the waistband and separate the denim from the cotton of his underwear, so when I shimmy them over his hips I won't take his briefs with me.

He helps and then sits down. I lower his jeans to the ground and free his legs. They're covered in soft, light blond hair. The swim trunks are in his hand.

"I'll be right back. Change while I'm gone?" I say, and then race back to my room and strip naked.

I wrestle my body into my bathing suit and return to him.

Raine is wearing the trunks when I walk in. He's lying on his side, curled up in a fetal position on the bed. I pass by into the bathroom and turn on the hot water. This guest room has the most generous shower, a walk-in with multiple heads.

When I return, Raine's eyes are closed. I brush back a clump of his matted hair. "Hey, are you still awake? You still want that shower?"

"Yes," he murmurs and grimaces when he tries to sit up. He clutches his head with his hand, and manages to get upright. Taking him by the arm, I gently lead him into the bathroom and underneath the warm water in the shower.

I wet my hair and push it back out of my way then position him under the spray. "Can I wash your hair for you?" He bites his lip and nods. His vulnerability breaks my heart. "Let's rinse the blood out first."

He turns his back to me and tips his head back. The warm water cascades through his hair turning it from tawny-blond to brown. Gently, I guide the water from his roots to his ends to get rid of the dried red reminder of his beating, careful not to put too much pressure on his skull and the tender lumps and stitches I feel under my fingers.

I squeeze shampoo into my hand then spread it through his hair, lightly rubbing it up into a rich lather. I focus on running the soap through his hair without spending too much time at the roots. "You can rinse now."

The lather snakes down the hollow of his spine in a soapy river.

"Conditioner?"

He nods.

I spread a small dollop through his hair, and rinse. With that done, I turn my attention to his body. Soaping up a pouf with shower gel, I start at his shoulders and work my way down the muscled landscape of his back until I reach the swim trunks.

Unprompted, he turns and I wash his arms and his chest, avoiding his purple ribs. Moving the pouf lower, I glide it over his sculpted abs down to his waistband and stop. To my artistic eye, even injured, I can't help but appreciate every line, curve, and ripple that I touch. I'm having trouble imaging what could drive a father to break and batter his own son like this.

"Can you . . . ? Um, never mind." I discard the idea of asking him to lift his leg. He's unstable enough on his feet, no reason to endanger him further. Instead, slowly, I sink to my knees in front of him, draw in a breath, and hold it. My face falls in line with the healthy bulge hidden underneath the swim trunks. Warmth unrelated to the heated shower spray spreads across my cheeks. *Lord, help me.* Pushing away my discomfort at being this intimately close to him, I cast my eyes downward. Brownish-blue bruises and scraped skin cover both kneecaps. His injuries tug at my heart. Carefully, I run the soapy ball over one well-defined leg and then the other.

Something close to relief fills me as I rise.

Switching to a face cloth, I take the corner and gently dab the ugly bruises on his face and the cut on his lip. He takes my hand as I finish, and brings it to his lips. I suck in a breath.

"Thank you," he says as his lips graze my knuckles.

"Can you finish from here?" I whisper.

"I think so." He swallows. "Will you . . . ?"

"Just tell me what you need." My voice is soft and encouraging despite the sudden rigidity of my spine.

He hooks his thumb inside the elastic waistband of the swim trunks. "Will you help me take these off? You don't have to look."

Oh, Sweet Jesus. "Sure, take this." I hand him the pouf and step behind him. Better getting an accidental eyeful of backside than . . .

Sinking to my knees, I stare at the tile and reach up to find the thick elastic band by touch. He helps me glide them down over his hips, and I take it from there. My fingers gently graze over the soft hair on his legs as I work them down to the shower floor.

"Thanks," he says, stepping out of them.

Keeping my eyes averted, I place the trunks in the back corner of the shower and step out of the steamy water. My heart rate slows as I hit the cooler air of the bathroom. Grabbing two towels on my way out, I wrap one around my wet bathing suit, and fashion the other into a turban around my head before heading for the door.

"Jillian?"

"Yeah?"

"Will you stay in here until I'm done? You know, just in case . . ."

"Okay." I plant myself on top of the closed toilet seat. I want nothing more than to get the cold, wet spandex away from my body, but I'm more concerned about Raine. My comfort is a small price to pay for his safety.

His masculine form moves stiffly behind the curtain of steam clouding the shower glass. I hear him groan a couple of times over the sound of the pounding spray.

The water shuts off, and he peeks around the glass door. "Can you bring me my duffel bag? Please."

"Sure." I ease off the toilet seat and out the door. It's sitting right where he left it on the side of the bed. I loop my hand through the handles and put it down outside the bathroom door. He peers out through the crack, and slides it inside. "Do you need my help?" I ask softly.

He hesitates before saying, "Thanks, but I can manage from here." I can't help but think he's too embarrassed to ask, but decide not to push him.

"Will you be all right for five minutes while I change?" I ask as he closes the door.

He nods and the door shuts with a soft click.

I return in yoga pants and an oversized T-shirt. He's curled up on the duvet in pajama bottoms and a clean T-shirt with his damp hair fanned out on the pillow. He watches as I walk in. His black eye is taking on a yellowish hue.

"Is there anything I can get for you?"

His head shakes imperceptibly, and his eyes close. For some reason, I can't let him sleep uncovered. Retrieving a blanket from the closet, I place it on top of him then turn off all but one small light visible through the crack in the bathroom door.

Crouching down next to him, I whisper, "I'll be back in an hour or so, just to make sure you wake up."

"Okay."

As I approach the threshold, his voice comes from behind me. "Jillian?"

"Yeah?"

"Will you stay with me?"

Thank God the darkness hides the surprise on my face. Warmth floods my chest. I can't remember the last time I comforted anyone.

"Sure." I set the alarm on the nightstand, and slide in behind him on the queen-size bed. Without hesitating, I snuggle into the hollow of his back and rest my hand on his hip, offering him my warmth. He smells fresh from the shower, the scent of my lavender shampoo clinging to his damp hair.

He takes my hand, twines his fingers into mine, and pulls my arm more tightly around him until my hand rests next on his stomach. His gesture ignites both my desire and my need to protect him.

"'Night, Jillian," he whispers, and drops off to sleep. He breathes in a steady rhythm, and after my heart quells, I soon follow.

Chapter 14

Raine

I REACH UP TO grasp my throbbing temple and groan. My eyes open into slits. Sun streams underneath the half-closed shades and I wince from the brightness. I'm desperate for something to dull the pain.

A soft hand touches my naked back. I remember being too hot during the night and the searing pain of removing my T-shirt, and then later, pulling the blanket back over me when the air-conditioning got too cold.

"You awake?" Jillian asks from behind me and removes her hand.

"Barely," I mumble. My skin tingles where her fingers grazed me.

"Roll over and let me see your eyes," she says, all business. "I want to check your pupils."

I roll onto my back and try to ignore the agony in my ribs. "Can you tape me up this morning?" I grit out through the shooting pain.

"Oh, God. I'm so sorry! I forgot to do it last night."

"It's okay, so did I."

My eyes feel heavy, and I know one is in dire shape from the way it won't open all the way. It hurts when I breathe, but at least I didn't puncture a lung. Been there, done that the last time my ribs were broken. That really was a sports injury.

I look up to find Jillian hovering over me. Her eyes meet mine, but she's assessing them, not gazing into them with interest. God, I must look a mess. I can't believe she even allowed me into her home. Not to mention, I must've been tripping last night when I asked her to take a shower with me. She must think I'm a nut case.

"They look good," she says, and I close them again.

Her fingertip travels over my cheek and my eyes snap back open. The feel of it is so intimate, something stirs down lower. I bite my lip, willing it to stop. On top of everything else, I don't want her to think I'm a sex-crazed lunatic. You'd think I hadn't gotten laid in a year.

My eyelids slide shut again. I still can't believe I'm here. I can't believe that piece of shit who calls himself my father came at me with a billy club. Who does that? Sick motherfucker. Nice bonus to know he also wishes my mom aborted me. I feel the frown etch deep between my eyebrows. Jillian's finger traces the furrows. I want her to stop, but I don't want her to stop. This connection feels good, but I realize I might be imagining the whole thing. We still barely know each other.

She clears her throat and takes her finger away. "Are you in pain? Can I get you some ibuprofen?"

"That would be great," I say and then cough. I regret it as pain spears my midsection.

She eases off her side of the bed. "Try not to move until I get back. Your appointment is in ninety minutes. Will you make it?"

"Yeah." My mouth is dry and gritty. The thought of getting up is unbearable. I hurt worse now than when I went to bed.

Before I know it, Jillian's back, helping me to sit up.

I swallow the two pills, and drain the glass. The cold water soothes my parched throat.

"Ready for me to tape you?" She takes one of the rolls of tape she's brought with her and pulls out a thick strip.

I eye her warily. "Where did you learn to tape up broken ribs?"

She smiles. "Jenny's field hockey games."

The pressure of the tape feels good.

When she's done, we agree to meet downstairs after I turn down her offer to help me get dressed. I'm still choking down my embarrassment from last night.

Twenty minutes later I'm sitting with Jillian in her kitchen at the island. Orange juice, a plate of eggs, and toast sit in front of me while Jillian just drinks coffee—which I despise. I drink tea, like my mom. But rather than ask for it, I skip it this morning.

"Talk to me. Last night wasn't the first time your father . . . hit you." Jillian raises her mug to her lips, and takes a sip. She makes it a statement rather than a question.

I take a swallow of OJ and grunt. I'm not sure I'm ready for this conversation. Revealing my sordid family history isn't high on my list of favorite subjects. Not to mention, it usually dredges up my fury over my father's betrayal. Because of him, I am where I am, rather than where I should be.

Jillian arches a brow at me. "I'm listening."

"Did you just give me a 'mom' look?" I say, frowning.

She narrows her eyes. "That would be impossible, since you already told me I wasn't old enough to be your aunt or your mother. Or are you taking that back?"

The way she says it makes me chuckle. "No. I'm not taking it back. If you were my aunt or my mom, I'd have to protect you from all my horndog friends."

"Was that a backhanded compliment?" she asks as her golden eyes sparkle.

"Actually, it was a front-handed compliment. Will you do me a favor? Stop obsessing over your age. You're an attractive woman, period. If you're thinking men my age won't date you, think again. True, some won't, but I can guarantee you, plenty will. As I recall, I asked you to dinner, didn't I? Now, let's move on." I finish with a wave of my hand.

Her head snaps back and her mouth falls open. "I'm not sure I know how to respond to that."

"Don't. That's the whole point. You don't need to respond to it. Just accept it, and feel good."

She shakes her head like she's clearing it. "Well, okay then." She gives me that serious look again. "I think you were about to tell me about your father."

"Not really." I take a forkful of eggs before they get cold and chew. I don't owe her an explanation.

"*Raine?*" Okay, that was definitely a "mom" tone.

"*Jillian?*" I mimic and finish my eggs and the rest of my toast.

She releases a breath and throws up her hands. "Fine."

I'm being an asshole and I know it. I release a breath of my own, put my fork down, and pop up off of my barstool. "Jillian, let's get something straight before I answer your question," I say more defensively than I really mean to. Not thinking, I run my fingers through my hair and wince as I pace in front her, unable to keep still. "I'll tell you when and if I'm ready, but not out of obligation. If I tell you, it's as a friend, because I choose to and because I want you to know. But let me be clear: I'm not a stray cat you found on the side of the road. And I don't want your pity. If you offered me a place to stay based on that, then I can't stay here. I'm not a charity case. That's not what or who I am."

Jillian's eyes are wide and her lips are parted. I can't tell if I've pissed her off or just surprised her. Scowling, I continue to pace nervously with my arms crossed over my chest. "Say something, Jillian. I need you to say something . . ."

Her hand shoots out and she grabs my forearm. "Stop, please. Just stand still for a moment." She doesn't look pleased with me, and now I'm the one who's surprised.

I freeze, hoping I didn't go too far. "What?"

Her eyes soften. "I don't think that's what you are . . . a

charity case. But I do think you need help, and I don't want you to be afraid to ask for it. I'm happy to help you. You can stay here as long as you need to."

I dig into my pocket and pull out the wad of cash I made last night and start to count it. "I'm not a freeloader, Jillian. I can pay you some rent. I think I have a couple hundred—"

She grabs me again, this time more firmly. "No. I don't want your money. I don't need it. I just want to give you a place to stay while you need one. Okay? All I ask in return is respect for me and my home. And if it means that much to you, I'm sure we can think of something appropriate at some point."

"It does. I may not have much, but I have my dignity and I have my word."

She squeezes my forearm gently. "That's enough for me, and that's more than a lot of people have to offer."

Her answer warms my insides. I fight the urge to pull her into a hug when she drops her hand. She doesn't understand how much this means to me. Those things were never enough for Vanessa, or anyone else for that matter, not by a long shot. Whenever Vanessa looked at me, I couldn't help but feel she was sizing up my future potential. Like an investment in her portfolio. Nine times out of ten, I felt like I came up short.

For the first time in months, I can breathe. And I feel safe here. But I meant what I said. Now there are two things I won't do to keep a roof over my head: pimp out my body or my dysfunctional family history.

Jillian glances at her watch. "You know what? I think we need to save the rest of this conversation for later if I plan to get you to your doctor's appointment on time."

We move to leave the kitchen and she stops me. "I won't make you tell me."

I give her a crooked smile. "I know."

Chapter 15

Jillian

I GLANCE AT RAINE in the rearview mirror as he follows me back to my house in his pickup. We stopped by the bar on the way home to pick up his wallet.

The doctor cleared him of any further head injuries and gave him enough painkillers for his ribs to last a couple of days. I popped up to see Vera quickly while Raine finished his appointment, but not before I shared my displeasure with the doctor about the hospital missing Raine's broken ribs in the first place. Vera was awake, and I was thrilled to see that she was doing even better. She was drifting off to sleep when I left. I almost feel optimistic.

I dial Kitty.

She picks up on the first ring. "Hey, Kitty. Don't kill me, but I need to cancel for later." I have a standing invitation every Sunday for dinner, a family tradition for as long as I can remember.

"Why? What's up?" my sister asks.

I take a deep breath and pray for minimal prying. "I have an unexpected house guest who's not feeling well."

"Who's staying with you?"

My jaw tightens. "A new friend. Someone with some cracked ribs."

"Jillian . . . Is it a man? I'm not sure I like the sound of this," she says with an unmistakable note of disapproval.

"Kitty, I'm old enough to make my own decisions. He's not an axe murderer, so please stop mothering me."

"It's not that young gigolo Jenny told me about, that cover model, is it?" she says in a low voice.

My hackles rise. "I'm sorry, what did you say?"

"Jillian. I think you need to stick to men your own age. It's like you're dating someone who could be your child, for Heaven's sake!"

My face has to be beet-red because my cheeks are suddenly on fire. "I'm not dating him! He's just a friend. Why the hell am I justifying myself to you? I can date or screw whomever I want as long as he's over the age of eighteen. I'll call you later." I disconnect my Bluetooth, wishing I had something to throw at someone. Instead, I slam my hand on the steering wheel. Other than making my palm sting, it barely takes the edge off. How dare she make me feel like a pedophile! And for her to insult him? What the hell was that about? A gigolo? Hardly. I consider myself a pretty good judge of character, and he hasn't given me that impression at all.

I pull into the garage and Raine pulls in front of the bay next to me, parking on the driveway. I make a mental note to dig up Robert's opener for him.

"What's the matter? You look pissed," he says as we walk into the kitchen from the garage.

I give him a wan smile. "My sister said something that did just that — pissed me off. I hung up on her."

His shoulders tense. "Jenny's mother?"

"She's the only sister I have. Why?"

He strolls over to the refrigerator and opens it. "I don't think Jenny likes me."

My eyes narrow at him. "Why do you say that?"

"Jillian, there's no food in here." He turns with a jar of mustard in his hand and arches his black-and-blue brow at me. "What do you do? Eat it on bread?"

I plant my hands on my hips. "Don't try to deflect my question. Why do you think Jenny doesn't like you?"

He straightens up and faces me, and then sweeps a hand over his bruised face. "She stopped me in the driveway after the photo shoot and shared her unflattering opinion of me. That I should stay away from you. What would someone like me possibly have to offer you beyond some eye candy to hang on your arm?" There's no mistaking the hurt and anger laced in his words.

My blood slowly boils as anger toward my family rises. He leans on the island with slumped shoulders. "I thought about staying away, not coming back. But I couldn't do it. I wanted to see you again. It's true, financially, right now, she's right. I don't have much to offer anyone. But I'm not interested in you because of your money, and hopefully the fact that I don't have any won't stop you. Money isn't everything. Of all people, I should know. Those other things she said? They're not true. That's not me at all."

He hangs his head, and asks quietly, "Do you want me to leave?"

My heart squeezes, and I want nothing more than to take away the layer of pain that seems to define him.

I walk around to meet him and pull him into my arms. "No. I definitely don't want you to leave." He wraps his arms tightly around me, rests his cheek on my hair, and lets out a deep breath. I melt into him, and the hard muscles of his chest feel good against me. His arms are strong and warm. I yearn to kiss him, and to comfort him — woman to man.

"Jillian?" he whispers.

"Yes?" I move my head from under his chin and look up.

His eyes are glassy blue marbles as he gazes down at me. He swallows. "Thanks for believing me." I'm suddenly aware his lips are only inches from mine. My breath catches. A moment later, they come down and tenderly press to mine. He closes his eyes and the feel of his lips are soft yet firm. He squeezes me tighter in his arms, and his tongue parts my lips and enters my mouth, probing and caressing in the most gentle, sensuous dance. I follow his lead and relax into one of the finest kisses I ever remember experiencing. Raine's hands travel my back as his mouth becomes more insistent, and my body reacts with a rush of warmth and a clenching need. My hands find his hair and twist into the tawny softness of it. They meet in the back of his neck, and I pull him closer, mindful of his injuries.

He moans and I join him until we break away, breathless. My hands shake. I just kissed a man young enough to be . . . I stop myself from going there. Instead, I just admit that I loved it.

He rests his forehead next to mine. "Jillian . . ."

"Yes?"

"I'll be back."

"Huh?"

"There's no food in this house. Unless we both want to starve to death, I need to go to the store if I plan on cooking anything. My only other option is throwing you down on the kitchen floor and making love to you until I'm blind. But I'm thinking we need to start slower since I'll be staying here for a while, and I don't want to screw this up."

He releases me, and I stand there dumbstruck, rooted in place. His hand snatches his truck keys off the island and he heads for the door.

"Raine?" My head is swimming and I don't even know why I've called out his name. Only that I feel giddy, and I want confirmation that I didn't just imagine the last five minutes.

He turns. "Jillian?"

On impulse, as a display of trust, I rush to my purse, and take out the credit card I use just for groceries. "Here. You cook and I'll pay for the food. Deal?"

A slow smile comes to his lips. He takes the card and stuffs it into the pocket of his jeans. "Deal."

He turns to go.

"Raine?"

He spins on his heel. "Jillian, you're making me dizzy."

"Did you mean to kiss me?" I blurt.

A rakish smile forms on his lips like the one he used in the studio. "Yeah, and I plan on doing it again. Now let me go so I can get back and cook us a meal."

Chapter 16

Raine

"WHERE DID YOU LEARN how to cook like this?" Jillian asks, wearing a look of disbelief as she dips her fork back into the chicken marsala.

I can't help but smile. I finish chewing before I answer. "My mom," I say and offer a silent prayer of thanks to her.

"Really?" Jillian's brow wrinkles and she smiles back.

"Don't sound so surprised."

"I'm just wondering how she managed it."

I shrug. "She paid me to learn. Growing up, to earn my allowance, I had to cook three meals a week. She taught me everything I know. I never realized how valuable a skill it was until . . ." I let my voice trail off, clipping off the "she died" part, and look away. If I start to talk about my mom, it will unlock my whole sordid tale. One question will lead to another. I'm not ready to pop the top on my can of worms. Jillian's already seen evidence of one of my largest secrets. I'm wearing the black and blues to prove it, and my dad's nasty revelation last night just added to my dysfunctional family history.

Jillian reaches her hand out and covers mine. "Just tell me, Raine. I promise nothing you confess, short of having murdered someone, will change my opinion of you." Her eyes are warm and encouraging. I find comfort there. Funny, it's easier for me to share my desire for her than to talk about my past.

I just shake my head and find I can't speak.

"Do you have any siblings?" Jillian asks gently before she takes another bite of her meal.

I'm comfortable enough answering that one. "I'm an only child."

She props her elbow on the granite and gives me a contemplative look. "Hmm. That fits. I'm the youngest. It's just my sister Kitty and me. She's eleven years older than I am."

I appreciate that she's offered me something about herself in return.

"Have you always lived in Morristown?" she asks.

"No, Mendham. I moved to Morristown after high school." I put down my fork. "Does it matter? Can we not do this?"

"People don't normally have this much trouble talking about themselves. I just want you to know you that you can trust me. When you're ready, for each story you trade with me, I'll trade you one of mine. Okay?"

"Okay, but not tonight. I've been down this road before. There's a lot I'm angry about, Jillian, and I want you to be ready for that."

"Have you ever seen someone professionally?"

I look down and bite back my frustration. "That takes money I don't have."

"Fair enough."

When we finish eating, she clears the dishes and I help her load the dishwasher. We share a comfortable silence. The stifling pain in my ribs surfaces again. I reach for the prescription I had filled while I was at Kings. Jillian brings over a glass of water before I even manage to get the cap off.

"You didn't have to do that."

She shrugs. "I was a wife for a long time, and old habits die hard." She turns to put the remaining items on the counter away. I think about what she said and suddenly long for the thoughtfulness and kindness she gives to me. I'll confess, in this way, she reminds me of my mother—the only other woman who had those qualities. But it's new in this context, not something I've ever experienced in a potential relationship. Not that I'm an expert by any stretch.

I sneak up behind her and wrap her in my arms, inhaling the soft feminine smell that clings to her hair. She tenses at first and then relaxes. "Thank you. I appreciate the way you treat me."

She turns in my arms to face me. Her hand brushes over the stubble on my cheek. "You deserve it. Don't ever let anyone tell you differently." Her lips touch mine briefly and she lets me go.

"I need to do some work tonight. Will you be all right?" she asks.

"Yeah, fine. I have a ton of reading and a new project for class."

"Are you working tomorrow?"

My expression changes as I worry about my cash flow. "No. I can't work with Mikey for at least a week until my ribs heal, and I don't have any hours at the bar until this weekend."

Her eyes take on a mischievous glint. "Classes are on Wednesdays and Thursdays, right?"

My lips turn up in a smile. "Where are you going with this?"

"How would you like to come to my shore house by Spring Lake for a few days while you heal? I'm on deadline and have to write, but there's plenty to do there on your own. There's only a couple weeks of good weather left, so it would be like the last hurrah for the season before it starts to get quiet."

There's a hopeful look in her eye, and God knows I'd enjoy some sun. "Yeah, let's do it. But I'm not sure how much time I want to spend in public. I look like I've been hit by a train. I think I scared a few people when I was in the checkout line." Before I forget, I dig my hands into the pockets of my jeans and pull out the credit card she gave me.

"I have a private deck facing the ocean. You don't have to leave the premises if you don't want to. The sea air will do you good."

I place the card on the counter.

It catches her eye, and she slides it back at me. "Put it in a safe place for the next time. You doing the cooking would be the best trade for a room I could ever imagine. If you ever meet my family, you'll quickly hear stories about my general aversion to kitchens and cooking anything more than eggs."

I give her a genuine smile, and a lump forms in my throat as I take the card back. I'm happy to have a way to repay her. Her small act of trust touches me. So does her hint of inclusion. "I'd like that... to meet your family someday." *Although I'll have to win Jenny over first.*

From the direction of the conversation, it doesn't sound like Jillian plans to kick me out anytime soon. Her earlier invitation seemed open-ended, but I don't want to take that for granted. I'm hoping I can impose on her for at least the same month I had planned on staying with my fucked up father.

But being here could definitely change things, and I'm not sure whether it would be for better or worse. Then I realize there's something I need to know and only one way to find out.

"Wait here for a minute. I'll be back."

Jillian gives me a puzzled look. "Okay."

I walk back to the guest room, take the signed release out of the pocket in my duffel, and return to the kitchen. Jillian's waiting for me on a stool next to the island.

Without a word I hand her the form.

She takes it between her fingers and frowns. Her golden eyes search mine. "Does this mean you'd rather not go to dinner?"

My heart suddenly aches—in a good way—and I smile. "Not at all. Does that mean you really want to go?"

A blush spreads across her cheeks. "Yes, I want to go." She reaches for my hand. It's small and soft inside my palm. For the first time, I'm embarrassed my hands are rough and calloused. But it doesn't stop my heart from beating faster.

"Is it okay if we wait until after my face heals?" I ask.

"That would be fine." She nods and slips off the stool. "Now I really have to go to work. Say goodnight later?"

"You got it."

We head our separate ways. The aches and pains in my body don't bother me as much now that Jillian has given me a ray of hope and something to look forward to.

Chapter 17

Jillian

TAP. TAP. TAP. My fingers glide over the keyboard and transport me into the world of Becca and Drew, who've been chattering away in my head since I sat down. Now that the synopsis is behind me, I'm back to working on the first draft of my novel. I've skipped backward in the plot—but not too far back—to work on a scene toward the beginning of the book. The part where Becca looks up in Boston's South Street Station and spots a man who she believes is Drew—only he's five years older than when he supposedly died.

The chill traversing my spine is Becca's. But her emotion is fueled by the amplified feeling I had when I saw Raine planting trees. In my case, too much time had passed for me to believe, even for a second, that I was staring at my Drew—unless he'd stopped aging. In the book, Becca never sees Drew's dead body. Part of me wishes I could say the same. Instead, I carry the unpleasant memory of Drew's wax-like corpse in his casket and the definitive knowledge he isn't ever coming back.

It's been almost twenty-five years, and I still find it difficult to think back to that time, even to lend it to Becca's past. I'm saving that part—the beginning of the book—for last, since it's the most difficult part of my life to face, even in fiction.

Here's hoping that it doesn't trip me up in the end.

I shudder and feel my breath hitch whenever I get too close to those memories. Especially the emotional numbness and the near catatonic state I lived in as I moved mechanically from the accident to the funeral, and then to the weeks that followed when I started college. The imprint of those weeks and months surrounded in a painful fog is ingrained on my soul. I still don't remember how I made it through them. Therapy barely helped. Journaling and immersion in schoolwork proved marginally better, but in the end, there was no escape. Grief engulfed my entire freshman year, suffocating me. I don't remember breathing again until the next summer.

The truth is I never fully recovered. Rather, I learned how to bury the pain enough to go on living and tried not to dwell too much on what I'd lost and why.

I caress a pair of girlish purple leather diaries sitting on my desk for inspiration. Every moment I spent with Drew up until the day he died is captured inside them—from the opening day bonfire where we met as camp counselors to the night before the accident and everything in between. Flower petals from my prom corsage, concert tickets, notes passed in class, and a dozen other things are all interspersed among the pages. I took them out of storage after Robert died and read them cover to cover at least twenty times, letting them take me back to that world. The one in which Drew was still alive.

Cracking open one of the diaries where an envelope is lodged between the pages, I reread the entry remembering the day . . .

I drop my cheerleading gear inside the door and race for the phone in the kitchen, picking it up on the third ring. "Hello?"

"Hey baby. Anything come in the mail today?" Drew asks.

"Um . . . don't know. Hang on a sec." I put the phone down on the floor and backtrack to the front door to the pile of mail lying where it fell when the postman shoved it through the mail slot.

I gather the pile and take it into the kitchen. "Let me see . . ." I thumb through the envelopes and food store flyers. My heart thumps in my chest when I spot it. "Yes, something from Villanova." It's our first choice school.

Drew breathes into the phone. "Me, too."

"Did you open it?" I ask anxiously, as the white creamy envelope shakes in my hand.

"Nope. Wanted to wait to see if you had one. Open it on three?"

"Wait! What if one of us doesn't get in?" I ask.

"Then we wait for the rest of the acceptances to come in, and we go to the school that accepts us both," he says, impatiently.

My stomach tightens. "What if... you know... that doesn't happen? If none of them do?"

"Come on, Jillian. No way that can happen. We're both in the top 10 percent of our class in one of the best high schools in the state. Our test scores are freaking fantastic, you cheer, I have baseball ... seriously, they'd be lucky to have us." His words are encouraging, and there's no mistaking I'm the worrier in this relationship.

I blow out a breath. "You're right. On three."

We rip open our envelopes. I squeeze my eyes shut, open the paper, and then look. As soon as I see "We are pleased to offer you ..." I have to squelch down a squeal of delight.

"What does yours say?" Drew asks. From the breathy quality in his voice, I can tell he's holding back good news.

Just in case, I answer calmly, almost sadly. "I got in."

He releases a breath. "Me, too."

I release my squeal of delight, and jump up and down. We hoot and holler into the phone until we're both hoarse.

We're laughing as I collapse into the wall, and slide down into a heap on the kitchen floor.

"This is it, baby. The first step to the rest of our lives together," Drew purrs into the phone. I love that he's so romantic and has never once thought we were too young to be this committed to one another. Part of it has to do with his reaction to his parents' divorce, and not wanting to end up like them. The other is a strong hunger he has to live his best life and thinking that includes me.

Me? I can't imagine loving someone more. I feel lucky to have found him, lucky that he's mine.

I close the diary and sigh.

In my mind's eye, Raine reminds me of an older version of Drew — a physical representation of who he'd be if he had lived. What I didn't count on is that Raine would be able to sneak under my defenses so easily because of it. I can't deny how attracted I am to Raine or how much my heart yearns to embrace him. But I struggle to sift through my emotions and separate my growing feelings for him with the echo of love in my heart for Drew. At times, they still seem almost inseparable.

I channel my inspiration into crafting the encounter between Becca and Drew — the tension, the confrontation, the dialogue, and the conflict. I stop typing after I fast-draft it and sit back in my chair satisfied. As part of my process, I set it aside, and pull up the last chunk of scenes I worked on. It's further along in the plot and less fraught with my own personal experiences.

Another hour passes, and I decide I'm done for the night.

Before I shut down, I check my email. I see one from Brigitte and open it.

How's your first draft coming? I'll need it in eight weeks, so chop-chop! Before you ask, I'm still working to sell them on the book cover design.

Well, don't keep me hanging. How was the date with the lawyer?

I groan, and craft a reply.

Glad to hear the publisher is pleased. But tell whoever you're working with at the publishing house to get a life, it's Sunday! Take the same advice for yourself. I appreciate your perseverance on the cover design. I don't plan to give up on it.

As far as the date? Awful. Actually, it was worse than awful. I'm surprised it took his wife as long as it did to divorce him. Seriously, he was a callous asshole and older than my grandfather. If he's forty-eight, then I'm twenty-one.

Going to visit Aunt Vera tomorrow and then head to the beach house for a couple of days to write.

My fingers hover over the keyboard, tempted to add

something about Raine. On second thought, maybe it's better if I keep him to myself for a while from those who don't already know he's here. Not to mention, if I tell her he's living with me, she might worry he'll become a distraction. I can't lie. I'm worried about that, too.

Call me if you need me . . . J

I hit SEND.

My lips press together. Speaking of Vera and people who already know about Raine, I eye the clock. Nine-thirty. It's still early enough to check in with Kitty, plus I owe her an apology for snapping at her earlier.

I dial.

She answers on the first ring. "The prodigal sister returns," she says and sighs.

I roll my eyes. It's clear who Jenny inherited her melodrama from. "Oh, for Pete's sake, Kitty, I only talked to you this afternoon. It hasn't been that long. Did you have a chance to see Aunt Vera since we spoke?"

Her voice takes on some excitement. "Jenny and I went over after dinner. We ran into the doctor, and he said her kidneys are responding and she may be off of dialysis soon. Isn't that wonderful news! I figured I'd let you cool off and surprise you tomorrow morning."

"That's fantastic news, Kitty!" Her words fill me with relief, and for the first time since Vera's admittance into the House o' Death, I feel truly hopeful.

"From your mouth to God's ears," Kitty says. "Jillian . . . I'm sorry about making you angry before. You know, about your house guest."

"Thanks, and I'm sorry I went off on you," I say and release a breath. "But I need you and Jenny to trust me on this one."

"We love you, Jillian. We're allowed to worry."

"Maybe, but you're not allowed to nag or judge."

"Fine." She relents, but I can tell from her tone she's not happy. "So how is your *house guest* doing?"

"Healing. That's all that matters. And you'll be pleased to know he's an excellent cook and has volunteered to man the kitchen while he stays here. He made chicken marsala for dinner. It was fabulous."

"How long does he plan on staying?" I hear suspicion in her voice, and I don't like it. "As long as he wants," I say, resisting the urge to snipe at her.

She *humphs*. I can picture the look of disapproval written all over her face. "I guess you'll be bringing him to dinner next Sunday?"

"Wow, Kitty. Way to make a question sound like an accusation. If he's welcome, yes, I'll bring him. Otherwise, I'll see you for Sunday dinner when he moves out—whenever that turns out to be."

"Of course, he's welcome," she says more pleasantly, and I sense defeat from her side of the phone.

A triumphant smile pops to my lips. "Fantastic. You have a week to get used to the idea and figure out how to be cordial to him. We'll be at the beach house for the next couple of days, since I need some uninterrupted time to catch up. I'm on deadline."

"You're taking him with you?"

I pull the receiver away from my ear and give it an incredulous look. *Didn't we just hash this out?* I place the phone back at my ear. "It's either that or leave him here on his own. Frankly, I'd like the company and the hot meals."

"I give up. Sleep with whomever you want. Just don't come crying to me when he breaks your heart."

My mouth drops open. "Kitty, I'm not sleeping with him! I'm giving him a place to stay. He's cooking. We're friends. End of story." Okay, I admit I'm downplaying the situation. I'm not sleeping with him . . . *yet*, and we're just friends . . . *for now*. But is it really necessary for her to give me all this grief just because he's younger than me? Okay, probably by two decades. Whatever happened to: "I hope you meet someone nice and fall in love again?" Does that only apply to men within a certain standard deviation of my current age?

"Whatever you say, Jillian. But someone his age is bound to eventually leave you for someone younger once the novelty of an older woman wears off."

"You would know this how, Kitty? Your vast experience with younger men?" My hand strangles the phone, wishing it were Kitty's neck. "And thanks for the vote of confidence! I'm glad I have no other qualities that would attract a man other than a quick romp in the sack to satisfy his curiosity of having sex with an old hag!" I say in my own defense, but I can't deny she's tapped directly into my deepest fears.

"I didn't mean it that way, Jillian. Let me quit before I say anything else to make you angry. I'll let you know if anything changes with Vera while you're gone. 'Night, sweetie."

I smolder. "Thanks, Kitty. I'll *probably* talk to you tomorrow . . . if my old arthritic fingers can still dial the phone."

I hang up, drained from the conversation and ready for a snack. Pushing away Kitty's words, I shove down my insecurities. Raine makes me feel a lot of things, but he doesn't make me feel like a novelty. I wonder what he's up to. The house is big enough so that I can't hear him, but knowing that he's somewhere close by makes the house feel more alive.

Thinking back to sleeping by his side last night fills me with warmth. It felt so good, reminding me how much I missed the intimacy of sharing my bed and feeling needed. A twinge of disappointment settles in the center of my chest at the prospect of sleeping without him tonight.

I switch off my laptop and snap off the light behind me as I leave my office. Rather than head to the kitchen like I intend, my feet carry me toward Raine.

Chapter 18

Raine

I'M RELAXING ON the guest room bed and leafing through the internship paperwork Nessie dropped off at the bar last night when my cell phone rings.

I glance at the number. Speak of the devil. What the hell could she want? I decide to be civil and ignore the fact that she probably cheated on me with Mercedes dude before we split up.

"What's up, Ness?"

"Are you okay?" she says, an edge of panic in her voice.

I sit up straighter. "Huh?"

"Your crazy father called me! He's looking for you." She's afraid, I can hear it. Vanessa knew enough about me to know what my father was capable of, although she never witnessed it firsthand during the time we were together.

A shiver runs up my spine. "He called you?"

"Yeah. I mean, he sounded normal, but I know you said he could come off that way sometimes."

My stomach drops. "You didn't give him my number, did you?" Whenever I call him, I block my phone number so he can't contact me directly.

She sighs. "No. I didn't. We may not be dating anymore, but that doesn't mean I'd throw you to the old wolf." She sounds almost nice, like the old Ness I thought I once loved. I'm thankful that she did me a favor.

"He told me you were in the hospital last night and wanted to make sure you were okay." She sniffs in disbelief.

A sudden head rush leaves me feeling faint as my heart kicks up painfully against my ribcage. "How did he know I ended up in the hospital?"

"Holy shit! You were really in the hospital? I thought he was lying," she says in a high-pitched wail.

I have to move the phone away from my ear. "Ness, don't yell! You almost busted my eardrum."

"Sorry. What happened? Are you okay?" she asks with renewed concern.

I draw a hand over my bruised face without thinking and wince. I choose to avoid any details until I figure out what she knows. "I'm fine. What did he tell you?"

"He said you never came home last night after work. He called around to the local hospitals today and found out you were admitted to Memorial Hospital after a bar fight. He wondered if I knew where you were."

That lying sack of shit! Of course, he didn't tell Ness he was the one who'd put me there in hopes of lulling her into telling him something.

"And?" I ask with exasperation.

"And what?" she snipes. "I don't know where you are! All I told him was that I'd seen you at work last night."

I breathe easier. That's good.

"So where are you, anyway? He said the hospital told him you went home with your *aunt*. I thought that was odd since they all live in Sweden."

My jaw tightens, and my relief turns to dread. "I'm staying with a friend." My safe haven suddenly feels threatened. I need to tell Jillian. If the hospital gave out her information, we could be in for an unwelcome visit. On the other hand, if my father thinks he can come within a football field of Jillian . . .

The thought of him touching her soft skin or even looking at her makes my hand clench into a fist. Let's just say I'd kill to keep her safe.

"Oh, *really*? Someone old enough to be mistaken for your freakin' aunt?" she says incredulously. "Getting a little desperate there, aren't you?"

My blood pressure shoots up until there's heat rising off my cheeks. Vanessa would never be half the woman that Jillian is.

"Back off, Nessie," I growl and grip the phone hard.

"You always did have mommy issues," she says with a trace of evil glee.

That's it! I fucking snap. "I have issues? Me? How about we talk about your issues? Oh, wait! I don't have the whole fucking night to list them!"

"At least sleeping with someone twice my age isn't one of them," she snarls.

Chapter 19

Jillian

"WHY ARE YOU being such a bitch?" he says. His words are muted through the guest room door. My hand freezes mid-knock and my heart unexplainably sinks.

He pauses, I assume, to listen to her response — whoever it is.

"*What?* Ness, I really don't need your bullshit right now, or ever again, for that matter."

My stomach knots. His use of a nickname tells me he's close to her ... girlfriend close. Or, given the nature of his words and what he told me the other day — ex-girlfriend. Either way. *Great. Just fab.*

Another pause.

"You know what? That's none of your goddamn business," he snaps. "I—"

The floors creak as Raine paces briskly inside, his bare feet stamping across the wood floor.

"*What?*" His footsteps abruptly stop. "Okay, that's enough! Why do you make everything sound so cheap? You don't even know her!"

My ears prick up on high alert as blood pumps in a heavy rhythm under my breast. Who "her?" Me "her" or another "her?"

"Don't ever say something like that to me again. Wait, let's do one better. Don't ever call me again," he snaps. "Ha! I'd cut my own dick off before I'd stoop low enough ever to fuck you again."

My eyes pop wide at the vehemence in his voice followed by a small stab of triumph. Ex-girlfriend. Definitely. The sound of his cell phone slamming onto a solid surface in the bedroom echoes through the door two seconds before he opens it and I stumble into the room.

His face twists into a scowl. "Jillian? What're you doing?"

My mouth suddenly goes dry. "I wanted to know if you, um, wanted something to eat." *Crap.* I regret the words the moment I speak.

His eyebrows fly up. "You're offering to cook after our conversation earlier?" Crossing his arms over his chest, he says, "or were you hoping I would?" The anger I heard in his phone call is still evident, but waning.

I shrug and glance briefly away. "I can make us something."

His mouth twists into a half smile, and then he reaches out and spins me around to face the kitchen. My shoulders tingle from the touch of his fingers. "I can't wait to see this. Okay, Julia Child, lead the way."

I stop when we reach the stairs leading to the lower level. "Before we go to the kitchen, do you want a tour? I realized I never showed you around."

He grins and gives me a pointed look. "You're stalling."

My eyes widen with innocence. "No. Really, I'm not." Well, maybe I am. "Come on."

I lead him down past my studio to the gym and flip on the lights. It was Robert's more than mine while he was alive. The gym is fully outfitted with multiple sets of free weights and every flavor of exercise equipment imaginable, including a full Universal Gym.

Raine whistles and walks past me to the weights. "Sweet."

I clear my throat. "My husband used to have a personal

trainer come to the house. I haven't been down here much myself since he died, but God knows, I probably should be. You're welcome to use it all." I'm assuming he must work out to stay in the shape he's in.

He picks up a forty-pound weight, winces, and places it back down. "How did your husband die?" he asks softly.

I stare at his back and try to swallow back the dryness in my mouth. "Heart attack."

He turns to face me. "I'm sorry. How old was he when he died?"

"Forty-eight," I say with a tight smile.

His face softens. He strolls back over to where I stand, and places his hands on my shoulders. "I have an idea."

"What's that?"

He lowers his head and touches his forehead to mine. "I can be your personal trainer. But I want you to know that you have a warped perception of your own body. You're beautiful, and I like you just the way you are. That said, I believe in fitness. I'll help you get more fit with the understanding that there's nothing wrong with the way you look. Deal?"

My cheeks grow warm, but not as warm as my heart. I'm speechless. How is it that he knows the right thing to say? "Deal."

"Great. Meet me here at eight tomorrow morning."

My eyes go wide. "Tomorrow? That soon?"

He folds his arms over his chest with a self-satisfied smile. "No reason to wait. Besides, I need to earn my keep. We can get on the road after a workout and a shower. I'm no pushover, Jillian. I'm going to make you sweat."

I don't need a workout for that. Watching him look at me that way is enough to make me sweat.

"But, but, but—"

He raises his bruised eyebrow. "But what?"

"Your ribs," I blurt.

He shakes his head. "I don't expect to do a workout

myself. My ribs won't stop me from training you."

"You're enjoying this, aren't you?"

"Immensely," he says, wearing a broad smile.

My shoulders slump. "Fine, you win. Eight o'clock. For the record, I still like the cooking trade better."

He chuckles, takes my hand, and pulls me into the hallway. "What else did you want to show me?"

I perk up. "Do you like to watch movies?"

"Sure, who doesn't?"

I redirect him two doors down, past my studio, to the home theater.

"Wow, this is great!" he says and scans the room, taking in the rows of cushioned movie seats, and the large projection screen against the back wall. Decorated in red and purple velvet, the room has the feel of an old-time theater, complete with a full-size popcorn cart and a beverage refrigerator.

"Robert was a movie buff. He built a complete library of films with over three thousand titles," I say, feeling like a tour guide. I pick up a small portable tablet, which is part of the built-in entertainment system, and hand it to him. "You can browse through the films on here."

"Jillian, this is incredible. I could stay in here for days," he says, awestruck.

I smile. "Then this will be the first place I look for you when I can't find you upstairs."

His eyes light up. "You wanna watch a movie? We could bring our snack down here. You know, that masterpiece you volunteered to cook," he teases.

I poke him gently on his good side. "Don't be a wiseass."

He laughs and folds his arms around his ribs to protect them.

"I was thinking something closer to cheese and crackers," I say.

"Sounds good."

This time I take his hand and lead him to the door. "Come

on. Let me show you the rest of place before we come back."

There's nothing else on the lower level to show him except the utility room, which I skip, and I lead the way back upstairs.

He already knows how to get to the kitchen, so I show him the rest of the 2,500 square feet on the first floor: the great room, a formal living room, dining room, laundry room, and my office.

I walk into Robert's old office last. Darkness fills the large bank of floor-to-ceiling windows along the back wall. The rest of the walls are painted white and contrast with the ultramodern black leather furniture. Huge, framed black-and-white architectural photographs hang on the walls. The only splash of color is provided by some pillows on the sofa. After Robert died, I packed up all of his work-related items, and stripped the room down to its essentials to give it a "just decorated" feel. It made it easier for me to walk by when it didn't look lived-in.

Raine stands frozen in the doorway. "This is amazing."

I smile. His reaction warms me, and I'm struck with a thought. "You can work in here if you'd like."

His eyes focus on the desk as his fingers tightly grip the doorjamb. "Was this your husband's office?" he asks softly.

I nod.

"What did he do? I love the artwork," he says, standing frozen, like he's hesitant to enter.

"Real estate developer. And thank you. Robert's father hired me out of college. Those photographs were my first project for his real estate conglomerate." I arch a brow. "You can come in, you know."

"They're amazing," he says, his feet slowly traveling over the threshold as he looks around. "If you're serious, I'd really like to work in here."

Clapping my hands together, I say, "It's settled. Now, let's go get that snack."

I walk past him, and his hand grasps my arm to stop me.

He gazes into to my eyes and swallows. "Thanks, Jillian. This means a lot to me."

His emotions are palpable. They take me by surprise, and I wonder why it means so much. It's only an office. I suspect his reactions will continue to surprise me for a while until he's willing to open up and let me in.

By the time we finish with the second floor tour, he knows where my bedroom is and has seen the three remaining guest rooms. On our way back downstairs, I show him where to put his dirty laundry.

He throws up his hands and shakes his head. "No way. You're not doing my laundry. I'll do it myself."

I shrug. "Have it your way." I pull down an extra laundry basket from the shelf and hand it to him. "Here. At least take something to put it in."

"Thanks." He takes the basket from me.

Confident he knows where to find everything now, I say, "Drop that off in your room and meet me downstairs . . . if you still want to grab a snack and watch a movie."

His mouth twists into a smile. "See you in three."

When he enters the kitchen, I'm already putting some cheese and crackers on a tray. I grab a glass of wine while Raine takes a bottle of water, and we head back down to the home theatre.

I choose a seat in the middle, and Raine settles in next to me. When I hand him the tablet for the entertainment system, he puts it on his lap and looks at me. His expression is pained. "Jillian . . . my ex-girlfriend, Vanessa, called me before."

"Oh?" I brace myself, thinking I might not want to hear what he has to say. I'm enjoying his company and don't want anything to ruin it.

"My father called her."

The hairs on my arms stand up. That wasn't what I expected. "And?"

He looks at me, and there's fear in his eyes. "He knows I was admitted to Memorial, and they told him a woman claiming to be my aunt signed my release."

My throat tightens and I gulp. "Are you afraid he might try to find you?" Even as I ask the question, I think of the Beretta I have locked in my desk drawer. But I don't think it will be necessary.

His body appears to close in on itself, and he looks away. He dips his head and nods. "But I'm more afraid of him getting close to you."

I rest my hand gently on his shoulder. "I asked the nurse to make sure that my 'ex-brother-in-law' didn't get my new address. She told me the hospital's privacy policy prohibits that anyway."

His head pops up and his face fills with relief. "Really?"

Before I can stop my hand, I run it over his hair and kiss the side of his head. "Really." Times like this I'm torn between wanting to protect him and wanting to make love to him.

When his eyes meet mine, it's clear he's thinking something more romantic. An unmistakable look of desire blazes in his eyes. He curls his hand around my neck and draws me into a kiss. A thrill shoots through me. His lips start firm and gentle and then build into a fiery insistence. I melt into him with growing urgency. His fingers work into my hair and cradle the back of my head; while he twists his body into me, his other hand touches my cheek. His tongue dances with mine, and my body ignites with burning need.

I want to wrap my arms around him and pull him closer, but I'm afraid to touch him where he still hurts. Instead, I touch my hand to his leg.

He moans and pulls his lips away. "Let's pick a movie before I start something I can't finish without puncturing a lung," he whispers and his breath warms my cheek. "Jillian . . . I meant what I said today. I don't want to screw this up. I want to take you on a real date."

I release a deep sigh and brush back a piece of his hair. "What do you want to watch?"

He sits back in his seat, touches his ribs, and grits his teeth.

"Something where they blow things up."

"Ribs hurt?"

He squeezes his eyes shut for a second and nods. I wonder if I would've let him go further if he had tried. I can't deny that I want him, but I like the idea of knowing there's a date ahead of us. The anticipation excites me. The kind of excitement that's been absent from my life for longer than I can remember . . . The kind held within the pages of my purple diaries.

"I'm game for whatever you choose," I say. We settle on a classic Bruce Willis *Die Hard* movie, and I transfer our snacks to the flip-up trays attached to each seat.

I darken the lights using the remote. Before the opening credits roll, Raine takes my hand, and entwines his fingers through mine. My heart flutters. He doesn't let go until the movie ends.

Chapter 20

Raine

A DAMP TOWEL WRAPPED around my hips, I stand in front of the mirror and groan as I study my injuries. The rainbow around my eye is fading, but not fast enough for my liking. I still look like shit and can't believe Jillian can look at me without feeling revulsion. Before my shower, I popped another pain pill and removed the tape from my ribs, revealing the multicolor hue that's glaring back at me from the mirror.

I'll have to take it easy when I train Jillian this morning. I feel a little less like road kill today than I did yesterday, but maybe that's just the meds.

It took all my willpower not to follow Jillian to her room last night. Waking up with her yesterday morning spoiled me, and I secretly hoped she would want to stay with me again last night. But I keep telling myself that it played out as it should have. Now that I've kissed her, I'm not sure I could've just stuck to sleeping next to her.

As impulsive as I want to be, I need Jillian to recognize I'm not just some horny young guy looking to get laid or that I'm out to use her. She needs to choose me . . . To be sure. I can't afford for her to think she's made a mistake while I'm living here.

Selfish? Maybe. Stupid? Definitely not. She's my only good option for the next four weeks, and we both know it. That means leveling the playing field as much as I can by paying my own way even if it's only through cooking and personal training duties. I also can't deny that I need her in more ways than one. As wacked as it sounds, and as much as I need her roof over my head, I want her company and to feel her touch even more.

I put on my workout clothes—a T-shirt, shorts, and sneakers—and then search through my drafting tool kit until I find a ruler. One of my other boxes contains my clipboard. All I need now is some string. I find that in the kitchen, make myself a mug of tea, and head down to the gym. There's no sign of Jillian.

The clock on the wall says seven fifty-five. I glance at the equipment and jot down a quick thirty-minute routine. Once I figure out her level of fitness, I can increase it to an hour. Four times a week should be more than enough.

"Hi," she says.

I look up and see her standing in the doorway with her arms crossed. She's wearing some stretchy-type biker's pants, a T-shirt that falls below her hips, and sneakers. Her lush brown hair is tied in a ponytail.

"Morning. You're right on time." I drain my mug.

She takes a deep breath and comes inside. "How'd you sleep?"

I capture her gaze. "Not as good as the night before. You?"

Her cheeks turn pink, and she tries to hide a smile. "Same."

"Maybe we should do something about that," I say, unable to resist my urge to flirt.

She shifts on her feet. "Maybe."

I pick up the ball of string. "I want to take your measurements so we can track your progress in inches as we go."

Her jaw drops and a look of panic crosses her face.

"Measurements?" She shakes her head vigorously. "Nope. No way."

"Why not?"

"That's too intimate. No, I don't want you to see . . ." her voice trails off, and she turns away.

I toss the ball of string to the ground, and stride over to her. I spin her around to face me. "Jillian? What did I tell you last night?" I ask calmly.

She won't look at me.

I tip her chin up. "There's nothing I'd like more than to gaze at your naked body. Now, don't be ridiculous, and let me take your measurements."

With a deep sigh, she says, "Fine."

I smile in triumph.

She purses her lips and pinches me. "Stop looking so smug."

"Hey! Don't hurt the help." I retrieve my ball of string.

She points at it. "Where did you get that?"

"You know, that vast wasteland you call your kitchen. Now hold your arms out."

"Don't expect me to be happy about it." She obeys, puckering her lips in a sour look. I wrap the string around her biceps and then measure it against the ruler. I write down the measurement on my clipboard then repeat it on the other side.

"Have you ever done this professionally?" she asks as I measure.

"No. But I've been weight training since high school." My lips turn down. "Let's just say it came in handy." I can see in her eyes she catches my drift, so I don't need to elaborate.

"I need to do your waist. Can you lift up your shirt for me?"

"Can't you just feel underneath to measure it?" she pouts.

I roll my eyes. "No."

Her jaw tightens and she lifts her shirt. I weave the string around her, and write down the number in inches.

"Hips."

She meets my eyes. "Let me guess. You want me to push my shorts halfway down my ass?"

I smile. "Yes."

She elbows me on my good side, and I flinch.

"Will you stop enjoying this so much!" she says.

"Hey, come on! I don't enjoy you elbowing me, Jillian," I say with less humor this time.

"Good. I'm trying to make this as uncomfortable for you as it is for me." She rolls her spandex shorts down to expose her hipbones. I stand behind her and wrap the string around her. I lift the back of her shirt and pause.

"You have a tattoo." I stare at the lacy scrollwork she has inked across her lower back.

"Um . . . yeah," she says. "Your point?"

I mark the spot on the string between my fingers with my left hand, and use the index finger on my right hand to trace the design. "My point is that it's sexy as hell," I growl, and picture myself making love to her from behind. "When did you get it?"

"My thirtieth birthday," she says. "Robert wasn't thrilled about it, but I decided to do it anyway. I'd wanted one since I was a teenager." She bats my hand away and drops her shirt before she turns to face me. "I was a little surprised that you don't have any. It seems to be a trend with guys in their twenties."

"How would you know? You haven't seen me fully naked yet." I give her a mischievous grin.

She raises her eyebrows. "So, you're hiding yours someplace intimate?"

I fess up. "Nah. I don't have any. There's never been anything meaningful enough for me to want to mark my body with for the rest of my life."

"Huh. Fair enough," she says, resting her hands on her hips. "So, should we get back to the task at hand? You know, taking my measurements and then getting me into shape?"

"We're done with the measurements, unless you want me to measure your chest? I kind of thought I'd be pushing it if I asked. Besides, I like it just the way it is." I wiggle my eyebrows at her.

She grins. "Will you stop already? I can't believe you'd pass up a chance for a cheap feel."

"There'd be nothing cheap about it. But in all seriousness, let's get to work." I explain my plan to her. We'll use a combination of weights, equipment, and core exercises to target her abs, arms, and thighs. "By the time I'm done with you, we'll be able to bounce a quarter off your abs."

A look of dread fills her features. "That sounds like a pretty tall order."

"Nope. Not so. Give me thirty days, and I guarantee at least a couple of inches. I'm also planning on increasing the lean proteins in our diet, so that should help, too. But tell me now if I need to hunt down all the sugar in the house and put it under lock and key."

She narrows her eyes at me. "Don't even think of going near my secret stash of Godiva, or I might have to hurt you."

I laugh, and still clutching the clipboard, I throw up my hands. "I wouldn't dream of it. You're doing enough damage to me already."

We start with the hand weights next to the weight bench. I discard my clipboard.

"Since I'm going for tone, we'll start with low weights and high reps." I flex my arm to demonstrate. "If we wanted muscle, we would use high weights and fewer reps." I grab the three-pound weights and hand them to her.

She gives them a dubious look and sighs. "Okay."

"I'll take you through a full set of chest, back, and arms, and then we'll repeat. And stop glaring at me like I'm about to torture you." I say, addressing the daggers she's throwing in my direction with her golden eyes.

She *humphs* at me and mumbles, "Sorry, I'm feeling

caffeine-deprived."

"I'll make you a cup of coffee when we're done, but let's focus for now," I say sternly.

"Meanie," she says under her breath.

I take her through one set of upper body exercises with ten reps each and then move her onto the mat for abs. She lies down with her knees pointed to the ceiling while I hold her feet.

"Rather than sit-ups, I want you to do Pilates crunches. The secret is to protect your lower back." I run my fingers around my middle. "You work the whole core this way. A tight core equals tight abs."

She pouts and points at my abs from her vantage point on the mat. "Will I have a six-pack when I'm done?"

"Let's take it one step at a time, tiger. If you're serious, that'll involve some serious weight training."

After struggling through crunches, leg lifts, and roll-ups, Jillian has murder in her eyes. "Son of a bitch! You're killing me."

"Hey, don't insult my mother." I help her up, and point to the Universal gym. "Wait until you're finished with the thigh exercises before you say that."

An unladylike growl rises from her throat. "I think I might hate you."

"Come on. Admit it. I'm too cute to hate." More glaring from her at me. We do inner and then outer thighs with twenty-pound weights.

"Are we done yet?" Jillian moans, draped over the seat, looking spineless.

I glance at the clock. It's only been twenty-five minutes. "Stop whining. One more set of free weights, and you'll be free to go."

When she finishes, she collapses onto the mat and lies down on her back. "I might not be able to walk tomorrow — or lift anything — or sit down."

I chuckle. "Wait until the day after."

She narrows her eyes and does something very un-Jillian: she flips me the bird.

"No need to get hostile about it." I'm only mildly offended. I ease down onto my good side next to her and prop myself up on my elbow. Beads of dampness dot her upper lip.

"You did well," I say softly.

She cups my cheek with her hand, and gives me a small smile. "You're a good trainer. But it was fun giving you a hard time."

"Thanks . . . and I noticed." Her words make me feel good, valued.

Her hand drops away from my face. "Coffee. Shower. Pack. Go. That's my plan from here. Did you want to follow me down to the beach house or meet me there?"

I shrug. "Follow you, I guess. You'll be writing all day?" I'm hoping to spend a little time together.

Her eyes show a sliver of disappointment, like she's read between the lines of my question. "Unfortunately . . . but maybe we can spend some time together tonight. I have to get some of this draft done to meet my deadline."

"Not a problem. I have a project for school to bang out." I run my finger down her arm. "Do I get to read any of this masterpiece you're working on? I mean, I'm kind of like Drew, aren't I? I'd like to get to know this dude I'm representing."

Her lips move but no sound comes out, and the look in her eyes is a cross between fear and horror.

"Um, was that a weird request?" Didn't seem like it to me.

"Uh . . . no. It's not a weird request. It's actually a nice request. It's just . . . um, it's . . . Robert was never interested in reading my work," she says, and shakes herself. "Can I think about it? It's only the first draft, so it might still suck."

"It's up to you. I'm just saying I'd be interested, that's all."

"Thank you, it means a lot. I really do appreciate your interest," she says, trying to push up into a sitting position before she looks at me pathetically. "I might need help getting up."

I chuckle and get to my feet, mindful of the dull ache in my side. If my ribs weren't a problem, I'd scoop her up off the floor and carry her out of here just for the hell of it. Instead, I offer her my hand. "We need to keep this routine up every other day. If we're not back by Wednesday, maybe we can take a run or something to keep our momentum."

She snorts. "No need. The shore house has a gym, too."

"Sweet." I can't wait to get back into my own routine once my ribs allow it. I miss the gym in the townhouse complex where I lived with Vanessa. But that's the only thing I miss. Funny, I haven't missed Vanessa at all.

Chapter 21

Jillian

I CLUTCH THE PAGES tightly to my chest. "You're sure you really want to read them?" I ask as my fingers twitch nervously.

After driving the hour and ten minutes to get to the beach house this morning post workout, I had a very productive day. Over dinner, I decided to take Raine up on his offer and explained the whole concept of beta reading and critiquing. Still, the thought of anyone, especially him, reading my first draft paralyzes me. But until this morning when he offered, I never realized how much I resented that Robert had never once asked. Granted, I assume Raine's request has more to do with his curiosity about Drew, his doppelganger, than my actual writing. Why else would he volunteer to read a romance novel? Most men would rather have their fingernails removed one by one.

He fluffs a square throw pillow before he lies down on the couch in my office and shoves the pillow between his head and the rolled arm, propping his feet up on the other end and crossing them at the ankles. His brow shoots up and he reaches toward me, wiggling his fingers. "Gimme. Unless you don't want my opinion."

I do want it. My face flushes. What will he think of Drew?

There's nowhere to hide; my words are bare on the page for him to judge. I sigh and peel the pages away from my body. Walking over, I hand him the latest scenes. At the last second, I snatch them back. "Wait. There's a love scene in here."

He shakes his head and sniffs. "Hand 'em over. I've been fucking since I was fifteen. I think I can handle it."

"No need to be crude about it." I thrust the pile at him.

He stares at me with wide-eyed innocence and points at his chest. "Me? Crude? That coming from a woman who flipped me the bird this morning." He rolls his eyes. "Jillian, my point is that you don't need to worry about my sensibilities," he says, air quoting *sensibilities*.

I glare at him. "Yeah, that reminds me. I can barely lift my arms after this morning, and muscles I didn't know I had are having a rebellion in my thighs."

"Your thighs, huh?" he teases with a sexy growl.

I forgive him for his comment and my thigh pain. How can I not? He's a combination of adorable and hotter than hell, and he's stretched out in front of me making me wish I were twenty years younger and a lot hotter.

Giving him a wry smile, I offer him the pages. "Here." He grins and takes them.

"Pen?" he asks.

"What do you need a pen for?"

He looks at me like I'm mentally challenged. "To ... make ... notes ... in ... the ... margins."

I'm tempted to hand him a crayon. Too bad I don't have any.

I stamp back the five feet to my desk and toss a pen at him. "Catch." He fumbles for it.

"Hey, Lady, you could've poked an eye out with that throw." He glares at me and uncaps the pen.

I smirk and look at my laptop, ready to start the next chapter. But a few seconds later, I peek over at him. His blond brows are knit together in concentration. The bruising on his face is starting to fade. He chews the end of the pen as he reads. I try to get back to work, but the thought of his eyes on my work make me feel like I've been tied up and left naked for his personal viewing.

Every once in a while, he stops to scribble some notes on the pages. I do everything in my power not to ask him what part he's reading when he bursts into laughter and writes what seems like a paragraph. My blood pressure suddenly escalates. What the hell could he be laughing at? There isn't anything funny in those scenes!

The words on the screen start to blur together. My hands hover over the keyboard without touching it. Nothing. I write nothing for a full hour as he reads through fifty pages.

More rustling of paper from the couch.

"Done." He swings his legs over the edge and onto the rug, and then walks over and slaps the pages on my desk.

"Well?"

He answers with a sexy smile and a wink and then heads toward the door.

"Where are you going?"

He stretches and yawns, his T-shirt rising up over the low-slung waist of his jeans with frayed bottoms. Smooth, taut abs peek through. *Get a grip, Jillian.*

"I'm going out to sit on the deck, and then I'm going to hit the sack." He gives me a rakish smile. "'Night, Jillian."

"'Kay, 'night." I'm torn between wanting him to stay to keep me company and wanting him to leave so that I can read his damned comments.

The moment he disappears from view, I flip through the pages. My trembling fingers rattle the paper. I take a deep breath and read his first comment. His handwriting is better than I expect. Legible even.

"First, I hate bony girls. Do you know what it feels like to get jabbed by a rib when you're having sex? Probably not. Why does she have to be fashion-model thin? Give me some soft curves any day. Second, she's

too young. This would be sooooooooo much hotter with an older woman and a younger guy. Don't you think?''

What the . . . ?

My thighs tingle unexpectedly at the same time I grit my teeth. Is he serious? I move to the next comment.

"Okay, sorry Jillian, but Becca is a bitch. I wouldn't sleep with her. Seriously. I wouldn't. Next . . .''

I move to his next comment.

"Now, I'm offended. But don't be offended by what I'm about to say. Drew is a pussy. Let him be the man, not Becca. She's got bigger balls than he does. It's plain embarrassing. She's got him so whipped. I just don't feel it's authentic or real. AND . . . AND . . . there is NO WAY his dick is staying that hard that many times in one night. How can ANY guy ever live up to this? This is setting very unrealistic expectations for women. Not to mention, this guy is too much of a wimp to deserve a cock that big (I'm just saying).''

My stomach clenches. Holy shit! Didn't he realize I'm in the business of women's fantasies? A muscle in my jaw jumps as I grind my teeth.

I march straight out onto the deck into the darkness with the wrinkled pages clasped in my hand. A gentle breeze carries the salt air of the ocean over to greet me. The sweet smell of pot hits my nose a moment later, and stops me dead. The red tip of a joint smolders between Raine's lips.

"You take drugs?" I blurt.

He chuckles. "No, I don't *take* drugs. I smoke a little weed from time to time to relax. There's a big difference. And it doesn't interfere with my pain meds." He holds it out to me. "You want a hit?"

God, I feel old.

I shake the pages at him. "Are you fucking serious?"

He giggles. "I'm always serious when it comes to fucking," he says and then mumbles. "I just wish you'd notice." He already sounds stoned.

"What are you saying?"

"Nothing. I'm not saying anything." He pats the seat next to him. "Sit, Jillian. Relax. It's late."

I plop down and sulk. "So, you hate Becca and Drew?"

He inhales and turns away from me to exhale. "No, I don't hate them. I just don't think they're real."

"So what would be *real* to you?"

"Why don't you ever use my name?" he says, annoyed.

I frown at him in the dark. "What?"

"*Raine*. You never say my name. I say 'Jillian' like every other sentence when I speak to you . . . at least that's the way it feels. But you never say, 'What do you think about that, *Raine*?'"

I sit back in my chair, again with my mouth agape. He unwinds me in a strange way. If I stop to think about it, maybe he's right. Rolling his name over my tongue has an intimate feel to it. It's not that I don't want to enjoy the sensuous texture of it through my lips, because I do. The truth is I'm not ready to fully surrender to this fantasy. I wish *real* meant that I could trust that he'd be interested in me for more than one date. His living arrangement is temporary, I can't forget that. But it's so damned tempting.

"I'm sorry, I didn't realize . . ."

He tamps out his joint, places it in a small tin box, and snaps it shut. Getting up, he reaches down to me, and says softly, "Give me your hand."

My heart skips a beat. Without thinking, I offer him my free hand and he pulls me to my feet. I'm in his arms, pressed against the hard lines of his chest, before I can react. His breath warms my cheek. "I'm real, Jillian. Me. If you're interested in finding out what that means, let me know. I'd be happy to show you." He kisses my forehead and lets me go. I stand frozen.

Like right now?

He leaves me standing there, and I listen as his footfalls recede down the hallway toward his room. I'm tempted to follow.

If it was only that simple.

Our kisses are burned into my memory. Every detail: from the taste, to the feel of his lips, to the warmth of his body, to the rush of heat that courses through me whenever I revisit them in my mind. One minute I want to throw myself into his arms and be done with it, and the next I'm afraid of what a stupid, irresponsible decision that could turn out to be for me. It's almost a guaranteed path to heartbreak. I keep reminding myself not to let my feelings seduce me into believing one date could turn into a future together . . . or permanently fill the emptiness in my heart.

But at some point, I'll have to commit . . . one way or the other.

Chapter 22

Jillian

"THAT'S NOT A WORD!" I yell at Raine. The Scrabble board is between us on the living room carpet. After a frustrating day of writer's block at the keyboard following Raine's comments last night, I gave myself the night off to spend some time with him, and to rethink Becca and Drew.

"What? Yes it is!" he says with conviction, looking up at me with wide, innocent eyes. He's lying on his side with his elbow resting on the ground, cradling his tawny head in his hand.

"There's no *x* in *tricks*, Raine!"

"Yes, there is! 'Silly, Rabbit. *Trix* are for kids,'" he replies.

"That's a breakfast cereal, not a word!" I laugh.

"So? That counts."

I roll my eyes. "No, it doesn't."

My cell phone rings and I lunge for it on the coffee table without getting up. I topple over when I overextend my reach, falling on the carpet and kicking the Scrabble board.

"Ticklish?" Raine grabs my bare foot without waiting for an answer and passes his finger over the bottom.

He's found my Achilles' heel. I let out a high-pitched squeal of laughter.

"Tickle, tickle," he teases.

133

I hit ANSWER, hoping I don't pee myself.

"Jillian? It's Kitty . . ." I pull my leg from Raine's grasp. My face goes slack and my blood turns to ice when I hear the tone of her voice. It's the same tone she used when Dad died.

I rest my face in my hand and brace myself. "What is it, Kitty?"

Raine sits up. I feel the heavy weight of his gaze on me.

Kitty sniffles and I know. My heart pounds. "Vera had a stroke. She passed away a few minutes ago." Her voice breaks and she sobs. "Can you meet me at the funeral home tomorrow morning?"

I don't need to ask her which one. I know that, too.

I bite down on my hand as my eyes fill. Another one gone. Death 5, Jillian 0.

"Yes." I say through a choked breath. "What time?"

Raine's fingers dig into my shoulder. "What is it?" he whispers. I can't look at him. I suddenly can't get enough air into my lungs and I shake him off.

"Ten?" she says through her tears.

"Okay. I need to go." I choke back the lump in my throat.

"Will you be okay?"

Of course I won't be okay. "Yes. See you tomorrow." I say, and hit END.

"Jillian? What happened? It is your aunt?" Raine asks. His shoulders are tight and the desperate look on his face begs me to answer.

I clasp my hand over my mouth and nod. Then I run.

My lungs compete for air between my sobs as I race out the front door into the cool night. The waves crash on the surf on the far side of the boardwalk across the street. I dash out, avoiding the oncoming headlights, over the gangplank and onto the beach. The tang of the sea air fills my senses and a light breeze blows my hair into my face. The sand feels cool against the soles of my feet, sending a chill through me.

I collapse onto the grainy surface and pound it with my fists, letting out a scream of frustration and loss.

To me, each death is like another star winking out in the sky, one by one, carrying me closer to darkness and to my own death. Life keeps being stolen from around me.

Warm arms envelop me from behind and pull me close until I sit between Raine's legs, and his body shelters mine. He wraps the blanket I keep on the couch around us, creating a cocoon. Then he kisses the side of my head and rests his chin on my shoulder. I welcome the sudden warmth on my gooseflesh-covered skin.

"I'm sorry I ran away," I say, wiping my eyes with the back my hand.

He doesn't speak; he just hands me a tissue. His thoughtfulness touches me and I blow my nose. "Thanks."

The surf pounds the sand farther out in front of us.

His breath is warm on my ear. "The day I came for the photo shoot, you asked me who I sat for to have my portrait painted. Do you remember?"

I freeze when I realize he's about to tell me something about himself—unprompted. I don't know what to say. My mouth refuses to operate, but my hand squeezes his forearm in encouragement. I nod. His uncanny knack for diversion interrupts my grief.

"It was my mom," he says. "She was an artist." He swallows before he continues. "She died in my arms when I was eighteen. It was spring, right before I graduated high school. She had pancreatic cancer. I still miss her," he whispers, and his voice hitches.

My heart lurches. I feel his pain as much as if someone sliced my heart open with a blade. I reach my hand up behind me and caress his cheek. "I'm so sorry, Raine. I understand."

I draw in a deep breath and drop my hand. I share something in return. "I lost my mom to cancer too—breast cancer—when I was fourteen. Vera was mom's twin sister. She and Kitty have been my surrogate mothers ever since. They raised me with my dad. He died four years ago of a heart attack, like Robert. It's just me and Kitty now."

Raine squeezes me tight and buries his face in my neck. "I didn't know," he mumbles. "I would have told you sooner about my mom. I don't want you to go through this alone. I'm here for you."

"Thanks, I appreciate that." I twine my fingers with his under the blanket and suppress a sob in reaction to both my grief and his empathy. Subconsciously, I think I always suspected that she was the one tied to his grief. It explains why he never speaks of her in the present tense. "You were close to your mom, weren't you?"

"Yeah. We were close. She was the one person who really believed in me . . . encouraged me to follow my dreams. You know what was worse than her dying?"

"What?"

"Knowing she was going to die and not being able to do anything but watch that fucking disease steal her life for eight months. Let's just say I'm a little too good at tapping veins," he says, his breath warm next to my cheek.

"You took care of her?"

"Yeah. At the end, she gave up on the chemo and refused to go back to the hospital. Nurses came during the day, and I helped at night if she needed me. The last month was the worst. She needed a lot of morphine."

My heart aches for Raine. "I'm sorry." Kitty, Vera, and Dad shielded me from that with my mom. I probe tentatively. "Is this when things became difficult with your father?"

His chest expands behind me and he releases a deep sigh. "They were always difficult, but after she died everything went to shit and a whole new level of difficult."

"You don't have to tell me if you don't want to."

"How's this? I'll tell you my story if you tell me about Drew . . . the real Drew."

The salt air breeze makes my hair clump and stick to my cheek.

"Only if you go first," I say, sweeping back the piece

closest to my mouth.

"You drive a hard bargain, lady." He kisses the top of my head and snuggles me even closer into him. "My dad worked in banking. We lived in a big house in a good neighborhood. You know the ones? Enough rooms to get lost in, but close enough to your neighbor's to spit and hit it?" His voice fills with resentment, and I already know this story doesn't have a happy ending.

"You grew up with money?"

"Pretty much."

"What happened?"

He inhales deeply and his body clenches around me. "Like I said, things between me and my dad went off the rails long before my mom died. Ever since I turned twelve, he's looked for reasons to punish me. But never in front of my mother. She wouldn't have stood for it. Clever bastard. He was opportunistic. He'd wait for me to fuck up somehow—like the time he caught me skateboarding on the new wood floors in the upstairs hallway—and then use it as a chance to teach me a lesson, knowing I'd lie about the bruises to cover my ass and not upset my mom. Lucky for me he traveled a lot, so it wasn't something I had to deal with every day.

"He didn't use a closed fist until I was fifteen. The day he caught me in bed with my high school girlfriend he punched me for the first time. Really punched me. There was hate behind that punch. That was the day I vowed I'd never let him beat me again. I talked my friend, Mikey Petrillo, into teaching me how to box, and I started weight training like a madman. Once my father realized I could defend myself, things settled down, for the most part. He didn't stop criticizing me, but he thought twice before raising his hand to me."

"Did he ever... touch your mom?" I ask, trying to delicately piece together the extent of his father's domestic violence while sidestepping any judgments about his sexual history and the humiliation he must've felt.

He shakes his head violently. "No way. He loved my mom. She walked on water as far as he was concerned. That's the only saving grace in this whole shit show. He would've cut off his own arm before he touched her. He saved all of his frustration for me."

"I'm sorry, Raine. No one should have to endure that kind of behavior," I say, despising his father even more. I can only imagine the depth of the damage a relationship like that could have on Raine.

"Thanks." He kisses the side of my head. "Things snapped again right after Mom died. I was a mess for most of the summer. But my dad was worse. He hated the fact that he wasn't there when she died, and he resented the hell out of me for being there."

"Where was he?" I ask, finding it odd he wasn't by his wife's deathbed.

"Atlantic City, maybe? I don't know for sure. A couple of months before she passed away, we figured out my dad had a gambling problem. He'd lost his job six months earlier. But that was only part of it. He was a recovered alcoholic for over twenty years, and he never picked up a drink while she was alive. His sobriety ended with a scotch after the funeral. Drinking transformed him into a violent drunk—like he needed more of a reason." He snorts. "By then, I just wanted out. I was on my college countdown, waiting to leave that August."

Raine's story sounds like he's describing someone else's life. I suddenly see the train coming and prepare for the wreck. I clasp his hand tighter. "Where were you supposed to go to school?"

Pain fills his voice. "Princeton. For architecture." Then it clicks. His reaction when I showed him Robert's office. An ache hits my heart.

"Tell me the rest," I whisper and squeeze his thigh.

"I opened a letter the first week of August. It said my tuition was overdue, and if it wasn't paid on receipt, I'd lose my place in the freshman class. I was furious. I confronted my father . . ." Raine falters.

The breeze swirls and mingles our hair around us, brushing my cheek. I ask softly, "What happened?"

His lips rest near my ear. "I didn't realize he'd just downed a fifth of scotch when I went storming in. I waved the letter at him demanding to know why he hadn't paid the bill. I knew he had my full, four-year tuition in a trust account. Rather than give me an answer, he punched me in the face and almost broke my nose. At the same time, he told me he'd drained my college fund. The money was gone, and the house would be in foreclosure by the end of the month. We got into a full-blown fist fight. I thought I'd won but made the mistake of turning my back on him. When I went to leave, he hit me in the back of the head, and then proceeded to kick the crap out of me. I ended up in the hospital for a week."

He tenses around me again while my heart squeezes over how he was treated.

"I hate him, Jillian. He stole my future," he says through gritted teeth.

"What happened after that?" I ask gently, knowing there was more, but not better.

"After I left the hospital, Mikey let me move in with him in Morristown while I got my head straightened out. It was too late to get financial aid. I was screwed. So, I took a year off and worked for Mikey during the day and got loaded every night until I worked as much of the anger out of my system as I could."

I think about what he just said and frown. "Wait. How did you have access to that much alcohol at eighteen?" The legal drinking age in New Jersey is twenty-one.

His shoulder grazes mine as he shrugs behind me. "Mikey was twenty-three and kept the fridge stocked. Then I got a really good fake ID."

I stop myself from saying anything for fear of sounding judgmental. Instead, I ask, "How did you end up back with your father recently?"

He snorts. "It was out of necessity. My father isn't always in a drunken state of rage. When he's not drinking, he's bearable—like he was before my mom died. After the confrontation about school, he begged my forgiveness and swore off drinking. Despite my hating his guts, we've been in touch on and off. I even helped him pack up and move after the foreclosure. He works in a local bank now and stays sober enough to keep the job. But put a drink in his hands, and he turns into Mr. Hyde."

"Why did he hurt you, Raine?"

He hesitates. "I don't really remember what happened before he nailed me on the back of the head. It could've been anything. He gets delusional when he drinks."

"There was no place else for you to go?"

He shakes his head next to mine. "My ex-girlfriend Vanessa basically kicked me out of her townhouse the day I met you in the hospital parking lot. We'd lived together for two years."

I draw in a sharp breath. I didn't expect that. "You lived with Vanessa up until two weeks ago?" Based on the conversation I'd overhead, I would've never guessed the longevity or seriousness of their relationship. But what do I know?

"Technically, but the relationship had been tanking for months before that. We didn't end on good terms." He squeezes me. "Hey, you promised to tell me the Drew story."

I'm still stuck on the live-in girlfriend revelation, feeling a little jealous. *Vanessa?* I wonder what she looks like. I knew I disliked her from their conversation and now I dislike her even more.

I shiver against him. "Can we go back inside where it's warmer first?"

"I'm not keeping you warm enough?" he asks, sounding offended.

"It's not you. The breeze is blowing up underneath the blanket."

Raine gathers me under his arm, and we head back to the house. I think of something and pinch his butt through his jeans.

"Hey!" he flinches.

"For someone smart enough to get accepted to Princeton, I can't believe you tried to con me with the word *Trix*!"

He chuckles and pulls me closer. "It was worth a try."

My heart swells with more than appreciation. I realize he's given me solace and helped me to contain my sorrow. At least for tonight.

Not only that, he's slipped further into my heart; and, for the first time, there's no echo of Drew.

Chapter 23

Raine

"IT'S TIME FOR that drink," I say, and open a bottle of Shiraz I found in the wine rack next to the refrigerator. I pour it into the two glasses on the coffee table while Jillian, still cold from the beach, huddles under a blanket. My ribs hurt like hell, but I'm out of meds. I'm hoping the wine takes the edge off the pain.

Her dark, windblown hair frames her pink cheeks, giving her a free and wild beauty. Other than the haunted look in her eyes, I've never seen her look sexier.

I move the Scrabble board and all of our letters to the dining room table, dim the lights, and then position myself on the couch behind her. I pull her back into my arms, and she lets me hold her again like I did on the beach.

Her aunt's death stirred up my pain, and I couldn't watch her suffer without releasing the pressure inside me. I thought telling my story would be difficult, but once I started talking, I didn't want to stop. With each word, my burden grew lighter. I guess it makes sense. Every moment I spend with her, the less broken I feel. I'm making a leap of faith that she won't use it against me, and hope that I've earned some trust in return.

Now if only the desire in her eyes weren't mixed with

doubt. It's getting impossible to resist throwing her over my shoulder and carrying her off to the bedroom to wipe away her worries. She has no idea how close I came to that last night on the deck. But at least I still have enough sense in my head not to ruin this by doing something stupid and turning her off. I need her to know that my desire to take her on a date has nothing to do with a quick score or keeping a roof over my head.

For now, I'll take that she's returned every kiss I've ever given her.

I hand her a glass, enjoying the warmth of her body in front of me. "Tell me about Drew."

She takes a sip and hands her glass back to me. I put it on the coffee table and she starts.

"After my mother, the second person who died on me was Drew. I was eighteen, the same age as you when you lost your mother."

My arms tighten around her and air rushes from my lungs.

"He's dead?" I feel sick. I hadn't realized that when she said she loved him the other day. I thought he was a high school or college boyfriend who went on to have another life. I suddenly feel bad for some of the comments I made about him in her manuscript.

She nods. "We met the summer after my junior year at a sleepover camp up in Sussex. We were both counselors." Jillian's voice takes on a dreamy quality as she speaks, and her words give me chills. Her head rests on my collarbone, and I snuggle her under my chin. "Drew had just moved to New Jersey from Colorado. His parents had gotten divorced a few months earlier, and he came back east with his mom. We caught each other reading the same book one night, and I knew we had to be friends. When I found out he lived in my town and would be finishing high school with me, it sealed the deal. By the end of the summer, it had turned into more than friendship . . ."

She pauses and a hard knot sits in the middle of my stomach. "Did you have sex with him?" I ask, preparing myself for the answer even though it's kind of dumb being jealous of a dead guy.

She pinches my leg. "Ow! What did I say?" I'm kind of at a loss.

"Only a guy would ask if we had sex instead of if we fell in love," she says, clucking her tongue at me.

My face grows warm. "I can't help it. It's the DNA I've been dealt," I reply, whining in defense of my gender.

"To answer your prying question, yes." Her voice gets dreamy again. "Right before school started. He was my first . . . We fell in that crazy kind of love that only new hearts can have—when everything feels raw and immediate. When you have no idea what forever means, yet you believe in it with a strength and passion that's tied to your ability to live and breathe. I think you lose that as you get older."

I listen to her words and realize I've never had that before. The kind of love that makes me do crazy things or believe in the possibility of forever.

My heart sinks. *If we get together, does that mean she can never have that with me?*

"We were inseparable, even when it came to college. We applied to the same schools, hoping to go together. The day we both received our acceptances to Villanova was one of the happiest days of our lives. We dreamt of our future, of getting married when we graduated college, having kids, the whole fantasy."

The hairs on my arms lift. I dread where this is going, because it can't end any way other than him dead. "When?" and "How?" are the only questions left to answer. I'm almost sorry I asked because then I'll know her pain, and I'd never wish that type of loss on her.

Jillian sighs and reaches down to touch my leg. She rubs it unconsciously, like she's soothing me. "Anyway, it was the summer after my senior year, and we were on the way to a party—just a bunch of us getting together for a barbeque before we all left for college. Drew's mother's car was in the shop, so I took my dad's. We had the music turned up, and we were singing to the radio. I'll never forget the song—Bon Jovi's 'Wanted Dead or Alive.' We'd seen them in concert earlier that summer before school ended. Drew had an amazing voice. . . ." Jillian's voice trails off.

I swallow and brace myself for what's coming.

"The woman who hit us had a heart attack and ran the red light. Her foot hit the accelerator. She struck the passenger side in the middle of the intersection." A sniffle escapes Jillian, and her shoulders shake next to me. "I walked away with only cuts and bruises, but Drew wasn't so lucky. He was pronounced brain dead at the hospital. He died three days later."

I rock her in my arms.

"It was my fault," she whispers, and I stop rocking her.

"No, it wasn't, Jillian." I frown. "What you told me just now? That wasn't your fault."

"I should've paid more attention." She whimpers.

Her guilt assaults me and triggers my anger. "Things happen, Jillian! Shit happens! You didn't make the woman have a heart attack. You didn't do anything wrong. That's why they call it an 'accident.' " Of all the screwed up shit that has happened to me, there's one thing I know . . . it hasn't been my fault. I very clearly know who's to blame.

She's crying now, and it shatters me. I hope it's not because of what I said.

"It's okay," I whisper, and kiss her hair. The smell of the ocean clings to it. "I'm sorry about Drew. It's a profound loss. All I can say is that I think I understand." I squeeze my eyes shut and rock her again. For the first time, I realize that Jillian lost a piece of her future, just like me, at the same point in her life. Her loss draws me so close to her emotionally that I feel my soul sink inside her skin until we intersect in a way I find hard to describe. More than that, it gives me a sense of peace I never thought I'd find.

My mouth dries out when a thought strikes me with sudden clarity. Before I can stop myself, I ask, "When you look at me, do you see only Drew?"

She turns in my arms. Her eyelids are red and puffy, and her eyes look like golden glass. She captures my gaze and holds it. I hold my breath. She touches my cheek. "Not anymore, Raine. I don't. I see you. Just you."

Her fingers tenderly pull my face toward hers and then her lips are on mine. Soft, full, and insistent. Like a dam breaking, the tension disappears inside me and I grip her arms and crush her into me. I ignore the pain in my ribs and explore every inch of her mouth, unable to get enough. My cock hardens so fast, I'm almost dizzy from the shift in blood flow.

Jillian's eyes pop open and she stops kissing me. She backs away and glances down at the bulge in my pants.

I flush, suddenly embarrassed. "Sorry. You have that effect on me."

Her eyebrows lift. "I do? Really?"

I look at her through half-closed eyes. *"Really."* I pull her back on top of me, wanting to keep her there.

Her eyes shift uncomfortably away, and she lays her head on my chest so I can't see her face. "Raine?"

"Hmm?"

"How old are you?"

I tense underneath her. "This again? Why does it matter, Jillian? I'm old enough to legally vote, drink, and have sex in every state of the union."

She turns to look at me. Her voice is weary. "Just answer the question. Please . . ."

I'm afraid if I do, we'll lose this moment. Not that she doesn't already suspect my age, but saying it out loud takes away any cloud of speculation.

I release an exasperated breath, and consider lying. Saying I'm older, but then what? Any trust I've earned by the time she finds out the truth would be at risk. *Fuck it.*

"I'll be twenty-five in December." That's three and half months from now. It's practically around the corner.

She averts her eyes, and then she moves to crawl off me. My fingers bite into her arms, and I narrow my eyes. "No, I'm not going to let you do that. I'm the same man I was five minutes ago. The same man you kissed."

She stops trying to get up, and her eyes meet mine. They're filled with a mixture of pain and longing. I'd give anything to get rid of the part that is pain. This shouldn't be so complicated. Every minute it takes me to get her over this hurdle is agonizing. I want her so badly. I'm not sure I'll make it until our date—three days from now. We agreed over dinner that it would be on Friday night, but with her aunt's death it could easily be longer.

She licks her lips and swallows. "Raine . . . I'm afraid," she whispers.

My expression feels as heavy and pained as hers. "Of what? Of me?"

"No. Raine, you don't understand. I'm afraid that the next time I'm sitting here like this—in mourning—it will be when I lose you."

My mouth drops open, and I stare, weighing her words. Could she possibly feel that much for me already? Could she feel what I feel? Crazy, I know, but my heart hasn't beat this fast for anyone . . . ever, and the thought of not being with her sucks the air from my lungs.

"If I get a taste of you," she says, "I'm afraid that I'll get so caught up in you that I might lose myself." Tears well in her eyes, and my chest constricts. "I don't know if I can handle that. You have your whole life ahead of you . . . . Eventually, you'll want to find someone younger to spend your life with."

She tucks her head back on my chest.

"No, look at me." Gently, I tip up her chin. "I'm not that shallow, and I'm not just passing through, Jillian. I want you, don't you get that? I'm not planning an exit. I'm willing to let this take us wherever it leads. I'm here for you, and I want to prove myself to you, but I'm not going to beg, Jillian. I'm willing to wait until you're ready. But I'm warning you, I won't hold back. I'm going to give it all I have . . . everything. Because we're worth that, and I want you to do the same. If you can't, then I want to just stay friends. It'll kill me, but I'll do it. If that's what you want. Just promise you won't push me away."

She gives me a weak smile. "That was some speech."

I run my fingers over her sea-blown hair. "I meant every word. I know it's impossible to promise never to hurt someone, but I know I'd do anything I could to avoid hurting you. If your age bothered me even a fraction of how much it bothers you, I wouldn't be pursuing you . . . us."

She brushes her finger over my bottom lip. "Is that what you're doing? Pursuing me?"

I throw my head back on the pillow propped up behind me. "Please tell me you're kidding."

"I'm kidding." She chuckles and kisses me lightly on the lips before pulling away. "Thank you . . . for being here and for sharing your story with me. And for listening to mine." She moves to get up, and I wrap my hand around her arm.

"Where are you going?"

Sadness returns to her eyes. "Shower and then to bed. I have to leave early to make it to the funeral home by ten."

"What time should we leave?"

She touches my cheek. "You can stay here if you'd like, and then go to class."

My brow tightens. "Are you trying to get rid of me?"

Her eyes soften. "No. I just don't want you to feel obligated."

"I already told you. I want to be there for you," I say, and my voice goes quiet. "Unless that's not what you want." Grief is a funny, but individual, thing. If it were me, I would want her there. Maybe she's different.

"Be ready at eight," she says and kisses the tip of my nose.

"We'll pack everything up and you can follow me back to Chatham." She crawls off me and heads to the door.

"Jillian?"

She turns.

"Please don't be afraid of me. Promise you'll give us a chance?"

She nods and disappears through the doorway. It takes all my willpower not to get up and follow her again. I wish we were at the point where I was an invited guest in her bed. Instead of her heading to the shower alone, I'd be with her. Afterward, we would slip naked between the cool sheets, and I'd hold her in my arms all night after we made love.

For whatever its worth, that's my idea of Heaven.

Chapter 24

Jillian

"SO WE CAN PICK up the ashes on Wednesday?" Kitty confirms with the funeral director while I sit silently next to her, clutching a damp, balled-up tissue.

I can't bear to look at him. I can't believe the last time I sat here was two years ago; it feels like yesterday. I zone out as Kitty talks through the logistics of the wake which will be held on Saturday. Per Aunt Vera's very specific orders:

My wake shall be no longer than one hour in length and done for those who must stare at my dead corpse for closure. Personally, I'd skip if I could get away with it. So for Heaven's sake, don't make people go. I'd much prefer those I love to attend the memorial service to celebrate my life. I also kindly request that someone is designated to have a drink for me, make that two, before my ashes are cast into the sea.

I almost chuckle inappropriately when Kitty reads it aloud, hearing Aunt Vera's irreverent tone in my head. Vera hated funerals almost as much as I do. She couldn't bring herself to be buried in the ground, turning to "worm food," as she liked to call it. Vera wanted a memorial service at her church, and then for her ashes to be spread into the ocean which she loved so dearly. Kitty and I already decided the service would be held the following Saturday. Afterward, we'll transport her ashes down to Spring Lake as a family.

I move through the rest of the appointment in a fog and feel guilty that I've allowed Kitty to bear most of the burden. But that's always been the nature of our relationship. I defer to her as my strength and pillar — the child to her mother.

"Thank you. I guess we're all set. See you at one o'clock on Saturday," Kitty says, and stands. I mindlessly follow suit. The funeral director leads us out of his office. We each shake his hand, and then Kitty hooks her arm through mine as we exit to the parking lot.

"Is this ever going to stop?" I ask Kitty, not really expecting a reply.

She squeezes my arm. "It's an inevitable part of life, sweetie. You've just had more than your fair share for your age. Will you come back to Vera's to pick out an outfit and some pictures with me?"

I'm torn. I want to, but I don't want to. My emotions are a big, tangled mess inside me. I'm desperate to crawl away from my grief and focus on something with a spark of promise. I find myself craving my next moment with Raine, wanting to curl up in his arms and take shelter from the world. But I realize how selfish it is to saddle him with my sorrow and use his strength as my own. I'm fully aware that my sadness makes me even more vulnerable to his charms and susceptible to making bad decisions. In truth, he's really the last thing I need right now with Vera's death and the deadline for my novel looming, but he's the only thing I really want.

Despite all that, I give Kitty the only right answer. "Of course I will."

In order to prevent Raine from driving me here and sitting in the car to wait, I promised him that I wouldn't be gone too long. I'll text him when I get to Vera's and ask him to delay lunch.

"I've scheduled the clean-out for after the memorial service," Kitty says, "so you have a while to decide if there's anything you want."

"Thanks." I have a copy of the will in my files at home; I already know she left me a painting of the ocean—which I plan to hang at the shore house—and a small bit of money that I don't need. There's nothing more that I want, other than some family photographs.

We stop at my car, and I take Kitty into a tight hug. "Thank you for everything. I wish I had your strength."

Kitty pulls back and looks at me aghast with her warm, chocolate-brown eyes. "Jillian, you're one of the strongest people I know. You inspire *me*. Strength isn't your issue, sweetie; trusting and giving yourself credit is."

My lips part in surprise. I never knew she felt that way. "I don't feel strong."

She nods. "But you are. It's one thing to lose parents, but I've watched you lose the only two men you've ever loved. Not only did you survive, but you've thrived. I sometimes don't know how you've done it."

The truth is that I haven't. I've hidden.

I give her a weak smile. "Neither do I."

Within an hour, we've picked out a nice ocean-blue dress for Vera's wake and rounded up a collage's worth of pictures which Jenny will mount on poster board for us.

I turn off the ignition in the garage, glad to be home. When I walk into the kitchen, I find Raine sitting at the island working on his laptop, and the smell of something delicious coming from the oven.

He looks up and gets off the stool to greet me. "Hey, how did it go?"

Wrapping me in his arms, he holds me inside his warmth. I vow never to tire of feeling his muscled chest next to mine. Energy seeps back into me, and as much as I want to stay locked inside his embrace, I push away and eye the oven. "What are you making?"

He smiles. "Comfort food. We're breaking the diet for today. Homemade mac 'n' cheese."

My stomach reacts with a grumble. "Yum."

He sits back down in front of his laptop and picks up the timer. "Ten more minutes."

My deadline niggles at me. "I'm going to head to my office. Come get me if I'm not back by then, okay?"

"Sure."

I move to leave.

"Jillian?"

I turn back to him. "Hmm?"

He swallows, and tension works its way into his shoulders. "No pressure, but did you still want to go on our date Friday night? With everything... you know. If not, the bar called and asked me if I wanted to take some extra hours."

For a fraction of a second, I wonder if he's having second thoughts before I realize he might be having financial concerns. "Yes, I still want to keep our date for Friday night... but I'll understand if you need to make some extra money."

He looks at me like I'm crazy and smiles. "Over a date with you? No way."

My heart flutters, and warmth fills my chest. "Then it's confirmed. You and me. Date. Friday night."

I leave him in the kitchen and fire up my laptop in my office. I study my outline and sit paralyzed until Raine brings me a steaming bowl of his macaroni and cheese.

"I thought you were going to call me?"

He shrugs. "I figured this would be easier." He hovers over me, waiting until I take a bite. I blow on my first spoonful. My taste buds ignite when it reaches my tongue. "Holy crap! This is the best mac 'n' cheese I've ever tasted." I shovel in another spoonful while trying not to burn the roof of my mouth.

His face lights up with delight, and he leans in to kiss the top of my head. "Enjoy. I have to leave early to meet my project group." There's worry in his eyes when he steps back to look at me. "Will you be okay tonight?"

I smile. "Yeah. I'll be fine. See you when you get home."

"'Kay," he says, and disappears through the doorway.

My fingers sit immobile on the keyboard. Becca and Drew have gone silent in my head. Ever since Raine's comments they've stopped talking to me. I resist the urge to panic. The road to finishing this first draft suddenly looks a hell of a lot longer.

Dammit. I should have never let Raine see those pages.

I stare at the blank screen and sigh. Since my characters refuse to speak to me, I'll tap into my personal well of grief. Maybe it's time to write the scene where Becca loses Drew. If Kitty's right, then I'll have the strength to get it onto the page. And if I get stuck, all I have to do is think about losing Raine, and the words should come.

Chapter 25

Jillian

"OH, HELL, NO," I hear from behind me.

I turn away from the mirror to see Raine striding through the doorway, looking mouthwatering with his hair sweeping down to his shoulders and wearing black tailored dress slacks, a silky button-down, and leather loafers. His face is almost completely healed with only a faint shadow around his eye.

"What?" I glance down at my outfit—a peasant skirt, a flowing top, and high-heeled sandals. He passes me and enters my closet. I hear him flipping through the hangers, and my face screws into a frown. "What are you doing?"

He pops his head out and holds up a short skirt. "I've waited an eternity to take you on a date. Can you please take pity on me and show some leg?"

"What's wrong with what I'm wearing?"

"You seriously don't want me to answer that question." He tosses the skirt onto the bed, and disappears back into my closet.

"Hey! Get out of my closet!"

He emerges with a pair of superhigh heels and a clingy top and tosses them onto the bed on top of the skirt. The shoes were an impulse purchase five years ago . . . for bedroom use only. Before Robert was diagnosed with ED when we were willing to try anything.

I plant my hands on my hips. "Are you nuts?"

He wraps his arms around me, pulls me close, and lays a kiss on my nose. "Yes, about you. Now, will you please put on something that doesn't resemble a potato sack?"

The blue of his eyes shines, and I melt against the hard planes of his chest, resting my pelvis against his. A smile escapes me. "You're a piece of work, you know that?"

"I do."

"Modest, too."

"Totally."

I eye the clothes on the bed and release a heavy sigh. "I'm not sure any of those fit." I give him a mischievous look and kiss his bottom lip. "By the way, those shoes aren't meant for going out in public."

A deep chuckle rises from his throat, and he puts lips to my ear. "I guess that's why they call them 'fuck-me' heels," he whispers and nips my earlobe.

A rush of warmth floods my core. Maybe we should skip dinner.

With a good-natured grin, I push him away. "Get out and let me change."

He grins back and closes the door behind him.

I look at the bed again and shake my head. Crap. I'll look like I belong on a street corner. I pass the bed, scoop up the shoes, and head back into my closet. I swap the bedroom heels for ones that are sexy, but slightly lower, and decide I can live with the skirt and top. Luckily, they fit.

After a three-sixty in front of the mirror, I pluck a thong from my underwear drawer and trade it for my bikinis. I smile, glad that I'm still smooth down below from the Brazilian.

Another glance in the mirror. Better. Actually, not half bad, and no panty lines. My legs have some color from lying out over the summer, so I skip the pantyhose.

I fluff my hair and give it a good shake.

There's a knock at the door. "Jillian, we need to leave if we're going to make our reservation."

"I'm almost ready." I yell through the door. "Be out in a sec."

With a deep breath, I open the door.

Raine fills the doorway and his eyes widen. "Wow! Now that does you justice." He reaches out to me. "Come on."

"Where are you taking me?" I ask. He's been tight-lipped about our destination, refusing to tell me even with my incessant prodding. I'm glad I insisted on keeping our date. Being with him is the only thing that makes me feel alive lately.

"Be patient. It's a surprise."

He drives my car, and we park in the center of Morristown. He escorts me into Roots, an upscale steak house. It's dark and clubby inside. I'm touched, but also concerned that he's spending so much on dinner. I've been here many times, and it's not inexpensive.

He holds the door open for me and then gives the hostess his name.

She smiles pretty at him, sending a shiver of jealousy over my skin. We follow her to a table for two.

Raine holds my chair out for me, and the waitress leaves us with two large one-page menus.

He rubs his hands together nervously. "Is this good?"

I smile, and reach my hand across the table. He takes it in his and I give him a squeeze. "It's wonderful. Thank you."

He beams at me. "I'm glad you like it. I wanted to take you somewhere nice for our first real date."

The servers approach; one is introduced to take care of our drinks, and the other for food.

"Would you like a bottle of wine?" he asks and glances at the menu. We settle on a Shiraz and our servers fade away with our order.

I lean forward and fold my arms on the table. "Is this where we ask each other first date stuff?"

He grins. "Makes it a little hard when we already know hundredth date stuff about each other."

"There's got to be something you'd like to know."

He gazes into my eyes and gives me a sexy grin. "There's definitely one thing, but I'm hoping I find that out later."

His words make me quiver. I confess, I've reached the limit of our flirtation. I'm dying to run my hands and my tongue over his naked body so much that I can almost taste the delicate skin at the base of his neck.

"Besides that," I say.

He hesitates for a moment then leans forward. "If this is too personal, you don't have to answer it. Is there any reason you and Robert didn't have kids?"

I shift uncomfortably in my seat and arch a brow. "Can't we start with something easy, like my favorite color?"

"I said you don't have to answer it if it's too personal," he says coupled with a look of innocence.

Since I plan to strip naked for him later, too personal isn't the issue. "It's not so much that . . . it's complicated," I say.

His eyes spark with interest. "How so? Did you want them and he didn't, or something like that?"

I shake my head. For the first time, I wonder about Raine's expectations. Silly that I didn't think of it sooner, I know. But part of me doubted we would even get this far. "No. I . . ." The words get caught in my throat, so I clear it. " . . . couldn't."

"Oh," he says quietly. "I'm sorry. I guess it wasn't very sensitive of me to ask."

I open my mouth to speak, but the server chooses that moment to come and pour our wine. We each glance briefly at the menu and give the food server our orders. I opt for a salad and salmon, even though it's a steak house, and Raine chooses a NY strip.

When the flurry of wait staff is gone, I reach for his hand.

"Hey, don't feel bad for asking, okay? We tried for years, but something with my ovaries just made it difficult."

"Were you disappointed . . . not having kids?" he asks.

I pause and decide how much to sugarcoat my honesty before slowly shaking my head. "No. I wasn't," I say softly, and leave it at that. In my heart, I was relieved that it never happened for Robert and me. All those years, I tried out of obligation, not desire. Any desire I had for children died with Drew, I'm not sure why. Then again, a lot of hopes and dreams died inside me that day.

I surprise myself and add, "Not that it matters now, but I think it was a blessing in disguise. My sister, Kitty, she always knew she wanted children. Me? Not so much. I was never sure I really wanted them."

"That's too bad . . . I think you'd make a great mom."

"Thanks." I smile. Not really sure what else to say, I reach for my wineglass.

"Wait," he says and picks up his. His eyes sparkle. "I'd like to make a toast."

I raise my glass and my smile widens.

He draws in a deep breath. "To you, Jillian, for saving me in more ways than you know, and for making every day since then brighter. And to us, together, finally."

I clink my glass with his and take a sip. I don't want to ruin the toast or the night, but I can't leave our conversation hanging. "Do you want children, Raine?"

His face takes on a contemplative look, and then he narrows his eyes at me. "No you don't, Jillian. Stop looking for excuses and trying to convince yourself this is a bad idea."

I throw up my hands. "That's not why I asked." *Okay, maybe I was . . .*

He frowns at me and nods. "Yes, it is. Don't forget, we're pretty good at reading each other."

I release a breath and roll my eyes. "I don't want to argue. I was only asking a question."

He crosses his arms and gives me a pointed look. "Fine.

Yes, I'd like to have kids, but it wouldn't be the end of the world if I didn't. Satisfied?"

I try to hide my grin as my stomach unclenches. "Yes, and don't get mad that I'm asking you a first date question."

"First date, my ass," he mumbles.

"Speaking of your ass . . ." I wink at him.

He blushes, and although I get the feeling he'd like to stay mad, a smile creeps onto his lips. "What about it?"

"It's a work of art."

He chuckles. "So is yours."

"Liar." I smile.

"Nope. Do you know the first thought I had when I met you?"

I shake my head.

"*Nice ass.*"

"You're such a guy sometimes," I tease.

"I thought I was a guy all the time," he says, and flashes a rakish smile.

"You know what I mean."

My salad comes, and I push it to the middle of the table for us to share. "Did you mind being an only child?" I ask before I take a forkful of lettuce.

He shrugs. "Not really. I always had plenty of kids my age to hang out with." After a bite of salad, he adds, "I sometimes wonder if that's why my mom and I were so close. Since my dad traveled a lot for business while I was growing up, most of the time it was just us."

"Hmm. I sometimes feel like an only child. Kitty's always seemed so much older than me; even now she feels less like a sister and more like a mom. I always thought it would be great having another sibling closer to my age."

The server delivers our entrees. We manage to avoid any more controversial topics for the remainder of our dinner and find fun and enjoyable things to talk about. Light, uncomplicated things. His favorite color is blue and so is mine. He played varsity soccer in high school; I was a cheerleader.

We're studying the dessert menus when I hear, "Jillian Grant?"

I look up and paste a smile on my face. An older couple approaches our table in a flourish. I recognize them as former clients of Robert's. We've socialized with them in the past, but I haven't seen them since well over a year before Robert died. *What the hell is her name again? Something old-fashioned.*

I ignore Raine's eyes as they bore into me. While he's trying to get a read on who these people are, I'm busy trying to remember whether or not they attended Robert's funeral.

"How are you, dear?" she asks. "It's good to see you out and about. I was just telling Frank that I hardly recognized you sitting here with this handsome young man."

Frank stands politely behind her wearing a cordial smile. *Gladys. That's her name,* I remember, filling with relief.

My stomach drops when I glance at Raine. He's looking at me, waiting to be introduced.

I push down my discomfort, and tip my hand in his direction. "Gladys, Frank, this is Raine."

Gladys looks at him with a wrinkled brow. "I don't recall Robert mentioning you had a son."

Raine clears his throat, and says politely, "I'm not her son." The faint red on his neck tells me he's angry, and he's doing everything in his power not to snap. But telling her he's my "boyfriend" feels wrong. Instead, I pray for a rock to crawl under and say, "He's a friend who is staying with me."

When I glance at Raine again, he looks like he wants to lunge across the table and throttle me.

Gladys turns to him and eyes him like a piece of fresh meat. "Oh, *really?* What is it that you do, Raine? My daughter is about your age. She's a very nice girl."

He's right about one thing. We can read each other well, and from what I can tell from the look in his eyes, he wants blood. Mine.

161

He manages to give her a nice smile before he reaches across the table and squeezes my hand, hard. Then he looks directly at me with an icy glare. "I'm a paid escort, and I like my women a little older." His words slap me in the face, and my blood pressure vaults.

Gladys gasps and backs away. "We were sorry to hear of your loss, Jillian. It was so nice to see you again." They make a hasty exit. When they're out of view, Raine gets up and stalks out the back door. I bolt after him, catching him outside in the courtyard between the buildings and the parking deck.

I grab his arm, yank him to a stop, and scream, "What the hell was that all about?"

He rounds on me, and his eyes are blazing. "A *friend*, Jillian? I'm a *friend* who's staying with you? What the hell's wrong with 'he's my date'? Are you ashamed to be seen with me? Is that it?" His cheeks flush red as he paces and runs his fingers through his hair.

"No, of course, I'm not ashamed of you! How could you even say something like that?" I sigh. "I'm sorry if I didn't want to advertise our relationship to people who I wasn't even sure knew my husband was dead. I didn't do it to slight you or to marginalize my feelings for you. And thanks for embarrassing the crap out of me—and yourself." The heat rises in my face as the words pour out of me.

He stops. "I'm sick of giving up things I want. I don't want to do it anymore. I want you, Jillian, but if you don't want me, just tell me!"

I recognize the broken place he's coming from, and I hate that he can't see what's right in front of him. I take his face in my hands and pull him into a hungry kiss. At first he resists, but slowly he gives in until I'm enveloped in his arms and he takes control. His kiss marries his anger with fiery passion, and he buries his fingers into my lower back as he presses me so tightly against him, I can feel every separate ripple of muscle covering the front of his body. His groin hardens between us, pressing against my belly. My core tightens in response.

When he breaks the kiss, we both stand breathless in his embrace.

"I could never be ashamed of you, Raine. Never. And don't ever undervalue yourself like that again. Do you hear me?"

He kisses the side of my head and hugs me tight. "I'm sorry," he whispers.

My head rests against his chest. "I want you more than I want to breathe, don't you know that?" I whisper back.

"Me, too. I want you that way, too," he says and just holds me there against his beating heart. Finally, he loosens his grip on me and says, "Let's go back inside so the waiter doesn't think I ran out on our check."

I nod, and then remember I left my purse on the chair. "Good idea."

"Will you come with me somewhere before we go home?" he asks.

"Where do you want to go?"

"The Grasshopper for a drink. If you meant what you said, it would mean a lot to me. I'd like you to meet some of my friends." His request takes me by surprise . . . in a good way.

Chapter 26

Raine

I LEAD JILLIAN toward the front of The Grasshopper. I'm still shaken and a little pissed off from our fight outside of Roots. I don't think she even realizes how shitty it made me feel when she introduced me to those people. Like all those things Vanessa and her niece Jenny said to me were true. Good enough for only one thing, but not worthy of respect or acknowledgment.

Being out on a date with Jillian makes me proud; it would never occur to me to hide the fact that she's my date or someone I want to be in a relationship with. I have my arm around her as we approach the bar. I glance at her walking next to me. She looks amazing tonight. The skirt is hot, but her legs are even hotter.

"Hey, buddy," I say to my friend Sean who is manning the door. Big and burly, Sean has a baby face and a mop of red hair. From the neck up, he barely looks old enough to drink legally.

"How ya keepin', Mac?" he replies and fist-bumps me.

"Sean, this is Jillian." I smile down at her and pull her closer into my side.

Sean extends his hand to her. "Nice to meetcha, Jillian. If you decide to dump old Mac, I'll be waiting right out here."

He winks at me.

"Go find your own woman, man, and stay away from mine." I give him a good-natured tap on the shoulder. "Who's working the bar tonight?"

"Dekkie, Ryan, and Fi have it," he says, and gives me a pointed look. "You may be better off takin' a booth." I read between the lines. Probably better for me to avoid Fiona. I don't disagree. No reason for her to be less than civil, but then again, it depends on which side of the bed she woke up on.

I nod. "Good idea." I open the door and shuffle Jillian into the air-conditioned darkness of the bar. I lean in and speak into her ear over the noise. "I want to introduce you to Declan, he's one of the owners, and then we can have a drink downstairs where it's quieter."

She nods vigorously, and we weave our way through the crowd. Every seat is taken. I edge my way up and put Jillian between me and the bar to protect her from the crush around us.

Declan spots me and smiles. It takes less than a moment for his eyes to focus on Jillian, and his smile grows. I quickly scan behind the bar. I see Ryan, but Fi doesn't appear to be around.

Declan leans in halfway to meet us. "Mac, what can I get for ye and yer lovely lady?"

My lips touch Jillian's ear. "What would you like?"

We alternate, and her breath warms my cheek. "I'll stick with Shiraz."

I'm driving, so I order a Guinness, which will do less to damage my sobriety than another glass of wine.

When Declan puts the drinks in front of me, I wave a twenty at him which he blatantly ignores. He leans back over the bar and speaks to Jillian. "So, you must be the special lady Mac was hoping would come by last Saturday night."

Heat rises in my face. "Thanks a lot, Declan. Remind me not to trust you with any of my secrets."

Jillian turns and looks into my eyes. She smiles and kisses

my cheek and then returns her attention to Declan. "Tell me more."

"Not fair. You're not allowed to gang up on me," I say.

"Yer much better than the last one," Declan says to Jillian and spins his finger next to his head in the universal sign for "crazy." "From what I hear, she made extra money as the stand-in for the Loch Ness Monster. You know, he tends to like all things Scottish. Me, on the other hand, I gravitate to all things Irish. By the way, did you know you have a lovely Irish name?"

I roll my eyes and I wonder if this was a mistake. "Stop talking about me like I'm not here," I shout over the din, but Declan is too far gone having fun at my expense. That's nothing new. He's more than kissed the Blarney Stone, he's screwed it. He can talk more shit than a septic tank, but he's good people and has taken good care of me over the last few years.

Finally, he looks up and winks at me. That's his seal of approval. "Jillian, let me give you back to yer date before he asks me to step outside. It's been a pleasure. Let me know if there's anything I can do for ye."

I take her back into my arms and lead her downstairs with our drinks. "He can talk your ear off," I tell her and find a booth in a darker, quieter section of the bar.

"He's lovely, Raine." She touches her fingers to my face. "And he cares about you. I enjoyed meeting him."

Rather than getting into the booth, Jillian puts her drink down and sidesteps me. "Where's the ladies' room?" she asks. I point her in the right direction and slip into the booth.

I'm holding my glass of Guinness, gazing off into space, when another beer glass slams down in front of me. My butt flinches a quarter of an inch off the seat.

Fiona's wild red hair is practically standing on end. "So, is that the one you were waiting for on Sat'rday?" she asks. Her eyes are blazing.

I'm in no mood for Fiona. I scowl at her. "What if it is, Fi? I thought I made it clear my love life is none of your business. Can you please leave?" I search the crowd for Jillian. The last thing I need is any more controversy for one evening, especially when my intention is to take our relationship to the next level before the night is over.

She crosses her milky white arms over her chest. "I thought you weren't ready for something new."

I let out an exasperated breath. "I wasn't, but now I am."

Jillian arrives back at the table and smiles at Fiona before she slides in across from me. She offers her hand, and I tense. "Fi, I presume? I'm Jillian."

Fi takes it and smiles back. "You came across a good one here, Jillian. Treat him well." She casts a glance at me and then melts back into the crowd. My lips part in surprise, and I'm thankful to escape without a scene.

Jillian props her elbow on the table and rests her head on her hand, wearing a mild smile. "Old girlfriend?"

"How did you know?" I ask, stunned.

"Body language. I'm a writer. I notice these kinds of things."

"You're not upset?" I hold my breath.

She shakes her head. "No. It would be silly to be jealous of your past, and it's obvious you don't return her feelings."

I release the air pent up in my lungs. "Thanks."

She pats the cushion next to her. "Come sit with me."

My mouth turns into a smile, and I shift to the other side of the booth to join her.

"Now hold out your hand. I have something for you."

I hold it out, and she pulls it under the table. She places a small ball of cloth in my palm.

My eyes widen and my heart beats faster. "What is it?"

She leans in, pushes my hair aside, and takes my earlobe between her teeth and whispers, "My thong."

Thank God I wasn't drinking, or I would've spit out my beer.

My blood rushes south, and my groin fills and tightens. I

pocket the thong and pull her close. My fingers travel up her bare leg, and I plant my lips on her hair near her ear. "I'm so turned on right now."

She touches her lips to my neck, sending a shiver along my arms. "Let's go home after this drink," she says.

"Mmm. Absolutely." I can't get the thought of her naked under her skirt out of my mind. I rearrange myself and then lightly dance my fingers up along her inner thigh until my fingertips hit delicate, moist skin. I draw in a sharp breath, and I feel my balls contract in my pants. How the hell am I going to make it home without exploding?

For a second, the fact that she's hairless down there puzzles me. Then it clicks. Vanessa had gotten a Brazilian bikini wax once. It was the hottest thing I'd ever seen, besides Jillian's ass. My fingers trail so lightly between her legs that I'm barely touching her.

She closes her eyes and moans next to me. To touch her so intimately in public makes my breath hitch and my cock swell to capacity. I feel her open her legs a little wider. I run my finger along her plump, delicate skin. She's so wet for me. That's when I do it. Slowly, I sink my finger into her heat, and she sucks me inside. My heart hammers and my groin pulses as I work my finger in and out of the slick contours of her body.

I'm tempted to add another finger when she leans in and says, breathlessly next to my ear, "We need to go." I leave her wet warmth and tease her soft, swollen clit with my thumb. She moans again and digs her fingers into my shoulder as I shelter her from view.

As much as I want to run for the door and take her straight to bed, I'm not sure I can stand without alerting everyone in the room that I'm rock hard.

"Jillian, I need you to walk in front of me." I feel my cheeks redden.

"Okay," she says and licks her lips.

I slide over and back out of the booth. When she gets out, I step in behind her and we head for the back exit. I'm tempted to push her up against the side of the brick building, drop *trou*, and bury myself inside her right here. But my saner half sticks to pursuing something more refined . . . like keeping the rest of our clothes on until we're someplace private.

I open the door for her and then slip into the driver's side and start the car. I think back to our conversation over dinner. If she can't get pregnant, I wonder if I'll need the box of condoms in my nightstand after all. The thought of having sex without latex for the first time since I was fifteen makes me giddy. I can guarantee my own health, and after her eighteen-year marriage, I'm certainly not worried about hers.

Chapter 27

Jillian

"JILLIAN." Standing behind me, his breath is a hot whisper on my neck. I shiver as his hands clutch my shoulders and his lips softly kiss the nape of my neck. We barely made it into the guest room. One more step will put us at the foot of Raine's bed.

I let out a soft moan and melt back into him. The effects of the wine are wearing off. I still can't believe I handed him my thong at The Grasshopper, but I'm glad I did. I wanted to erase any doubts he might have had after the scene at dinner and prove to him that I'm committed to ending this night in his arms.

"Do you know how sexy you are?" he asks as his hand reaches around and sneaks into my low, clingy blouse until it finds its way under the cup of my bra. The calloused tip of his finger rubs over my nipple and my whole body clenches, making me acutely aware of my lack of underwear.

He stops. His voice is low and throaty. "Jillian? I asked you a question."

Words stick in my throat. My desire outpaces my feelings of desirability. His hand slips away from my breast. He presses me back hard against his body, and I gasp. His erection underneath his pants rests in the hollow of my spine.

"If you don't answer me, I'm not going to touch you. I'll ask you again. Do you know how sexy you are?" he growls.

"Yes." It's barely a peep, and I feel foolish. Of all the things I feel—crazed with desire is number one—"sexy" barely makes the list even after a couple of Raine's workouts this week.

His hand moves back inside my blouse, and his voice turns seductive, coaxing. Less animal. "Say it again for me, Jillian. Do you know how sexy I think you are?"

"Wait. That's a different question."

"Yeah, but it's the same answer." He nips at my neck playfully and rolls my nipple between his fingers and tugs.

I moan and grow slicker than I already am. I don't want to play games, I want him . . . now.

"Spread your legs," he says into my hair. His other hand travels down around my front and under my skirt.

I obey. His fingers slide between my wet folds until they touch my pulsing core. *Oh, my God.* He buries two fingers inside me and strokes while his lips trail kisses along my shoulders and his other hand works my nipple.

"Mmm. You're so wet for me, Jillian. I love it." He groans as he massages me inside and out, his hard length straining against my back.

My breath comes in short pants as the tension mounts inside me until a soft, guttural moan escapes through my lips. He removes his fingers and takes his hand from my breast, leaving me wanting.

"I don't want you to come until I'm inside you, Jillian," he whispers. He fumbles with his pants behind me, and I almost cry out in anticipation. He lifts my skirt, exposing my naked bottom. I lean forward and grasp the footboard, giving him full access. His fingers trace the tattoo at the base of my spine before he cups my ass in his hands.

"So sexy . . ." he whispers and positions his hot head at my opening.

I moan, ready for him to take me.

"Ask me to make love to you, Jillian. Say, 'Make love to me, Raine.' "

My anger flares alongside my passion. "I have to ask?"

"Yes," he hisses in a harsh whisper. "You have to ask. I want you to understand how much I want you, and how much you deserve to come until you scream. And I need to know that you want me, too, Jillian. That I matter."

His vulnerability unmasks itself and sneaks under my defenses. I swallow hard. Sometimes he amazes me, and I feel like he's the older, wiser one, while at other times, he touches my heart and makes me want to reach out and comfort him.

He rubs up against me, stiff and ready. "Do you want me to use a condom?" he asks in a throaty growl. "I'm healthy, but I'll use one if you want me to."

"No," I say breathlessly, not telling him I'm allergic to latex and have never been able to use condoms. What's the point? It's not like I can get pregnant. All I want is to feel his hot skin against mine.

"Mmm," he moans, "then say it, Jillian." He nudges apart my slick folds from behind with his blunt, velvet head and stops. I'm silent.

"Is it so difficult to meet me halfway?" His voice aches.

I give in, realizing how much he needs my validation and wants me to acknowledge his. "Make love to me, Raine," I whisper. "Right now."

"Oh, Jillian." He growls and thrusts deep. We both let out a moan at the same time as I arch forward even more. "Oh, baby." His hands grasp my hips, and he pumps fast and deep, filling and opening me with each stroke. "You feel too good." He slows and pulls me back against his body while maintaining a delicious pace. Stroking in, stroking out. Slow and easy. His hand reaches around, his fingers gently dancing over my nub. Touching, teasing.

"Raine . . ."

"I love it when you say my name." His voice is soft and sexy.

He pulls out and turns me around to face him and then kicks off his pants the rest of the way. His eyes blaze a bright blue and hold purpose. His lips connect with mine. Hungrily, he takes my mouth and conquers it. His tongue probes and caresses mine as he scoops me up and carries me around to the side of his bed. I feel like a feather cradled and supported in the corded muscles of his arms.

Laying me down, he pulls his shirt, still buttoned, in one fluid movement over his head. He stands before me naked for the first time. I've never seen a man so breathtaking. Smooth skin over hard, carved muscle. I've seen some of that in the shower his first night here and downstairs in the gym, but seeing him completely naked is different. Better. My eyes gravitate to his crotch. Surrounded by a curly thatch of blond hair, his thick shaft stands up and taps his stomach. My heart beats in a staccato rhythm under my breast. To me, he's perfection.

Without a word, he undresses me, discarding my clothes onto the floor.

He looks at me with longing. "You're so beautiful, Jillian. I swear."

I give him my best "come-hither" look, and his mouth twists into a smile as he kneels over me and knees apart my thighs. He lowers himself and his mouth hovers an inch from mine. His hair drapes down around the side of our faces. "Ask me again," he says softly. The warmth of his body heats me from above. "Please."

"Make love to me, Raine," I whisper.

"I thought you'd never ask." His mouth crushes down on mine, and instead of a passionate assault, he tenderly kisses me and slides back inside me. His mouth drinks at my lips, his tongue waltzing with mine, slow and sensuous. He moves slowly and deliberately, rocking his hips into me in a steady rhythm. I grow breathless, losing myself in his kiss while the pressure builds at my core growing hotter with every penetrating thrust. He dips his head and rests it on my shoulder as his fingers travel my body, sending chills over my skin.

"Does this feel good, baby?" he asks.

My eyes half-closed, I meet his insistent gaze. "You know it does, Raine. You feel unbelievable." I touch his cheek. "You're amazing, you know that?"

He smiles, and runs his finger over my lips before his kisses me gently. Then he positions himself squarely on top of me. He wraps one of my legs over his hip and then the other, without missing a stroke. I lock my ankles together tight in the small of his back. He throws his head back and moans. His abs bunch with each deep, penetrating stroke. Changing his angle, he slides over my core with every inward motion.

"Raine . . ." His name escapes my lips through ragged pants, and I arch off the bed. My body loses control in a sudden wave of sheer pulsating ecstasy and I milk his length as I come.

"Fuck . . . Jillian!" He holds me against him and thrusts hard and deep until his shoulders stiffen and his erection kicks inside of me, pulsing as he comes. Sweat covers us in a thin layer, and I collapse with my release, jelly underneath him. He lies with his full weight on top of me and breathes heavily next my ear. Still buried deep, he rolls to the side and cuddles me into him.

"Don't pull out yet," I say, "I want to enjoy you inside me as long as possible."

Our heads rest on the same pillow, and when he smiles, it's filled with satisfaction. "I'd never leave if I didn't have to."

I sweep a strand of his tawny hair back, and stare at his beautiful face. I love the life I see there.

"I loved that," he says and kisses my hair. His strong arms pull me closer, and he molds me to his chest. The succulent smell of his skin mixes with sex and fills the air around us.

"Will you let me hold you all night?"

My mouth opens and then shuts. For a moment, I wonder if I should. I already know a relationship with Raine may not be the best idea . . . but I no longer care about that. I care about him—no, that's a cop out—I think I'm falling in love with him, and I'm no longer going to get in my own way. I've done enough of that. Now it's time to let him carry me away. It's time to let myself get caught up in Raine.

"Is anything wrong?" he asks as his eyes fill with alarm.

I caress the smooth skin of his cheek. "Nothing's wrong. Not anymore."

Maybe I'll feel differently in the cold light of day, but I doubt it. If I made a terrible mistake sleeping with Raine then I'll own that mistake in the morning. For tonight, I'll sleep in his arms and enjoy it.

Chapter 28

Raine

FINGERS BRUSH THE HAIR from my face and coax me awake. My eyes flutter open, and a smile forms on my lips when I feel Jillian's lips tenderly touching mine. My arm tingles from where she rested her head when we fell asleep, finally, deep into the night. We must not have moved.

When I think about last night, my heart fills with enough happiness to explode. I want to jump up and strut around the room with pride, knowing we gave Becca and Drew a run for their money. I managed to make love to her three times. *Yeah, baby!* I'm usually good for two, but I surprised us both. Needless to say, I'm feeling pretty fucking good about it.

"Hey." I kiss her back. I'm aware of her legs entwined with mine and her breasts pressed against my side. It stirs me down below.

There's something in her eyes this morning I haven't seen before. A sense of peace mixed with happiness ... and something else. I feel loved or at least what I think it's supposed to feel like to be loved. Maybe I'm just delusional or wishing too hard.

"Good morning," she says softly and draws her fingertip across my bottom lip. "That was an amazing night."

I wrap her in my arms, and pull her on top of me. There's so much I want to say. I think about how to respond. We've come too far for me to screw it up now. I'm afraid she'll run if I tell her how I feel, so I compromise.

"It's the most incredible night I've ever had." I stare into her golden eyes. "I mean it."

A smile curls on her lips. "That was better than anything I could've written." She kisses my neck and nips at my earlobe. "I think you're setting unrealistic expectations for women."

I chuckle. "Only if you write about it." Then I squeeze her into me. "You're the only one who'll ever know for sure."

She raises her brow. "I'm not your first girlfriend."

But I want you to be my last, I think. "But you're the only one who has ever inspired me to give the best I have to offer." As I speak the words, the truth resonates inside me.

Her eyes soften, and she moves to speak, but stops.

"What?" I ask, clinging to her unspoken words.

Rather than answer, she climbs on top of me and gives me a devilish look.

"Don't start something you're not going to finish," I tease, looking up at her with half-closed eyes. She rubs her delicate, wet skin along my length, and it doesn't take more than a few seconds for my shaft to fully harden and for a moan to rise from my throat. I curl my hands around her hip bones, and shift underneath her as she straddles me. I seek out her opening, wanting to sink into her tight, sexy warmth. But she shifts away just enough so that I can't reach her.

She leans forward, and whispers back, "I wouldn't dream of it. Be patient for me."

I frown but do what she says. Her fingertips travel lightly over the skin of my shoulders before she sinks her lips onto the pulsing vein in my neck. It sends shivers down my back. She traces the strong beat with her tongue as she kisses a trail down to my collarbone.

I can't prevent the next moan that escapes through my lips. I press my pelvis up until my length grinds against her petals of swollen skin. I want in so badly, but she slides away. I almost whimper when she abandons me, and then her mouth hits my nipples one at a time, grazing them lightly with her teeth until they tighten into firm points. I want to scream in ecstasy. Instead, I sink my fingers into her upper arms, and push my head back into the pillow. "Do you know how good this feels?" I growl with my eyes closed. "Let me inside, Jillian. Please . . ."

"Not yet," she breathes.

I groan. "Not fair."

"Everything is fair," she says, dipping her hot tongue into the indentation in the center of my chest. My erection throbs with need, begging for attention. She ignores it, and her fingers travel along the ripples of my torso while her mouth blazes a trail to my navel. She bumps right into the sensitive tip of my cock with her chin before she gets there. Ha! She can't ignore me now . . .

My hands clasp her shoulders and I shudder as she takes me into her mouth. Her tongue circles my tip once then she releases me and moves on.

"Jillian . . ." Her name comes out as a plea. I'd do anything to plunge into her mouth right this second. Then she holds my shaft to the side, so she can dip her tongue into my belly button. I shudder again.

Holy shit. I'm almost at my limit for foreplay; it's like exquisite torture. I need to be inside her somewhere. She lets go of my cock and it springs back to the center of my stomach. She journeys down to the crease along my inner thigh, buries her fingers into my quads, and parts my legs wider. Her tongue darts down to touch my sack, and the next thing I know, she takes my balls into her mouth one at a time.

"*Sssss!*" My nerve endings explode with sensation, and I let go of her shoulders so I don't leave bruises and grip the covers in my fists. My hips jut forward off the bed. More blood pumps to my groin, filling it to a painful capacity.

She licks a trail up my shaft from root to tip, sending fire through my veins. My breath comes in gasps. "Jillian . . . you're killing me."

My eyes connect with hers as she hovers over the tip of my cock, wearing a knowing smile a second before she wraps her lips around me and swallows me up to the hilt. Surrounded in wet, hot bliss, I'm close to losing my mind. My balls contract and my toes involuntarily curl.

"Jillian! Shit." I pant and tangle my fingers in her hair. To avoid choking her, I let her take control and set the pace. Moans rise from her throat as she pleasures me. I've never been worked with such expertise in my life. Her tongue dances in rhythm with her hands as they alternate between massaging my balls with just the right amount of pressure and working my shaft, while her tongue tangos with my tip. My eyes roll back in my head as the pressure builds inside of me. It would be easy to just lie back and explode right here, but I don't want to. I want to take her with me.

"Mmm . . . Stop, let me inside you," I say in a throaty growl. If I'm not careful, I'll get lost in the emerging tide of my pleasure. My length kicks in her hand. "Stop . . . please."

She takes one last pull before she releases me. I groan as I fight with whatever shred of control I can muster to hold myself back. She slides up to meet my eyes. Her lips are plump and slick from working me.

I taste the salty sweetness on them as I take possession. My hands cup the soft skin of her sexy ass, and I position myself under her until my cock connects with her opening. With one thrust, I'm inside, surrounded by her satin heat. She cries out as I rock deep, caressing her from the inside. I focus on her pleasure first to warm her up, grazing over her sensitive center with every thrust.

My body demands me to drive harder. Instead, I ignore it and pull out.

A disappointed gasp comes from her when I leave. I wink, and with a quick roll, she's underneath me.

I return the favor she granted me and slide down her body until my face is between her parted thighs. My fingers reach up to find the hard peaks of her nipples, while my tongue massages her swollen clit.

"Oh, Raine..." she cries and clenches the muscles of her thighs against my cheeks. It gives me a thrill every time she calls my name when I make love to her. I inhale the sweet, musky scent of her laced with some of my salt.

"Raine!" She pulses under my tongue and her body arches off the bed. I lick at her tender folds as she comes for me. A satisfied smile touches my lips. We're as much in tune with each other in bed as we are out, and I love it. It's never felt this good or been this easy with any other woman. I'm convinced now more than ever that I'm meant to be with Jillian. Being with her makes me believe in the crazy love she told me about that can last forever.

I reposition myself over her, and sink back into her heat.

"Come with me," I whisper hoarsely. My arms flex around her, and I hold her tight so that her breasts press against my chest while I move slowly and deliberately enough to hook her for a second time and coax her to climax with me. I memorize every nuance of her lush warmth, and know she's close when I feel her swell again around me.

"You're amazing, you know that?" she pants.

I shake my head. "It's not me. It's us together. That's what's amazing."

It doesn't take long for the pressure to build inside me to the point that I'm holding on by a thread. A groan escapes me as I reach the breaking point. Within a split second, Jillian cries out and her warmth milks my length.

"Jillian!" I unclench my groin and spasm, letting go of all coherent thought and drown in the combined waves of our orgasms.

My strength drains from my body, and I collapse down next to her and pant. Still joined, I pull the covers over us, and roll onto my back, taking her with me. I turn boneless underneath her, enjoying the last of her warmth surrounding me before my inevitable retreat.

After I catch my breath, I kiss her long and deep. Drowsiness overtakes me, and I want nothing more than to fall back asleep and enjoy my new blissful existence. My eyes creep shut.

"Raine?" Jillian says, brushing my cheek with her lips.

"Hmm?"

"I have to get up . . ."

That's right, the wake is today.

"Five minutes and then a shower?" I ask in my satisfied state of sex-coma.

"'K. Five minutes," she says, and snuggles down next to me.

Big mistake.

I wake up to a screaming wail, and Jillian bolting from the bed. "Crap!"

The covers fall away. *"What?"* My heart jolts in my chest, and I sit up with my eyes still glued half-shut. "What's the matter?"

She races around the room collecting her clothes. "We're going to be late! It's twelve thirty!"

The wake starts at one. After a quick calculation, I'm scrambling. Shit! Ten minutes to take a shower and get out the door if we plan to be on time and not get pulled over for speeding on the way.

"Shower," I bark. "Downstairs in ten. Go!"

I see her luscious ass and tattoo practically fly out of the bedroom door as I haul my own naked ass straight into the guest bathroom.

Despite the fact that it's my fault we're late, a smile spreads across my face as I wash off the morning and remainder of last night. It was one of the best nights of my life, and I draw the conclusion that I wouldn't change a minute of it. Even oversleeping.

Chapter 29

Jillian

I HOLD RAINE'S HAND as we walk into the funeral home, and run my free hand over the bun at the back of my head, checking for loose hairs. Dressed in heels and the black dress I've relegated to funerals, I look like the appropriate picture of mourning. For a ten minute sprint, it was the best I could do. At least I don't smell like I just spent the night, and half of the morning, having sex.

"You look beautiful," he whispers next to me, dressed in black jeans and a black button-down. He told me he's saving his suit for the funeral. I'm still angry that I let him talk me into another five minutes of sleep which turned into an hour.

"Where were you?" Kitty's eyes flash at me. She looks matronly in her black suit.

The best defense is a good offense. I don't see my brother-in-law. "Where's Bob?"

She sputters in confusion, not sure whether to continue yelling at me or answer my question. "He took Vera at her word, and decided—and I quote—not to stare at her dead corpse." Her eyes shift to Raine, and she freezes. Blinking rapidly, her hand flies up to cover her mouth.

She obviously sees the resemblance. Even though he's been dead a long time, how could she miss it? His pictures are in the old family album she keeps in the attic. I took one out with the diaries when I started *Twisted Up in Drew* to keep on my desk. I put it away the day Raine came for the photo shoot in fear that he would see it and freak out.

"You must be Raine," she says in a muffled tone from behind her hand, offering her other in a handshake.

"Nice to meet you, Kitty," he says politely although I can see his discomfort.

"God, he looks just like Drew," she blurts, unable to take her eyes off of him. "I'm sorry, that was rude of me. It's just . . ."

"It's okay. Jillian's already told me about him. I guess I look more like Drew than I thought."

"Who's Drew?"

We all turn to look at Jenny.

I smile kindly at her. "Long story, sweetheart. I'll fill you in another time."

Guests start to arrive around us, and I stare up at Raine. "I need to go with Kitty and Jenny to stand up front."

He squeezes my hand and captures my gaze. "I'll take you up there and pay my respects." He tips his head toward the chairs. "I'll sit in the back until it's over."

My heart swells with gratitude. I'm glad he's here. "Thanks, sweetheart."

He kisses the side of my head and then ushers me after Kitty and Jenny toward Vera's casket.

I glance at Vera and my stomach clenches. The waxiness that I hate covers her, making her look like a facsimile of herself. With her spirit gone, all that remains is her empty shell.

We station Jenny a little closer to the door, while Kitty and I stand next to the casket. I accept people's condolences as they file by with kisses and hugs.

During a lull, Kitty leans over. "Brigitte sent a beautiful arrangement," she whispers and points to the biggest one in the room.

"She was so sorry she couldn't be here," I say. She texted me two days ago from Asia with her regrets for missing both the wake and the memorial service. On the bright side, her travel schedule dampened her efforts to hound me on a daily basis to complete my first draft. But if I don't get my muses back soon, I'm going to be in serious trouble with Brigitte and the publisher. I worry that my recent loss of inspiration may have something to do with my budding relationship with Raine and the promise of a life not restricted to paper.

By the end of the hour, even though it feels like over a hundred people have filed by, a healthy line still remains. The funeral director pulls us aside. "How would you like me to proceed?"

"How many people are left?" Kitty asks in a voice that's worried but not panicked.

"Maybe fifty more," he says.

"That's fine. It's not like we can turn them away," I say. Had she been asked, I doubt Aunt Vera would've actually made us enforce her "one hour" rule. My feet ache from standing in heels for so long in one place. I glance at the back of the room, and Raine gives me a little smile as he sits patiently and waits.

"I can't believe how much he looks like Drew," Kitty whispers.

I greet the next guest, and after he passes, I say, "On first glance, and maybe even second. But he's not him, Kitty. He's older, more mature, and much more complex." Even as the words pass through my lips, I realize how unbelievable they sound, but yet how true they are.

We accept our next set of condolences. "Thank you so much for coming," we say almost in unison. The elderly woman moves off toward the casket.

"He's so young," Kitty says softly and then sighs. "Does he make you . . . you know . . . *happy?*"

I glance at Kitty to make sure I understand her question. When I see the wicked spark in her eye, I know what she really means. I try to reconcile the fact that my prim and proper sister is actually asking about my sex life.

"Very," I say, trying to suppress a smile as I remember how I spent the morning.

"Lucky you," she says in a raspy whisper.

"Kitty!" I growl softly.

"What? Enjoy him if he makes you happy." She grips my hand. "Life is too short for regrets, Jillian. Maybe this could be your second chance. The one you didn't have with Drew."

I'm ashamed to say that in the beginning, I had wondered the same thing. Drew died the year Raine was born. As I'd assumed, there's an eighteen-year age difference between myself and Raine. If I believed in reincarnation, it would be easy to let myself get caught up in the metaphysical possibilities. But in the end, it would be unfair to Raine to think of him in those terms. Still . . .

"I honestly hope it lasts," she says sincerely.

So do I, Kitty. So do I. My only question is: Could it cost me my career? If my muses abandon me for much longer, that might become a real possibility.

After the last of the mourners file past, Kitty stares at Raine as he gets up and makes his way to the front of the room.

"You have my blessing, in case you wanted it," she whispers.

I smile at Raine as he approaches. "Thanks, Kitty. That means a lot to me."

In truth, I think Kitty's blessing will mean more to Raine.

Chapter 30

Raine

MY HEART POUNDS AS I sweep past my father's shabby rental in my truck. His car isn't there. It's not on the street or in the driveway. Just to be safe, I sandwich my pickup between some cars a few houses away to stay hidden from view. I turn off the ignition and wait for my pulse to return to normal.

I can do this. I rummage through the toolbox next to me on the seat and grab a slim flashlight, a box knife, and a pair of bolt cutters. That should be enough to get me where I need to go and to retrieve what I want. I toss the flashlight and bolt cutters in an empty backpack, and slip the knife into the back pocket of my jeans.

I step outside into the hot midday sunshine. It's Monday. If he didn't fuck it up, my father is still employed and should be at work for the next few hours. The fact that his car's not here is a good sign. It's now or never. Tomorrow, I'll be back at work, limiting any future chances of doing a little breaking and entering. But that's not the reason. It's only been a few days since my date with Jillian, but I feel hopeful for the first time in a long time. I'm ready to move on and leave my father behind me, but not without my mom's portrait.

My eyes dart around as I walk back toward my father's

house. Just as my fear wells up, I think about the life I want a chance to have with Jillian and it turns to resolve. I pass the house and walk down the driveway to the detached carriage house garage. Glancing around as I go, I'm relieved not to see anyone.

The backpack zipper slides open noiselessly, and I remove the bolt cutters. With one hard snip, the lock falls away and hits the asphalt. I kick it away with my foot and enter the hot, musty garage. Shutting the heavy door behind me, I enclose myself in the oppressive heat and flick on the flashlight. I look around to get my bearings. There's definitely less in here now than the last time I was here. Still somewhat organized in rows, the piles are lower. I weave my way among the boxes and around the stacked up furniture. Luckily, I know which box I'm looking for. The day we moved, I took a Sharpie and marked a red star on it in permanent ink. Rectangular and skinny, the box is shaped to hold a painting. But there are at least a hundred of them in that shape, all containing work from my mom's studio.

Sweat trickles down my back, and I sneeze, motivating me to find what I need fast and get out. I flip through the dusty boxes. My heart sinks lower as my flashlight passes over each one, seeking the red star and not finding it. When I get to the last box, I want to scream in frustration.

My T-shirt is soaked, and I have trouble breathing in the heated air. But I refuse to give up and make another pass through. When I get to the far corner of the garage, I spot something behind an old desk. Holding the flashlight between my teeth, I slide the desk forward.

My pulse races when I see the star. I pull the box over the desk and slit the tape holding the flaps together with the box cutter. Carefully, I slide out the bubble-wrapped painting. My face peers out from next to my mom's through the tiny plastic cushions. I punch the air in triumph and slip the painting back into the box.

As I get to the door, voices outside freeze me in place. I

listen over my pounding heart, and hold my labored breath. If I don't get out of here soon, I'm going to pass out.

I blow out the remaining air in my lungs when I realize they're speaking Spanish and it's not my father. Peering through the dirt-caked glass windows at the top of the garage door, I catch a glimpse of the next-door neighbors over the high wooden fence and slump with relief. My hair is plastered to the sides of my head. I feel faint. It's time to bust a move; I crack the door open as quietly as I can.

They yammer on in Spanish without noticing me. The door shuts with a faint squeak. Hunkering down low, I head up the driveway with the boxed painting and my tools.

I give the street a hasty look before hightailing it to my truck. Once the painting and backpack are loaded into the flatbed, I get out of Dodge as fast as I can. It's only when I reach the main road that I slow down and my muscles relax. The air-conditioning blows on my wet shirt and sends a shiver over my skin. I catch a whiff of myself.

"Whew!"

I need to shower . . . bad.

But I can't wait to show Jillian the painting. I'm not sure I can explain, even to her, how much it means to me. I carry some photographs of my mom—some with me in them, and some without—but they'll never be as special as this portrait.

When I pull into the driveway, I don't even bother to park in the garage. Instead, I pull up and park in front of the door next to where Jillian's SUV is parked inside. Like a kid on Christmas, I swell with excitement and retrieve the painting out from under the flatbed cover and carry it through the front door.

"Jillian! I'm back," I yell.

"I'm in my office," she replies.

I kick my shoes off inside the door and trek the awkward-sized box to her office. She peeks up over her laptop.

I light up, unable to contain my excitement. "I got the portrait."

She rises and claps her hands together. "I can't wait to see it."

"I'll show it to you, and then I need to jump in the shower." I lean the box against her desk, and wrinkle my nose. "I reek."

She giggles. "I know. I can smell you from here."

"Sorry. It was like a steam bath in that garage," I say apologetically as I slice carefully through the bubble wrap to unveil the portrait.

Pulling it out, I hold it up for her. It's done in an Impressionist style using pastel-colored paints.

She comes around to get a better look. Her fingertips pass over the canvas, and she glances between me and the portrait and smiles. "It's so special. I understand why you had to have it. It captures the bond between you perfectly. I love it."

Warmth floods my chest. I love that she loves it.

She beams at me. "Where do you want to hang it?"

I stare at her dumbfounded. It takes me a minute to process her question. "You want me to stay?" I swallow past the lump rising in my throat.

Her smile grows and she nods. "I do," she says softly.

I rest the painting against her desk, and take her in my arms. "I'm sorry to hug you when I smell so bad, but you just made me really happy."

"You can hug me any time, even when you smell." She squeezes me back. God, I want to tell her I love her so badly . . . but I'm afraid.

She leans back in my arms and gazes up at me. "Why don't you shower, and then, if you're up for it, I have some revised pages for you to read. I'm desperate for some help."

I loosen my embrace. "Sure." I dip my lips to meet hers for a quick kiss and growl. "Then maybe I can convince you to take a little 'research' break for your love scenes."

"You're going to wear me out if this keeps up," she says and cups my ass through my jeans before she lets me go.

"Ha. I'll believe it when I see it." I head for the door but lean on the doorjamb and glance back at her. "I'll think about where to hang the painting while I shower."

She nods and smiles broadly. "Take your time, there's no rush."

I smile back. As I round the corner to get to the stairs, a fist lands solidly in my face, and I cry out. I reach for my nose, and an arm locks around my neck from behind. Panic fills me as I claw at his arm.

"You little fuck," he says. Whiskey-filled spittle sprays the side of my face. "Did you think you could steal from me?"

"How did you find me?" I grit out as my windpipe starts to close.

"You think you're so smart? I saw your truck drive away, and I followed you here, you dumb shit. Now where's that fucking ring!"

Stars dance in my vision, and I struggle for air. "I . . . don't . . . have . . . it!"

"Did you give it to your girlfriend? Do I have to cut her finger off to get it back?"

The thought of him harming Jillian sets me on fire. I jam my elbow back with such force I hear a crack when it sinks into his ribs. Maybe I returned the favor. He grunts and loosens his grip on my throat. I twist away and fall out of his grasp, gasping for air. He hurls his body at me and drives me onto the marble floor, hard. The force jars my healing ribs, but I'm able to protect the back of my head. That doesn't stop the pain from radiating up my spine.

"Give it back!" he screams into my face.

Click!

"Don't move or I'll blow a hole in your worthless head," Jillian says through gritted teeth.

I look into her cold, serious eyes. Over his shoulder, she grips the gun in both hands with confidence and skill. I don't doubt for a moment she would kill him to save me.

My father's eyes grow wide, and he freezes. "If Raine gives me what I want, I'll never bother you again."

"I don't give a shit what you want. If you ever step foot in this house or touch Raine again, I'll make sure you end up dead. Do you understand *me*?"

This is the first I've seen of badass Jillian, and I love it. I love her even more. Sirens blare in the distance and grow louder.

"Right on time. Now, get up and keep your hands where I can see them," she says.

He rolls off me and gets up with his hands in view. I spring to my feet, ignoring my pain.

"Hey, *Dad*?"

When he looks at me, I wind my arm back and punch him squarely in the face with all my might. His head snaps back and he goes flying, landing in a broken heap on the marble.

My knuckles hurt like hell, but it was worth it.

"Well deserved," Jillian grins, and keeps the gun pointed at him until the police arrive a few minutes later. Then she flips the safety back on and sticks it in her waistband.

I look at her in awe with my mouth agape.

She shrugs. "Don't look so impressed. I have a license to carry," she says, and walks past me to answer the door.

"Hey, John. Thanks for coming," she says, greeting the plain clothes officer wearing a sport jacket. His salt-and-pepper hair is clipped high and tight, and he carries a few too many pounds around his middle.

He dips in and kisses her on the cheek. "You're lucky I was close by. Plus, you know I'd do anything for Kitty's little sister." He glances down at my dad, who lies moaning on the ground, and points. "I presume this is the douche bag who attacked you both?"

John turns to the uniform as he walks past. "Cuff this jackwad, Curt, and get him outta here."

Jillian catches my eye. "Hey, John. This is Raine ... my partner. Raine, this is Detective John Henshaw." My heart swells with pride, and I give a half-smile. After the disaster with those people at dinner, Jillian asked if she could use "partner" instead of "boyfriend," saying it felt more adult to her. I told her I was cool with it.

She glances over at my dad, still in a daze as he's being hauled out. I landed a great right hook, if I do say so myself. "And that's his father. I'll pull the disk from the security system so you can view the entire incident."

John turns to me with a friendly smile and an extended hand. "Nice to meet you. Wish it were under better circumstances."

"Pleasure," I say before turning to Jillian with pleading eyes. "I'm going to hit the shower if you don't need me."

"Go ahead. I'll get John the security disks so he can take them into evidence."

John waves his hand at me. "No worries, Raine. You and Jillian can come downtown later to make a statement."

I nod gratefully and head to the stairs. I take them one painful step at a time.

It's not until I shed my clothes and turn on the shower that I start to shake uncontrollably.

Chapter 31

Jillian

"JILLY, I DIDN'T REALIZE you liked 'em so young," John says, wiggling his eyebrows at me once we're inside my office.

I purse my lips and give him a good-natured shove. "Don't start with me. He's not that young. Well, maybe he is. But I don't care. He's really good to me and that's what counts."

"You're into assaulting detectives, too, I see," he says, wearing a broad grin.

"Only when it's warranted," I say and grab the CD from the disk recorder located inside my closet. Robert installed the security system a decade ago after a crazy client had stalked him. He bought me a Beretta, which I keep locked inside my desk drawer, and a Glock for himself, which is in my bedside table. John trained us both on how to use and maintain them.

"How's Kitten?" he asks shyly. John and Kitty were high school sweethearts, but Kitty broke his heart when she married Bob. John later married, but then divorced. Even after all these years, I still see the love he has for her in his eyes.

I hand him the disk and smile sadly. "She's been much better since the wake."

He grabs my arm. "What wake? Who died?"

My eyebrows knit together. "Aunt Vera. The memorial service is Saturday. Didn't Kitty contact you?"

John's face folds, and he shakes his head. "No. Jilly, I'm so sorry. Where's the service? I'd like to pay my respects."

"St. Theresa's. Ten a.m.," I say, disappointed that Kitty forgot to tell him. I wonder whether it was intentional.

John pushes the painting aside and sits on the edge of my desk. His eyes size me up. "And how are you, Jillian? How are you really doing?"

I shrug and release a sigh as I drop into a chair facing my desk. "On one hand, fantastic and never been better. On the other, one step away from losing it." I look down to study my hands. My calm cracks and I realize how close I was to pulling the trigger on another human being. "If I had seen him punch Raine one more time, I would have shot him, John. I swear I would've."

"What was he even doing here? Fathers don't come and randomly beat the crap out of their adult kids."

I shake my head. "I really don't know why he came here today." I glance at the painting, but I'm not convinced retrieving it was the end game. All that did was lead him here. He wanted something else. "He shouted something about a ring that he needed back, thinking maybe Raine gave it to me . . . I don't know."

John crosses his arms. "Your boyfriend has some older bruising on his face. How did he get it?"

I snort. "More work done compliments of his father. The man has a history of drinking and violence. Ten days ago, I picked Raine up from the hospital after his father cold-cocked him, giving him a severe concussion and broken ribs. I asked him to move in with me after that so he would have a safe place to stay. Supposedly, that was the first incident since he moved out when he was eighteen." *As far as I know.*

John purses his lips and narrows his eyes. "You love him, don't you?"

I nod, unable to avoid acknowledging what is so obvious.

The truth is that I don't want to hide it anymore, so I look him straight in the eye and confess. "More than I have a right to."

John smiles and nods his approval. "Good. Love is good. Don't waste it."

"That coming from an old curmudgeon like you?"

"Hey, don't let it get around." He gets up and waves the disk at me on his way to the door. "I'll make sure this gets in the right hands. In the interim, let me see what else I can dig up on this clown. I'll file a restraining order for good measure."

"Thanks. We'll be down in an hour or so."

"How's your book going?" he asks when he reaches the entrance.

I shrug, and run my fingers through my hair. "If I don't pick up the pace, you might have a homicide on your hands when Brigitte kills me." I'm only half joking.

He chuckles. "She's a tough one, that Brigitte."

"Either way, I should have some preliminary research questions ready for you in about two weeks," I say.

"I look forward to it. See you later, Jilly." He hesitates and then says, "Tell Kitten 'hi' for me, will ya?"

I beam at him. "You know I will, and thanks for everything."

As soon as the door shuts, I race upstairs and follow the sound of running water. The bathroom shower is filled with steam when I crack open the door. An alarm triggers inside me when I see Raine huddled in the corner of the walk-in shower with his arms wrapped around his legs. My stomach lurches. I strip naked as fast as I can.

"Raine?" My fingers graze his arm, and I drop down onto my knees next to him. The water cascades down over us. He lifts his head, and his eyes connect with mine. The look inside them is raw and wild. A wet clump of hair hangs down next to his cheek; I push it away from his face. He takes my hand and presses my palm to his lips a moment before he leans forward and wraps his arms around me, almost crushing me with his strength. His lips take mine. Urgent and hungry. The tiny stone tiles dig into my knees, but I don't care. His fingers firmly press me closer to him until there's no room left between us. The water wraps us in wet warmth, and I sip some of it as we kiss.

He pulls me onto my feet, and within seconds he's fully erect against my belly. My body responds instinctively. My core clenches in anticipation, flooding the juncture of my thighs with heat and preparing me to welcome him.

With his eyes half-closed, he whispers hoarsely, "I need you, Jillian." His lips seek out my jaw, devouring a trail down to the tender skin of my neck. "I need this," he growls, and steps behind me, pulling me back against the hard planes of his chest and his throbbing erection. I crave this raw passion between us. I know exactly what he needs, because I need it, too. I need to cleanse myself and exorcise the ugliness and feelings of rage that I experienced earlier. I can do that with Raine—we can do that for each other.

A primal urge drives me to spread my legs and rest my cheek against the tile wall. With my hands to support me, I arch back and offer myself to him. I hunger to feel his strength inside me.

His hands curl around my hips from behind, and he opens me with his thick head. In one thrust, he plunges deep, letting out a guttural roar as he enters. He thrusts into me with a wild abandon that he's never had before and utters my name between impassioned groans.

I push back into him, meeting his punishing rhythm stroke for stroke, enjoying the wet, delicious friction.

Without warning, he slows his thrusts and covers my back with his chest. Wrapping his arms around me, he pulls me up into a standing position against him. His length swells and fills me, rooted there inside me. He leans his chin on my shoulder. His breath comes in ragged gasps against my cheek.

"Jillian..." he says, and lets out a husky sigh. His lips

tenderly touch the base of my neck, and his movements inside me turn to a stroking caress. With a groan, he eases himself out, and turns me to face him. I whimper at his abandonment.

His eyes reflect a purposeful intensity, and he cups my cheeks gently as he kisses me deeply, exploring my mouth and taking possession. When he pulls away again, he presses his forehead to mine. His fingers weave into my hair, and I shut my eyes to keep out the water that's streaming down my face in small rivers.

"Jillian . . . I love you," he whispers.

My heart skips a beat and my eyes flutter open to meet his gaze. For a second, my breath catches in my throat.

His words hang suspended between us.

I rest my hands on his chest, and set my heart free. "I love you, too, Raine."

He closes his eyes, and crushes me in an embrace. "Oh, Jillian . . ."

My heart squeezes. I take him in my hand and glide my fist over his throbbing length. "Let me show you how much," I whisper, and kiss his lower lip.

His eyes open and flare with desire. He dips down and flexes his arms underneath my thighs, lifting me. "Wrap your legs around me," he says hoarsely.

I cross my ankles in the hollow at the small of his back, opening myself for him to enter. He presses my back against the chilly tile in the corner of the shower. Using the wall as leverage, he lowers me onto his erection until he's buried deep. He lets out a hiss, and his fingers sink deeper into my thighs as he moves me in tandem with his thrusts. I moan at the delicious feel of him filling me.

His rhythm is fast and urgent. A groan rises from his throat, and his lips find mine. He moves us away from the wall, so that we're freestanding, and plays my body like a Stradivarius. The precision of his movements stroke my core, and I feel the rising tide of my release.

He throws back his head, and grits his teeth. "Come for

me, Jillian."

I tip over the edge. "Raine!"

"I feel you." He shuts his eyes and thrusts harder. His face contorts, and he loses himself in the chase. When he cries out, his expression turns to ecstasy and his body pulses in time with mine. He backs us up into the wall, and collapses against me. My muscles quake as I unlock my legs from his around hips and slide down along his body.

He draws me closer, breathing hard against my ear. "If he had hurt you —"

"Shh," I say into his shoulder and hug him tight. The adrenaline rush from earlier begins to ebb, leaving my muscles weak and shaky. I hate to let reality ruin our moment, but we have an appointment downtown. "We'll talk about it later," I whisper. "I told John we'd be there in a little while."

Raine shudders against me before he lets me go and reaches for the hand shower. He rinses us and shuts off the water.

Within five minutes, I'm toweled dry and digging in my closet for something to wear while Raine gets ready in the guest room.

A smile touches my lips from the delicious ache that remains between my legs, a pleasant reminder not only of our encounter but of the words we exchanged.

I turn and stare at the empty side of my walk-in closet and sigh. It's time to see some clothes on that side, not to mention filling the other side of my bed. I've slept with Raine for the last three nights, but always in the guest room. I realize what I need to do to complete my surrender.

When I'm done dressing, I find him in the kitchen at the island having a snack.

He points to a plate with a sandwich on whole grain. "I figured you might be hungry, so I made that for you," he says, then takes a large bite from his.

"Thanks." I smile, and pull up the stool next to him. "What

do you think about moving into my room?" I say, and pick up my sandwich.

"I'd love it," he says, wide-eyed.

I finish chewing. "Good. You can move your stuff in when we get back."

He hooks his arm around my neck, and pulls me close enough to kiss the side of my head. "That means a lot to me, Jillian."

I brush a piece of his damp, tawny hair behind his ear. He's stopped wearing it back, knowing I like it loose. My gaze locks onto his. "I know it does."

"I hope you don't get sick of hearing this, because I'm going to keep saying it—I love you." His eyes shine such a bright blue. I don't think I've ever seen such a beautiful pair of eyes. Maybe it's the love in them that gives them their beauty, or maybe it's just because they belong to Raine.

"I love you, too, Raine." I cup his smooth cheek and sigh. "It's impossible for me not to love you." I surrender to the truth inside those words.

He takes my free hand and places his lips against my knuckles. His eyes never leave mine during the kiss. "You make me feel so good about myself, you know that?"

That he doesn't feel good about himself to begin with practically breaks my heart. He's blind to his own value sometimes. I'm committed to helping him find it and never doubt it again. When I look at Raine, I see a talented and loving man. And I don't see Drew, not anymore.

I shake my head. "You have a lot to be proud of. Don't ever let anyone take that away from you."

He kisses me lightly on the lips in response and settles back onto his stool. A moment later, he says softly, "I think I know where I want to hang the painting."

"Where's that?"

He takes a deep breath, and holds my gaze. "Robert's office."

I nod. "It would be perfect there. There's just one thing."

His shoulders stiffen. "What's that?"

"It's your office now."

He relaxes next to me and his lips caress mine.

Kissing Raine sustains me in a way I've never thought possible. I push away the fear that taunts me, telling me that I won't be able to keep him. That someday he'll leave me. That someday I'll experience something worse than another funeral. But for now, I force down the fear and give myself permission to put my heart at risk. I release my passion, and let myself drown in Raine for today.

Carpe Diem.

Chapter 32

Jillian

"ASHES TO ASHES, dust to dust..." The priest delivers the passage that Vera selected years ago when she planned her own funeral.

Her ashes sit on a pedestal at the front of the church encased in a shiny silver urn that Kitty and I picked out. Classic and beautiful, just like Vera.

Raine stands tall next to me in a black suit with his hair neatly tied back. His fingers are entwined tightly with mine. I take solace in his strength. He leans in and whispers, "Are you doing okay?"

I nod, clutching a wet tissue in my hand. He's checked in with me three times since I survived delivering the eulogy with Kitty earlier, and I don't mind.

We stand next to Kitty, Bob, and Jenny. At the end of the aisle is my Aunt Sue who is my mother's and Vera's younger sister, and the only living relative from my mom's immediate family. She flew up from Florida yesterday and is staying for the weekend. The rest of the cavernous church is filled with Aunt Vera's senior citizens group, and the many families whose children she taught as one of the longest-tenured Sunday school teachers at St. Theresa's. John is sitting in the back. I spotted him earlier when I was at the podium.

My stomach aches as loss fills the center. The finality of knowing I'll never hear my Aunt Vera laugh in that girly giggle she had, or watch her face light up as she tells me about all the "sexy bits" in the latest romance novel she read, or eat her apple cake, or cry on her shoulder, I feel more alone in the world with her gone.

I squeeze Raine's hand. He pulls me in front of him so that he can shelter me inside his arms.

As the final hymn ends, our row exits to the back of the church, and we form a receiving line for the mourners to file past and give their condolences. Raine stands silently next to me at the end of the line.

Like an automaton, I shake hands and receive kisses from people I know, and some that I don't. Some I met at the wake, some I didn't. Raine slips me new tissues as I need them.

John finally comes at the tail end of the procession of guests. Most of them have already scattered and gone to their cars. Only our immediate family, and Raine, will travel down to the beach house to transport Aunt Vera's ashes. Kitty and I will spread them after dark, once the beach is clear of tourists and sunbathers.

John greets Aunt Sue and then stops in front of Kitty. He gives Bob only a cursory glance.

"Kitten, I'm so sorry for your loss," he says. Bob steps away, half to give them privacy and half to hide his jealousy. I've watched this same dance happen many times over the years.

John's mouth is grim, but his eyes are kind when they rest on Kitty. He takes her hands in his and squeezes. She smiles sadly. "Thank you for coming, John. Vera was very fond of you."

I watch all the unspoken dialogue pass between them through their eyes. Kitty saying she's sorry and that she'll always love him, John telling her he'll never forget her and will always love her, too. I wish I knew the details of why Kitty made the choice she made, but even after all these years, she won't discuss it.

John leans in and gives her a kiss on the cheek, and tears glistens in Kitty's eye as she closes them for a moment at the touch of his lips. I suspect her tears aren't just related to Vera.

John clears his throat when he pulls away and moves to Jenny for a hug. "Sorry for your loss, Jenny dear."

She smiles kindly through her red-rimmed eyes. "Thanks, Detective Henshaw."

When he gets to us, he pulls me into a firm hug. His face is all business when he steps back. "Jilly, can you and Raine step away with me for a minute?"

His words send a tingle of worry down my back, and Raine stiffens next to me. We haven't heard much about the incident with his father since we gave our formal statements this past Monday. Thankfully, we haven't had any unwelcome visits, either. Raine's father was released from custody after being charged with breaking and entering and assault charges. We still aren't sure how he made bail given his lack of capital. The trial date is set for next month, and I'm eager to hear if John has any other news.

We walk around the corner into the courtyard.

John takes a deep breath and scrubs his hand over his face. "The last thing I wanted to do today was to bring you both bad news."

I feel the unmistakable prickle of hairs on my arms standing on end at the same time Raine tightens his grip on my hand so that I can barely feel my fingers. "What is it?" I ask and brace myself.

He turns to Raine, and says gently, "I'm very sorry, Raine. Your father's body was fished out of the Hudson River early this morning. Since my name was on his case file, they contacted me directly."

An involuntary gasp escapes through my lips, and Raine's body sways beside me.

John motions to the bench with his hand. "Let's sit. There's more," he says solemnly.

I glance at Raine, and his face is ghost white. "Will you be okay to hear this?" I whisper. He nods, but doesn't utter a sound.

John sighs. "I did some digging. Raine, did you know your father was let go from his job three weeks ago?"

He shakes his head. "No," he says so softly it's no more than a whisper.

"I also found out that your father took out some big loans with the wrong people. His gambling debt was sky high. He owed some serious coin to the tune of two hundred grand. At this point, even though it looks like a suicide, I suspect it was a hit. Let's just say, the person who posted his bail had connections. Either way, this just became a federal case, so I'll be turning over my files."

My eyes go wide. "John, what about Raine? Is he in any danger? His father thought he had something of value."

John shakes his head. "I honestly don't think so. But the Feds will probably want to talk to you both at some point."

"Do you need me to identify the body?" Raine asks quietly.

"No. He's been in the water for several days so you probably wouldn't recognize him anyway. Since he was in the system, we made a positive ID based on his fingerprints and identifying marks."

When I look at Raine, his head is hanging, his arms resting on his thighs. I know him well enough now to realize his reaction means he's deep in thought. With his father dead under these circumstances, there's a lot to think about. Or maybe he's shell-shocked. I'll find out once we're alone.

Raine lifts his head and asks, "Will I get a chance to see him?"

"Once they're done with the body, the funeral home can make their arrangements. It's probably best to speak with them," John says kindly. "I'm really sorry for your loss, Raine, truly. You'll have to forgive me for dumping this all on you here."

Raine nods. "I understand."

"When do you think they will release his father's body?" I ask, wondering if I should intervene on his behalf.

John shrugs. "Given the nature of his death? Two days, minimum."

I breathe a sigh of relief. One thing at a time. We'll deal with this on Monday. "Thanks, John."

"Like I said, sorry to bring this to your doorstep today, but I figured it was better coming from me than having the Feds show up at your house and surprise you."

"I appreciate that," I say.

Raine lets go of my hand and stands. He offers a handshake to John. "Thanks, John, I appreciate it, too." He seems stronger than he did a minute ago. I take that as a good sign.

"Any time, Raine. I'll be in touch."

As John walks away, I pull Raine into a hug. He rests his cheek on my hair. "How're you doing? Will you make it today?" I ask.

"Yeah, I think I will."

And I believe him.

Chapter 33

Raine

"DOES IT MAKE ME a bad person to feel relieved?" I ask, taking the steering wheel of my truck into a chokehold. My knuckles strain under the pressure, and my skin turns white. Rather than glance at Jillian, I keep my eyes glued to Bob's car as he exits the Garden State Parkway to get to Jillian's beach house. A negligible dose of sadness is laced with my relief. Once I became a teenager my father only elicited fear inside me, not love. I'm not sad for that man. I honestly don't feel any grief at all, only an airy numbness.

Jillian's fingers caress my arm and then drop away. "I don't think it makes you a bad person, Raine. Not in this case."

"I don't think he ever loved me, you know," I say. Instead of saddening me, my admission sets my teeth on edge. Anger wells up into my chest. I think back to what he said about wishing my mother had had an abortion. Without mincing his words, he told me he wished I never existed. What kind of depraved human being says that to his kid?

"That can't be true. I know it seems that way, but I think he was a sick, desperate man. Deep down in his heart, he loved you. It would've been impossible for him as a father not to," she says. "Raine... There's one thing I've been wondering..." She pauses and when I glance over, she's looking at me.

"What's that?"

"What ring was he talking about?"

My shoulders tense. I don't want to answer that question for more than one reason, so I lie. "I don't know," I say, and tell myself it'll be better for Jillian if she doesn't know.

"Why did he think you had it?"

I shrug, and feel like a shitheel for lying again. "I don't know."

"Hmm. Should we contact your grandparents?" she asks softly.

I breathe a silent sigh of relief that she's moved on and let go of the ring. But her question confuses me for a second until I remember that I haven't told her much about my family. Since I no longer have a reason to hold back, I blurt it all out, giving her the basics. "My dad's parents died in a car crash when he was young. He was an only child, like me."

"What about your mom's family?"

"They live in Sweden. I'll give them a call tomorrow to let them know." I shake my head. "I never told them what happened after mom died. They only know we moved, and I didn't go to Princeton, but not the reason why. They don't know anything about the drinking or the gambling. My mom wouldn't have wanted them to know, since they didn't like my father much and weren't happy she married him."

"When was the last time you saw them?" she asks.

"At her funeral."

"You have no other family in the States?"

"No. No one," I say, but the truth doesn't leave me as lonely as it did before I met Jillian. With her, I feel at home. Maybe I'll even be considered a part of her family someday.

"What brought your mom over from Sweden?"

Thinking of my mom brings a smile to my face. "Before she was an artist, she was an international fashion model. She met my dad at a party in New York City. The rest, you could say, is history."

"Really?" Jillian says with heightened interest. "What was her name? I started my career in fashion photography. I worked for one of the top photographers and did a lot of shoots for the big designers and retailers."

"Selka Nilsson," I say, and glance at Jillian for her reaction. "Her maiden name is my middle name."

Her mouth drops open and her eyes light up. "Oh, my God. I remember shooting Selka a couple of times. She retired in the late-nineties, didn't she?"

I smile, happy to make the connection between her and my mom. Knowing that they met, even in a professional setting, makes me happy. "Yeah. She decided she didn't want to leave me with the nanny when she traveled, so she quit and took up painting full-time. Some of her work was sold in local galleries and even in New York City where she had connections."

Jillian reaches for my leg and squeezes. "No wonder I thought she looked familiar, but now I see it. I see the resemblance," she says softly.

For the first time in a long time, I feel like I'm someone. I've always been Selka Nilsson's son, but the fact that it means something to Jillian gives me a new feeling of legitimacy.

I pull into Jillian's driveway next to Bob, and glance at the silver urn at Jillian's feet. "Ready?"

She nods and gives me a soft smile. When I reach for the door handle, she clasps my arm. "I won't say anything about your father, and don't feel that you have to, either. It's entirely up to you what you decide to share this weekend . . . But Kitty may ask us what John wanted."

I blow out a breath and frown. "Yeah. I know. This whole situation sucks. Can we just focus on you today?"

She leans over and kisses my cheek. "Just let me know what you need. Promise?"

"Yeah, I promise," I say, recognizing that we've spent the

day emotionally propping each other up. It doesn't escape me that together we make each other stronger.

She squeezes my arm and then rubs the urn. "Come on, Aunt Vera. I'll give you the place of honor on the mantel until later when we can give you a proper send-off."

Across the street, the beach is dotted with sunbathers, even though the sun isn't nearly as warm as last week when we were here. Jillian and Kitty need to wait until after dark to release Aunt Vera's ashes, when they're less likely to get arrested for violating the ordinance against disposing human remains into the ocean.

My stomach rumbles loudly, and I pray the caterer arrives on time. While Jillian worked this week, furiously attempting to rewrite Becca and Drew's story, I volunteered to line up the food for the weekend. Lunch should arrive any minute.

Jillian lets us all in and settles her Aunt Sue in one of the guest rooms. Kitty and Bob take another, and Jenny gets the third while I put my bag in Jillian's room. I can't get out of my suit and into jeans and a T-shirt fast enough. A headache forms behind my eyes and throbs as the pressure of the day and lack of food catches up with me. I drop onto the bed and open my wallet.

With a deep sigh, I squeeze my fingers into the tight compartment behind my driver's license and pull out the business card my mom gave me the day she died.

I flip it over and read the inscription in Swedish on the back. It tells me to call this number when my father dies. *Fuck.* Only half of me believes that the bastard is dead, while the other half wants to see him with my own eyes. As much as I hated him, it bothers me that I couldn't muster much of a reaction to his loss beyond relief. I never stopped mourning my mother, yet I can't squeeze out a tear for my father even when I think back to happier times. For some reason that leaves me feeling guilty and dysfunctional.

I slip the card back into my wallet where I found it and place my wallet back inside my duffel.

Monday. I'll call on Monday.

The doorbell rings on my way downstairs. Everyone is gathered in the open area that's a combination of living room, dining room, and kitchen. I meet Jillian at the door.

"Let me get that." I take the larger box from the delivery guy while Jillian follows, carrying the smaller one.

"I'll get the dishes," Kitty says. "Jenny, can you help me set the table, please?"

At Jillian's insistence, we brought an apple cake in remembrance of Vera. I gaze over at her urn in the center of the mantel among the large seashells and wish I'd met her before she died. She sounded like a great lady.

I stand at the counter unpacking when Jenny sidles up next to me. I give her a wary look. I still haven't forgiven her for being such a bitch to me in Jillian's driveway. If I wasn't mentally drowning under a mound of shit right now, I'd be inclined to try to make amends.

"'S up?" I ask.

"Can we talk later?" she asks in a low voice.

I arch my brow at her, and reply in an equally low tone. "As long as it doesn't involve any swearing."

She jerks her head back. "I didn't swear at you."

"I didn't say you did. I was talking about me," I say, realizing I might not have the energy to solve this today.

"I think I can manage that," she says and walks away.

Jillian comes over to grab a salad. "So, what were you two whispering about?"

"She wants to talk to me later," I say. "I'll let you know what she says." She smiles, and gives me a peck on the cheek. I follow her to the table with my food and sit down next to her. Then I brace myself. This is the first meal I've shared with her family, and I anticipate an experience somewhere between bearable and a root canal.

Aunt Sue is the first to dive in. "So, Raine, Jenny tells me you're in college. What are you studying?" Her eyes shift to Jillian and her eyebrows rise before she looks back at me with a polite smile.

And so it begins.

"Computer Graphics and Design," I say politely back, deciding to give her the short answer, and stab a forkful of salad. If I fill my mouth, maybe I won't have to speak.

Jillian jumps to my aid. "Raine designed an amazing cover for my next book, Aunt Sue. He's incredibly talented." She punctuates her sentence by squeezing my leg under the table.

I can't help but feel like I'm on display, but I remind myself that I'm here for Jillian. If this is the torture I need to endure to do that, then I'll endure it. But laying the burden back on Jillian isn't cool, so I put down my fork and volunteer "family-approved" information.

"I have a couple of years to go. I've been going part-time, so it's taking me a while. I was just accepted into an internship program at a design firm in New York City. They originally wanted me to start during the Christmas break, but they had a big project come in and asked me to start in mid-November."

I hear Jillian intake a breath next to me and glance over. I can't miss the surprise in her eyes. "You didn't tell me," she says, and tries to hide her hurt.

"It hasn't come up. Don't worry, I planned on telling you," I say, taking her hand under the table and hoping I didn't make too big of a relationship screw-up.

A throat clears, drawing my attention away from her.

"Jillian, you were gone a while with John. What did he want?" Kitty asks before she takes another bite of her sandwich. Bob's mouth drops into a frown next to her at the mention of John's name.

I'm poised to speak even though I haven't chosen any words.

"He's doing some research for me on my new book," Jillian answers, and I release a breath. Then her fingers clutch my shoulder. "And I've just drafted Raine as part of my research team."

I do everything in my power not to spit out my water. There's only one kind of "research" I've been helping with, and it's not for polite dining conversation.

" . . . Not to mention, he's turning out to be a solid critique partner on the new manuscript."

I make it through the rest of the meal relatively unscathed. When I try to help clear the dishes, Jillian, Kitty, and Aunt Sue kick me out of the kitchen. No use arguing with that group of women. I throw up my hands and head for the door. "Jillian, I'm going for a walk." I'm dying for fresh air and some time alone.

Jenny pops up from the sofa. "I'll come with you."

I think better of glaring at her and resign myself to her company. "Okay, come on."

"Don't look so unhappy about it," she snipes under her breath as we walk outside.

We step out into the sunshine and the sea air greets us. I fill my lungs and let the salty ocean air do its work.

Tipping my head at the boardwalk across the street, I ask, "North or south?"

"South," she replies, and follows me to the other side.

We walk in silence for a few minutes as the sea breeze whips at us. I'm glad I had the foresight to pull my hair back earlier. Not so much for Jenny, whose long hair is swirling around her in a silky cloud. I dig an extra elastic out of my pocket.

"Here. For your hair," I say.

"Thanks." She quickly braids the length, and uses the elastic to tie off the end.

"So what did you want to talk to me about?"

Her hand reaches out, and she pulls me out of the flow of foot traffic to the boardwalk railing. Her big blue eyes reach up to find mine. "Raine, I want to apologize. I was out of line for what I said to you when we first met." She pauses, and looks down at her hands. "The way you and my Aunt Jillian look at each other, I can see how much you both love each other. I saw it even then . . . before you both even knew. It's special . . . I think I was jealous, and I'm sorry."

My lips soften from a hard line into a half smile. "Apology accepted. Friends?" I say, and hold out my hand. My pent up anger toward her disappears, and my emotional baggage lightens by one suitcase. As a bonus, I feel like I'm one step closer to acceptance into Jillian's family.

She grasps it and smiles. "Friends."

I give her a full smile this time.

We walk another mile south, and she tells me about her troubles with her boyfriend, Russ, and her most recent job prospects. I know we're close in age, yet I feel so much older. Jillian fits me so much better than a girl like Jenny. And in hindsight, I see that although most of my girlfriends were older than me, they didn't have the maturity I crave. Most of them were just plain selfish. None of them were as loving and nurturing as Jillian, or made me feel as complete.

None of them before Jillian ever made me feel like I couldn't breathe without them. For the first time since I turned eighteen, I have hope that I can regain my future. Only it's better than the one my father stole from me . . . it includes Jillian.

Chapter 34

Jillian

"BUT RAINE, I can just ask the clean-out service to swing by—" I say from the passenger seat of my SUV as Raine drives us to the appointment he set up with the lawyer on the business card his mother gave him.

"No, Jillian. I can't let you do that," he says, shaking his head vehemently.

"Why not? It's no big deal. Really." I'm trying not to sound too overbearing.

A frown darkens his features. "I don't want you spending money on anything related to my father," he says.

We've been debating for most of the ride from Chatham to Bernardsville.

I blow out an exasperated breath. Being Swedish and Scottish makes him two kinds of stubborn. "Raine, a funeral is going to cost at least ten thousand dollars," I say. God, I should know. I'm an expert, and I'm only quoting him a price one step up from Potter's Field. Given Raine's father's financial situation, I'm doubtful there will be any money left to help Raine defray the cost.

We have an appointment with my friendly neighborhood funeral home this afternoon. He'll hear it for himself then. The sad truth is that, at this point, I should consider putting the funeral director on speed dial, or at least buy stock in them to make back some of my decade-long investment.

"I'm not giving him a funeral. I'm just getting him into the ground next to my mother because that's what she wanted. They bought a headstone and two burial plots before she died. It's shouldn't be that expensive," he says, trying to maintain his calm, but his rigid posture betrays his agitation.

"I understand why you feel that way. Are you sure?"

"Damn sure." His hands clench harder around the steering wheel, making the corded muscles of his forearms twitch.

"Fine." I throw up my hands. "Will you at least let me help you clean out his rental house?"

He glances over, and his face softens. "Yeah. Thanks."

We pull into the lawyer's parking lot.

"You have no idea what this is about?" I ask again. He took me by surprise with the business card on Saturday night after Kitty and I had returned from spreading Vera's ashes.

The weekend turned out better than I could've imagined despite being overwrought with an excess of emotions. We managed to do what Vera wanted us to do. She insisted that we celebrate her life by spending time together as a family looking at family pictures and remembering. We went to church on Sunday morning and then had a family picnic on the beach before we all left in the afternoon. It was Raine's first time experiencing a major dose of my family, and he did well. Really well. He seemed to enjoy himself despite the news about his father. I was especially pleased that he and Jenny made up. Now, if only I could make some traction with my novel . . .

He shakes his head. "I honestly don't know. I was so overwhelmed with grief when she handed me the card. I just did what she told me to do, and kept it in a safe place until my father died."

"Fair enough," I say.

The law offices of Brown, Nyland, and Row are on a tree-lined street in a building that looks like a two-story Victorian house.

The receptionist looks up wearing a warm smile. "Can I help you?"

"We're here for a ten o'clock with Silas Row," says Raine.

She checks her computer, and points to the waiting area. "Please take a seat, Mr. MacDonald. He'll be with you shortly."

We sit, and Raine flips the business card over and over between his fingers. The door opens just as I'm ready to lunge and take it away from him.

A man in his seventies steps out to greet us. He looks dignified, with a full head of perfectly coiffed gray hair and a well-tailored navy suit.

"Please come in, Raine," he says. We follow him through the hallway to his office, upscale, but far from lush. I take a seat next to Raine in one of the leather guest chairs.

The lawyer picks up a folder on his desk, and removes a sheaf of paper. Placing his readers on his nose, he peers down at it.

"Uh-huh. Okay, I've been left some very clear instructions from your mother," he says as his eyes travel over the page. He removes an envelope from inside the folder, and hands it to Raine. "You're to read this first before we proceed. I'll give you a moment of privacy." He leaves the office and the door clicks shut behind him.

Raine stares at the envelope. It's blank, but thick enough to contain a letter.

"Do you want me to leave?" I ask.

"No." He shakes his head, and proceeds to rip it open. He draws in a deep breath when he sees the handwriting. "It's a letter from my mom," he says quietly.

I glance over. It's written in Swedish like her note on the back of the business card.

He reads, translating it for me.

Dearest Raine,

216

I love you so much, and I'm sorry that I'm not there to say these words to you in person. You were my world, and I'm so very proud of you.

He stops. His bottom lip quivers, and his Adam's apple bobs as he swallows. I reach over and rub his back. "You don't have to read it to me," I say softly, but he shakes his head and continues.

When you and I discovered your father's problem, I knew I had to take action to protect you in case the situation became dire. Unless he forges my signature, your college trust fund should be secure.

Anger flares inside me when I think about how his father betrayed him. I add "forger" to his list of transgressions.

There are many things I kept from you about my relationship with your father since a child should not be burdened with such knowledge. Also, I wanted you to love and to respect him, like a good son should. I pray that when you receive this letter, your life is already productive and happy with a wife and children of your own. I pray that when you receive this gift, you will not be desperate for it.

Always in my heart,
Mamma

Raine folds the letter when he's done, and wipes his eyes. I take his hand and squeeze it.

Silas Row raps on the door once and reenters without waiting for a response, taking his seat behind the desk. He removes a larger envelope from the folder.

"Raine, before your mother Selka died, she called me and purchased a lump sum insurance policy on your father for two hundred and fifty thousand dollars with you as the sole beneficiary."

I expel a sharp breath as Raine leans forward in his chair and blurts. *"What?"*

Row nods solemnly and clasps his hands tightly. "Son, your mother and I knew each other a long time. She hired me when she first came to this country and started her modeling career. I did her first contract." He releases a long sigh. "I know more about your situation than I probably should. I'm going to go out on a limb here and tell you what I know. She did this because she didn't trust that you would be taken care of properly. Her biggest fear was that your father would gamble away his fortune and leave you a pauper. When you were a toddler, there were several 'incidents.' Selka threatened to leave him. He loved her enough to clean up his act, and as far as I know, he never broke her trust . . . until she was months from dying. Or maybe that's just when she found out. She couldn't be sure."

"Did my father know about this policy?" he asks.

Row shakes his head. "No, he didn't. Selka kept a secret rainy day account in her own name with money left over from her modeling days. It was the same account she planned on using to make her escape when you were a toddler. In the end, it was all she could get access to without his finding out. She converted it into a policy. In this form, the money could remain secret and safe until your father died. Her fear was that even if she designated you as the beneficiary on her bank account that he would somehow get his hands on it."

My heart warms with admiration for Selka Nilsson. I'm so pleased that her love reached Raine from beyond the grave with good fortune when he needed it most.

"Thank you," he says, holding the letter tightly in his hands. "I appreciate it."

"I just need your bank account information and your father's death certificate once it's issued, and then we'll get the funds transferred."

We rise from our seats, after wrapping up our discussion on next steps, and say our good-byes.

Raine is silent and hasn't spoken since we left Silas Row. I buckle myself into the passenger seat. "Are you okay?"

"Yeah. Just thinking." He starts the car and hands me the letter. "Can you hold this for me?"

I take it. "Absolutely."

We drive in silence. I give him time to be alone in his thoughts.

Instead of going home, he pulls into the cemetery on the border of Chatham and Madison. I've traveled a well-worn path through here since I was fourteen. I glance at him in confusion, wondering why he would bring me here of all places.

And then I know. We're going to see his mother. She must be here, too.

Chapter 35

Raine

"RAINE?"

I flinch at the sound of my name and look up at John Henshaw from where Jillian and I sit in the waiting room of the Chief Medical Examiner's office in New York City. Jillian squeezes my hand, and I squeeze hers back as we stand. Right or wrong, I'm here to see my father's body now that the damn Feds are finally gone.

True to John's word, they showed up at Jillian's door on Monday, three days ago, after we visited Silas Row and I took Jillian to visit my mom's grave. My brain feels like it spent the last few days inside a blender. They questioned us in painful detail. I told them everything I could which wasn't much, since I don't know jack. They didn't do much better with Jillian. She knows less than I do, yet she still had to explain how we met, if she'd ever met my father before he showed up that day in her house, why she owned two guns and a bunch of other irrelevant bullshit questions. Who knows how much value any of it had regarding their investigation. And they still won't let me anywhere near my dad's rental house. I haven't been back since the day I broke into the garage for the painting.

John runs his fingers through his salt-and-pepper hair with

one hand, carrying a file and a large bag marked "Evidence" in the other. "We could've done this back in Chatham."

"I told you. I want to see his body," I reply more calmly than I feel. It's not that I don't believe my father is really gone, but something inside of me hungers for proof. To know he's no longer a threat to me . . . or Jillian.

John's gaze shifts to Jillian with a raised eyebrow. She just nods and some silent message passes between them. I'm too wired on adrenaline to care or feel left out. It gives me comfort to know that if I asked Jillian she'd tell me. We share things now. I love that.

John blows out a breath. "Let's head downstairs then."

The elevator lets us out into a brightly lit hallway, and John leads us to another small cubicle-size waiting room with a video screen.

"You'll be able to view your father on there." He points to the screen as he's about to leave the room.

"No way. That's not going to do it for me. I want to see him in person."

"Raine—"

I cut John off and drop Jillian's hand from mine. "No, man. I'm serious. I *need* to look at his body." To make it real.

"I'm not sure that's a good idea until after the funeral director . . ." Jillian says tentatively with a look of unease in her eyes.

John swipes his face and gives me a hard stare. "Raine, it's not like it is on TV. Have you ever smelled a dead body before? It sticks with you. Trust me, Jillian's right. Wait for the funeral director to work some magic first."

My jaw grinds in frustration. I'm sure they mean well but after the week I've had, I don't want to be told what to do. "I don't care. I want to see him."

"Fine. Let me get approval." John presses his lips tight and leaves the room.

I lean up against the edge of the table, my arms locked across my chest. Jillian sits down in one of the chairs and stays silent. One glance and I see the concern engraved on her face.

"Say something, Jillian," I whisper, wanting her support. "It's not like I haven't seen a dead body before. My mom died in my arms."

She shakes her head, and says softly, "This will be different. He's been dead a lot longer. But if this is what you need to do then do it. I just don't want it to haunt you later. That's all."

Her concern touches me. I get it. He could be disgusting to look at. My mom looked like she was sleeping but it was clear that she was gone after her last breath.

"I can respect that. This might not make sense, but I need to see him at his worst. Not prettied up." My mouth hardens into an angry line. I'm pissed. Not at Jillian but at my father. For failing me, for not wanting me, and for stealing what he could from me.

John comes back five minutes later and beckons me to follow with a wave of his hand. "Come on."

Jillian gets up, but John wards her off with a shake of his head. "No, Jilly. You stay here. Hold onto these for me until we get back, will ya?" He hands her the sealed folder and the evidence bag.

She rests a hand on my shoulder, pulling my gaze to hers. "Raine?"

"John's right. I'll be fine." I lean over and kiss her forehead, my lips lingering there for an extra moment. No use dragging her through this. Plus, I want to spare her the nightmares if I can help it.

I follow John into the morgue. The stench of formaldehyde with an undertone of bitter cherries hits me as I walk in. It makes my head throb. For a moment, my stomach churns but not enough to make me heave.

Eight stations including steel tables, basins, faucets, scales, and other apparatuses stand in a line along one wall. A few people in lab coats stand idly by waiting for us to move through the room where they do autopsies. We pass some tables with corpses covered with opaque plastic sheets. Watching *CSI: Miami* growing up hasn't quite prepared me for the reality of seeing a morgue in person.

I breathe a sigh of relief when we walk into a cool corridor and close the door to the autopsy room behind us. John leads me down the hall into a room the temperature of a meat locker. The place where they store the bodies they're not working on. The chill cuts into me as we pass over the threshold.

John walks midway into the room and rolls out one of the numbered metal drawers that line one wall, revealing another corpse under plastic.

Even through the cold, I catch the aroma of death.

"You sure you really want to see this?" John says. This time his voice is compassionate.

I bite my lower lip and nod.

Slowly, John peels back the plastic.

John was right. Time in the water does harsh things to a body. My father's face is a grotesque mask. His skin is a mottled darkish grey with oversized wrinkles not normally found on a human being. More like that dog breed. Even lips that should look like mine, don't. A large piece of his ear is missing, nothing left but a ragged edge of bloated flesh.

I choke back my revulsion and the bile rising in my throat. None of his features are recognizable except for his eyebrows. The way the over-long hairs poke out in multiple directions like they're confused which way they should grow. But it's the mole on his temple that clinches it. That's all I need to see. It's him.

"Cover him," I say, swallowing past the lump in my throat.

John slides the plastic back over him and closes the metal drawer.

"You okay?" John asks.

"Yeah. Fine." At least emotionally. I thought maybe I'd feel something. But I don't. If anything, I feel even more disconnected than I did before.

John walks stoically beside me. Rather than walking through the room with the steel tables, we take a different route back to the viewing room where we left Jillian.

"Why didn't we come this way to the freezer?" I ask.

John shoots me a look. "Since you were so hell bent on the full experience, I figured I'd give it to you." He eyes my clothes. "You might want to change when you get home." I don't have to ask what he means. The lingering smell of death torments my nostrils.

Jillian pops out of the chair the moment we walk back in, her golden eyes carefully assessing me.

"I'm fine," I say, grabbing her hand and heading off her concerns.

"Let's sit," John says, pointing to the folder and envelope lying on the table. "Jilly, hand me that stuff." She slides it over to him. "I wrestled some intel from my guys in the NYPD and got the Feds to release all your dad's personal effects."

We settle around the table.

John holds up the folder. "This contains your dad's autopsy report. I was right. Even though we found his wallet, keys, and shoes at the point where his body was most likely dumped into the Hudson, this wasn't a suicide. The M.E. found a needle mark at the base of his skull by his hairline."

"But why would they kill him? He can't pay them back now that he's dead," Jillian asks. It's a reasonable question.

Shaking his head, John tents his hands on the table. "I dug a little deeper. Turns out Raine's father had a long history with the people he owed money to. He managed some of their off-shore investments back when he worked on Wall Street. From what I've gleaned from my contacts, for the last six or seven years he's been able to keep slightly ahead of his debts. About a year ago, the Feds tapped him on the shoulder and enlisted him as a snitch. They kept him paid up. But a couple of recent bad nights at the tables landed him right back in hot water. This time they refused to bail him out."

A hard knot forms in my stomach and I snap, "How come they never said any of that for the three fucking days they grilled us?"

John fixes me with a hard stare. "They wouldn't. This is all off the record. Me going out on a limb for you and Jilly, got that?"

My mouth drops into a frown and I feel like a shithead for shooting my mouth off. "Got it. Sorry, John. I appreciate everything you've done. Really."

John's demeanor softens. "There's something else you should know, Raine. Your father . . . I'm not sure . . ." He huffs and stares down at his hands for a moment. "Listen, I don't pretend to know about the issues between you and your dad. But I'm not sure he did what he did to you just for the reasons you think."

My jaw tenses. "What do you mean?"

"All I'm saying is he may have had another reason to keep you away . . . to create the hatred."

"What are you talking about?" I ask as tension radiates across my shoulders.

"*John?*" Jillian says, reaching for my hand and looking at him intently. "Tell us what you know."

He looks from one of us to the other before settling on me. "Your father made the deal with the Feds under the agreement that they keep you safe at all costs. He believed if he kept you estranged, his associates wouldn't use you as leverage. I'm not saying that what he did to you was excusable in any way or that he didn't have deeper motivations outside of these problems. Just that I think he cared about you in his own way."

I sway backward in my seat. *Could it be true?* That my father actually cared enough about me to want to keep me safe?

"Here are his personal effects." John stands and pushes the bag marked "Evidence" toward me. "The Medical Examiner will release the body to the funeral home tomorrow."

"Thanks. I mean it." I take the bag. The shoes inside make it heavy. Rising, I offer my free hand in a handshake.

Jillian meets him on the other side of the table and wraps him in a hug. "Thanks for doing this, for all of it."

He looks at her warmly and smiles. "As I always tell you, anything for Kitten McNally's little sister," he says, referring to Kitty by her maiden name.

Whenever he says stuff like that, it makes me wonder why they never ended up together. That's got to be a story worth hearing.

We all make our way to the First Avenue entrance and say our good-byes. Jillian and I head to where her SUV is parked in the Park & Lock across the street while John heads across town.

"You okay? You haven't said much since we left," Jillian says as we drive through the Holland Tunnel on the way home.

I'm glad I asked her to drive. My nerves are shot. I can't stop thinking about what John said.

"I'm here if you need me," she adds and gives me a gentle squeeze on the shoulder.

My heart swells and I muster a half-smile for her. When we get home, I might sleep for a week from the stress of the last few days.

"I know. Thanks for coming with me." I say and glance down at the bag on my lap. Without thinking, I open it. Keys, a beat-up pair of wing tips, and a wallet are all it contains. I slip out the thick rectangle of battered brown leather, and lay the bag on the floor. A strip of leather and a snap closure keep it shut. I flip it over in my hand, examining both sides. I don't remember ever seeing it or associating it with my father. Based on the thickness, for a moment I think it might contain some cash.

I unsnap it and look inside.

My father's driver's license is visible through the clear plastic window on the inner flap. On the other side, an ATM card pokes out of one of the credit card pockets.

In the billfold section, there are only two bills — a five and a one. What's making it so thick is a small insert with some pictures.

I take it out.

My parents' wedding picture is visible on top under the soft matte plastic. They look elegant and happy. I flip the little plastic page. A professional headshot of my mom is on one side and a picture of her pregnant with me is on the other. I'm not surprised his wallet is filled with her pictures. He adored her.

I turn the page again.

A small gasp escapes through my lips. It's a picture of my dad and me on the slopes in Switzerland when I was seven. The other is my class picture when I was nine. Both pictures were taken before his crazy behavior started. Before he not-so-subtly acknowledged I was competition for my mom's affection. A lump forms in my throat. Based on how I thought he felt about me, I didn't expect to see any pictures of myself.

I flip to the next page and freeze. There are two more pictures. Recent ones. All taken after the height of our conflict started. One of me as a senior in my varsity soccer uniform — my mom had the big one framed and kept it in her studio. The other of me receiving my diploma at my high school graduation. A tremor runs through me . . .

I turn to the last page. There's a small folded square of paper held between the plastic sleeve. Working my fingers inside, I retrieve it.

I unfold the paper and air drains from lungs when I see the block letters. I wrote it when I was six years old, one afternoon during a Swedish lesson with my mom. I remember how proud I was, and how big of a deal he made over receiving it at dinner that night.

My lip quivers as I stare at the letters until I can no longer see them through the hot blur of tears.

Pappa, Jag älskar dig. Raine — Daddy, I love you. Raine

After all these years, he never threw it away. Could it be that maybe he loved me a little bit after all?

Chapter 36

10 weeks later . . .

Raine

PLINK. PLINK. PLINK. I refuse to open my eyes as my hand slams around the top of the nightstand, searching for the goddamn alarm clock. Jillian crawls over me to reach it, and her breast lands in my face. I consider this the first thing to be thankful for today. A smile forms on my lips and my tongue darts out to say hello.

"Hey, I thought you had to get up," she says, half-asleep.

"I do. If I don't get the turkey in the oven, we'll be eating nothing but stuffing and string beans later," I mumble before I pull her nipple into my mouth and caress it with my tongue. I turn over onto my back without letting her go, and curl my hands around her hips. She moves one of her legs over my waist to straddle me.

"Mmm. The other one feels ignored," she moans from above. I switch sides, and run my hands up and down the hollow of her back until they settle on the round globes of her ass. My blood rushes south, and I'm ready for a proper good morning. I let her go and shift underneath her until I find my way inside and sink into a nice, hot welcome.

"Happy Thanksgiving," I say in a deep rasp and move underneath her. My lips find hers, and I kiss her deep before she breaks the kiss and her lips travel over my jaw and down onto my neck. I hug her close and expel a satisfied groan as I rock inside her and pick up my pace. I can't dally too long since I have a date with a turkey downstairs. There'll be plenty of time tonight for an extended play version of my thankfulness.

She moans, and her hand gently caresses my cheek. "I'm so thankful that I found you."

"Me, too, baby. Same here," I growl as the pressure builds inside my groin, and I head toward release. "Sorry for the quickie. I'll make it up to you later. I promise."

"Ooo, Raine . . . I might beat you there," she says, and then cries out and clenches around my length. Two seconds later, my body tenses before exploding in sensation. I ride the wave home and join her with a primal moan.

We rest for five breathless minutes with her on top of me, and my arms wrapped tightly around her. "That's what I call starting Thanksgiving with a bang," I say in a hoarse whisper.

She rests her chin on my chest, and looks me seriously in the eye. "All kidding aside, we have a lot to be thankful for today."

I squeeze her tighter. "I know."

With Jillian's help, I hired a dealer to run an estate sale out of my father's rental once the Feds let me in, and with the exception of my mother's paintings, I sold everything and donated what remained. Of the one hundred–plus paintings, I shipped half to Sweden to my grandparents to disburse among my mother's family and put the other half into storage until I can figure out what to do with them. I may sell some of them through my mom's old dealers, and the others I'll keep.

I gave my father a quiet burial, and he now lies at rest beside my mom. I've forgiven him as much as I'll ever be able to. More than that, I pity him. His old, shiny façade masked the life of an unhappy addict trapped in a personal hell. What really matters is that I have the closure I need to move on.

Jillian supported me through all these things. Every step of the way.

I push a piece of her thick mane of hair behind her ear. "I couldn't have made it these last few months without you."

She lays a sweet kiss on my lips and traces my lower lip with her fingertip. "Ditto."

I glance at the time. "Shit, I have to get up!"

An hour later, I'm running around the kitchen like a lunatic with the Macy's Thanksgiving Day parade on TV in the background. Underdog and Hello Kitty float by on the screen, keeping me company while I scramble around, hyperventilating. Why did I think it was good idea to invite Jillian's family to her house for Thanksgiving? The bigger question is: Why on earth did I think I could make the whole meal from scratch?

The turkey is safely in the oven, but the counter is covered in the ingredients I need for stuffing, cranberry sauce, apple and pear pies, and a sweet potato puree that I thought looked good. My laptop is open to the Food Network, and all the bookmarked recipes I found earlier this week are lined up in memory.

My fingers are woven into my hair, and I'm wearing a look of panic when Jillian comes into the kitchen. I'm about thirty seconds away from screaming at the top of my lungs.

Her face screws up in a frown. "Raine, are you okay? You look like you're about to snap."

"I need help," I say, feeling like a drowning man clutching for a life preserver.

She comes over to me and places her hands on my shoulders. Her golden eyes lock me in her gaze. "Relax. I'll help you. Take two deep breaths."

I blow my breath in and out twice. "Done."

"Feel better?"

"No."

"Sit." She chuckles and points to the stool.

I sit. She walks over to get a pen and paper and then settles down beside me.

"Calmly, tell me the temperature of the turkey and how long it takes," she says.

"350 degrees for six hours," I say, wringing my hands and bouncing my knee nervously up and down on the stool. "I put it in at eight a.m."

She jots it down. "Okay, tell me what else you're going to make, include the time it takes and the temperature." I recite my list of side dishes and desserts including the specifics she asked for with the help of the recipes on my laptop.

Done, she hands me the list. Thank God for double ovens. There's a grid of both ovens with start times, end times, and prep times all calculated.

"This is amazing," I say as I watch her roll up her sleeves and wash her hands.

"I'm going to be your sous-chef," she says. "Let's start on the sweet potatoes first, since they take the most prep."

My eyebrows fly up. "Have you been holding out on me?"

She chuckles. "My planning is great; it's my food that tastes like crap. Together, I think we'll be a kick-ass team and make a decent meal. Ready?"

I pull her into my arms and growl into her neck. "I love you."

"Hey, that tickles." She giggles, and clenches her shoulders up to protect her neck. "Love you, too. Now, let's get crackin'."

I frown and let her go. "Don't you need to work on your manuscript this morning?" A twinge of guilt passes through me. She's running way behind and probably going to miss her deadline.

She shrugs. "Becca and Drew can wait. This is more important."

"Thanks." I sigh gratefully and clap my hands together, feeling calmer and a little bit selfish. "Okay, let's do it."

By two o'clock, we're actually dressed and presentable with food ready in the warming drawers and on the stove by the time our guests arrive. Jillian is wearing a nice black dress, and I've changed into a pair of pants and a clean shirt.

Bottles of wine, nonalcoholic drinks, and appetizers are neatly lined up on top of the island. I replace the blare of the TV with some holiday music when the doorbell rings.

Kitty, Bob, and Jenny are the first to arrive. There's a young guy with dark curly hair with them whom I've never met before.

Jillian speaks up before Jenny has a chance to introduce him. "Hi, Russ," she says, and gives him a hug. "How's everything going out west?"

Russ lights up in Jillian's arms. "Great, thanks for asking."

Jillian turns to me, "Russ, I'd like you to meet my partner, Raine."

Russ extends his hand and I take it. I feel his eyes sizing me up.

"Nice to meet you," I say.

"You, too," he says tentatively, and moves deeper into the foyer.

Jenny walks in behind him and leans in for a quick peck on the cheek. I glance quickly toward Russ and lift my eyebrows at her. She rolls her eyes and shrugs. "Tell you later," she whispers.

I kiss Kitty and shake Bob's hand, and Jillian takes everyone's coats and hangs them in the hall closet.

Before we even make it to the kitchen, the bell rings again. Jillian answers the door, and it's her cousin, Cheryl, husband Joe, and their two little girls, who are three and seven.

The noise level jumps several decibels when we all get into

the kitchen. Jillian sets up Nickelodeon for the kids in the family room, while the adults cluster around the island to have a quick snack and catch up.

I jump when the timer for the turkey rings. Throwing on an apron, I continue to channel my best chef and fellow Scotsman, Gordon Ramsey. I take out the turkey, set it on the stove, and put in the pies.

Jillian comes over and whispers in my ear. "Do you need help carving?"

I look at the huge bird with chagrin. Nah, I could do this. I shake my head. "I think I can manage, why?"

She glances in Bob's direction. He's nervously stirring his drink, looking like he could use something to do. "I think it might make his day if you asked for his help," she says quietly.

I give her a wink and turn to Bob. "Hey, Bob, would you be able to give me some help with the turkey? I think it's a two-man job."

Bob's face lights up with purpose, and he makes a beeline around the island to join me. "Sure, Raine. No problem, buddy." I've never seen him so animated.

"Thanks, sweetheart." She leans over to give me a kiss and then glides off to mingle.

"Here you go." I hand Bob the knives and let him have at it on the carving board. "I'll arrange the slices on the plate as you cut."

"Sounds good to me," he says and attacks the bird with gusto.

Within five minutes, Bob has the turkey expertly carved and cleaned. "Awesome job, man," I say, truly impressed.

Jillian joins us, and we take the rest of the food from the warmer and set it up family style along the counter. Everybody fills their plates and meets at the dining room table. Cheryl delivers a paper plate to each of the girls in front of the TV, and we gather for an adult dinner.

Now that the food is served, I can relax. Tension drains

from my shoulders as I sit back and listen. The one thing I can say about Jillian's family is they aren't quiet. Everyone talks at once. Their conversations include a liberal amount of gesticulating with their hands punctuated by raucous laughter. It's so not what I'm used to, and I love it.

I sample the meal Jillian helped me make, and the food tastes amazing.

"Did you make all this yourself, Raine?" Kitty asks from across the table, ready to eat her next forkful of sweet potatoes. "It's absolutely delicious."

Cheryl chimes in from farther down the table. "Kitty's right. Bravo, Raine. Fabulous meal."

A blush rises in my cheeks. "Thanks. Jillian helped . . . a lot."

"Barely at all," she says and rubs my arm. "I only calculated the schedule and did some chopping. He did the rest. Great meal, sweetheart," she says, and my face reddens more.

"Thanks." I'm not used to being the center of attention.

"I thought Brigitte was going to be here," Kitty says to Jillian between bites.

"She's in Paris with her new boyfriend. He surprised her Sunday night. She's sorry she couldn't make it. But I think I can forgive her for ditching us for Paris. Lucky her," Jillian says. There's a dreamy look in her eye.

I lean over and whisper, "You want to go to Paris someday?"

Her smile is bright and airy. "Most definitely. Especially if it's with you."

"Then we will," I say seriously, thinking maybe we can swing it during spring break. The weather should be nice by then.

"Raine, how is your internship going?" Jenny asks.

I perk up. Another thing I need to be thankful for. "So far, so good. I'm helping with the big project they landed for a total redesign of the company's website and their international branding campaign." Lucky for me, the timing worked out perfectly. I started a week ago, after the landscaping season ended.

Her eyes spark with interest. "Do they have any entry-level positions open?"

I cut a piece of turkey. "I don't know, but I can find out for you." I feel bad that's she's still desperately looking for a job.

She smiles brightly. "Thanks. That would be great."

Russ leans over and whispers in her ear, and she frowns. I wonder what that's about, suddenly feeling protective of her . . . like a future uncle. A cool, young uncle.

"Jillian, how's the book going?" Cheryl asks.

She sets down her fork, and her face darkens. "I'm running a bit behind on my final revisions. But on the bright side, Brigitte let me know that the publisher is leaning toward using one of the covers that Raine designed."

"Really?" I ask as a spike of pleasure shoots through me.

She nods and squeezes my hand. "Really."

The dinner conversation buzzes around the table. It fills me with warmth to be included. When the timer rings for the pies in the kitchen, I lean over to Jillian. "You want more? I'm going to get seconds while I'm in there."

"Maybe later. I'm kind of full," she says, and presses her hand to her stomach.

I pick up my plate and head back to the kitchen. I smile when I see the feast covering the stove and counters. Jillian and I made this . . . together. It makes me proud that we could do this for her family, but I'm relieved knowing that I'm done in the kitchen for the day. Jillian, Kitty, and Cheryl pulled clean-up duty, while I've been deployed to take the guys downstairs to watch football after dinner. *Score!* No argument here.

I rescue the pies, and place them on the stove to cool.

I'm shoveling some stuffing onto my plate when Jenny walks in.

"Hey, Raine." She comes to stand next to me wearing a

frown, and crosses her arms over her chest.

"What's up, Jen? You look bummed." I reach for another slice of turkey. "What was going on with Russ out there?"

"He asked me to move to California with him," she says without preamble. Jenny and I have gotten closer since we made up back in September. For some reason, she feels comfortable talking to me about personal things. I'm glad, but I follow a strict "don't kiss and tell" policy when it comes to Jillian.

"And?"

"It's not like he asked me to marry him or anything," she says with an underlying tone of bitterness.

I put my plate down and look at her. "Do you want to marry him?" I ask, thinking it's a logical question.

"That's not the point," she snaps.

I throw my hands up in surrender. "Then what *is* the point? Help a poor, ignorant guy understand what's going on in your female head and where you're going with this."

"Would you shake up your life for no guarantees?" she asks.

I snort. *Is she kidding me?* "Jenny, my life has been shaken up since I left high school. Let me remind you—there are no guarantees. There are gambles, chances, and hope. You'll have to place your bets in life, there's no getting around it. For what it's worth, the best advice I can give you is to follow your heart."

She pouts. "But I could get all the way out there and we break up. Then what?"

"Come on, Jenny, really? You get on a plane and come home, or you make a life out there if you like the place. Point is, don't be afraid to do something because of how it might turn out."

"So you'd go?"

"Only if I wanted to be with the person who asked," I say.

She nods and gives me a peck on the cheek. "Thanks."

"Ironic, isn't it? You asking me for relationship advice," I say, grinning.

"Why? You clearly know what you're doing," she says with an appreciative glance, and walks out to rejoin everyone in the dining room.

I follow her a few moments later and sit back down. A bite of turkey is on its way to my mouth when Jillian sways into me and clutches my arm. Her face is a pale shade of green.

I drop my fork. "Are you okay?"

"I'm going to be sick," she says. Her hand flies to her mouth as she bolts from the table toward the powder room next to the kitchen. I race after her. The door slams shut before I get there, and I hear her retching on the other side. God, I hate that sound.

"Jillian, what can I do? Do you need my help?" I ask with my hand poised on the doorknob.

"No, don't come in," she says in a weak voice that carries a quiver. "I'll be okay."

"I'll wait out here then." I post myself against the wall with a mix of worry and relief. I'd go in if she needed me, but all it would take is one whiff and I'd have to fight back the urge to join her. Suddenly, I wonder . . . the food! But I ate everything, and I feel fine. What if it's E. coli? But we followed the safe handling instruction on the turkey.

I'm running over the possibilities when Kitty comes a minute later. "Raine, how is she?"

"She won't let me in. But I think she's done puking." I can hear water running in the sink.

"Jillian, do you want some crackers and ginger ale, sweetie?" Kitty asks through the door.

My brows draw together. "No one else feels sick, do they?"

"Jillian probably picked up a bug," she says, and gives my arm a reassuring squeeze. "I think the guys are ready to watch some football before dessert. Do you want to take them down now?"

"Not until Jillian comes out," I say, locking my arms across my chest. The water shuts off.

"I'm out," she says, no longer looking green but still a little shaken. "Kitty, crackers and soda sound good."

"I'll get them right away." Kitty skitters off to the kitchen.

I take Jillian's arm. "Do you think you're coming down with something?"

She presses her hand to her forehead. "Maybe. I feel a little dizzy."

My stomach clenches at the thought of her not feeling well. Worry is hardwired inside me after spending so much time with my mom when she was sick. "Can I take you upstairs?"

She attempts a smile and caresses my cheek. "I'll be fine. It's just a little nausea. Go take the guys downstairs. It's okay, really."

"You sure?"

"Yes. Go."

I follow her to the dining room, and reluctantly gather up the guys for the game. As I descend the stairs into the basement to the home theater, I can't help but feel something is off.

Chapter 37

Jillian

"JILLIAN, please let me in," Raine says from outside the bathroom door.

I press my cheek against the cold porcelain bowl, and hug it for dear life. This is the fourth day in a row that I haven't been able to keep down any food. The nausea gripped me hard this morning after I drank my coffee. The back of my throat still burns with the bitter residue.

"I'll be out a minute. I promise," I say in a harsh rasp. I cough up some acid and spit it into the bowl. *I hope I'll be out in a minute.* The wave of queasiness is receding, signaling that the worst of it should be over.

"I can stay home from work," he says. I picture him leaning his blond head up against the door. His voice is that close. I hate seeing the concern in his eyes and want to push him away. When I'm sick, my instinct is to crawl into a hole and hide like a wounded animal . . . alone. He, on the other hand, is the opposite. He loves when I dote on him, liking me close and there to comfort him. After the broken ribs, he's only been sick once. It turned into a two-day affair of chicken soup and tender loving care. I admit that I enjoy taking care of him, but I'm not the same, regardless of how much he wants me to be. I've given myself a pat on the back for not hurting his feelings over the last few days while he's tried to care for me, but I can tell it's stressing him out.

"No, go to work. I have an appointment with the doctor at ten. I'll be fine," I say as gently as I can.

"Will you call me after the appointment?"

"Yes, sweetheart. Right after I see him," I say to placate him.

"Please let me see you so I can say good-bye," he pleads.

"Just a sec," I say, and crawl onto my knees before I can stand. I wash my mouth out and then open the door.

He's standing against the doorjamb, his forehead etched with concern. His shoulders slump in relief, and he takes me in his arms. He's dressed for work in slacks and a button-down, and his hair is neatly back. "I hate leaving you," he says into my hair. "Call me later. Don't just text me."

I give him a kiss on the lips and meet the blue intensity of his beautiful, worried eyes. "Please don't stress, I'll be fine. I'll call you right away. Now, go before you miss your train."

He releases a breath. "Okay. I'll come home if you need me."

I give him a weak smile. "Raine, I love you. Go."

He lets me go, and reluctantly heads for the garage. "I love you, too. Going."

I breathe a deep sigh of relief when I hear the garage door close and his truck back out of the driveway. I pass my hand over my face and make my way up the stairs to dress.

God, I feel like shit.

My mind shifts to a black place as I size up the possibilities and pray I'm wrong.

Chapter 38

Jillian

"LUCAS, how the *HELL* can I be pregnant?" I scream at Dr. Lucas Wilson as I pace inside his office like a caged animal. My lungs seize in panic as the walls close in on me. I'm trapped in a nightmare with an eight-week-old fetus inside me, and I can't wake up.

No more than ten years older than me with a full head of salt-and-pepper hair and warm brown eyes, Lucas sits on the edge of his desk wearing a white lab coat over his golf shirt. He looks like he just stepped off the course right before my appointment . . . which he did. I rank on his list of patients — he's a family friend and my private concierge physician. An excellent general practitioner, lucky for me, he has a dual specialty in gynecology and obstetrics.

"Jillian," he says sternly with my file open, and his glasses perched on the end of his nose. "The fertility specialist said, and I quote, 'Patient has less than a 2 percent chance of conceiving based on her current condition affecting the production of her ovum. It is highly unlikely that she will be able to conceive a child.' They never said you can't get pregnant, they only said it was highly unlikely."

I clutch the sides of my head. "I tried for a decade and a half. I've never used birth control. How could this happen?

Why now?" *When I'm finally happy.* I'm torn between wanting to cry and wanting to break something.

"I understand your surprise, Jillian, but I would think—given how hard you've tried—that you'd be . . . pleased."

"*Pleased?* At thirty-three, maybe, but not at almost forty-three," I snap and sweep a hand over my face.

"I understand your concern. We'll have to watch you carefully given your advanced maternal age. I'd also recommend a genetic screening test in your fifth month." Lucas picks up his pen. "Let me write you a script for prenatal vitamins."

"No," I say through my clenched teeth.

"What do you mean, 'no?' " he asks, dumbfounded.

"I *mean* that I'm probably not going to keep it." I never thought I'd be confronted with having to make this choice, but, damn it, her I am.

A horrified look passes over his face. "What?"

"You heard me," I grit, clenching my hands at my sides. My fear and anger make me almost rabid. Doesn't he understand? *I. Don't. Want. A. Child.*

"Jillian, you can't be serious. What about the father?" he says quietly.

"What about him?" As soon as the words leave my mouth, I realize there is no way I can push this burden onto him.

Loneliness gores me, and I know. I'm going to lose him. If he doesn't leave, I'll end up pushing him away. I can see the train coming down the tracks, and I'm standing in its path unable to get out of the way.

Lucas blows out a breath. "Think long and hard before you make this decision, Jillian. But if you decide to move ahead, I'll only agree to terminate the pregnancy on two conditions," he says roughly. "Or you can find someone else."

"What conditions?" I ask, relieved that he won't flat out refuse on moral grounds. I don't relish finding a new doctor.

"You think about it for a week . . . and you tell the father. Obviously, the last piece is just a request. I'll have to take you at your word."

"Fine," I say as I grind my teeth. I grab my purse and turn to leave.

"Wait," he says.

I turn and glare at him, even though it's me that I'm disgusted with. I want to be anywhere but inside my own body right now. "What?"

He shakes his head. "I hope you ... decide to keep it. That's all."

"I'll be in touch," I say and shut the door behind me.

As I head to the SUV, I hear my phone *pling* with a new text. My jaw tightens, and I pull it out.

Don't keep me hanging. What did the doctor say? Call me. Love ya, Raine

I drop the phone back in my purse. I let the numbness spread through me in preparation for the pain that will surely follow. Right now, I need some distance. I need to be away from Raine. I need to think by myself.

On autopilot, I find my way home. I leave my purse in the car since I won't be staying long. I pack up my laptop and an overnight bag.

By the time I return to the car, there are two more texts and two voicemail messages.

Hey, where are you? I'm worried. Call me. Love ya.

Jillian, is everything okay? Please call me when you get this. R

Instead of listening to the voicemail messages, I delete them and text him back.

Will be in touch later. J

Then I turn off my phone. I need silence. I turn onto Route 24 and head for Spring Lake where I can be alone to think . . . and breathe.

Chapter 39

Raine

WILL BE IN TOUCH LATER. J

What the fuck does that mean?! I slam my cell onto my desk. Forget the fact that she's avoiding me; there's nothing warm or fuzzy about her message.

A pit of fear coalesces in my gut. I know something's wrong, I can feel it in my bones. Jillian has been acting odd ever since Thanksgiving, slowly withdrawing and pushing me away. I keep racking my brain. What did I do? Have I done something wrong?

Karen, another intern, looks up from her computer. "Everything all right?" she asks.

"No," I mumble, and before I can stop myself, I blurt out what's on my mind. "My girlfriend went to the doctor, and now she won't pick up the phone. I'm worried."

"What's wrong with her?" she asks while her fingers continue to fly across her keyboard.

"She's been throwing up like crazy since Thanksgiving."

Her eyes widen, and she stops typing. "Um, if you don't mind my asking, how long have you've been dating?"

I quickly calculate our time together. "Almost four months, why?" I eye her with suspicion before I figure out where she's going with this and shake my head. "No, not possible. She can't have kids."

She shrugs and resumes typing. "If you say so."

Yeah, I fucking say so. There's no way that can be it. If she didn't already tell me she couldn't get pregnant, I would've made that connection myself. I'm not an idiot.

A flash of doubt hits me, followed by a wave of discomfort. But what if . . .? Our first date at Roots and our conversation about her not really wanting kids comes back to haunt me. Still, I can't believe that's a possibility, and if it is? I could roll with that, and I'm sure she could, too. I shake off the thought and release a calmer breath. Like I said, there's no way that can be it.

"Hey, I need to jet early and get home," I say, as I log off the system.

"Okay. You coming in tomorrow?" she asks.

"Yeah, unless something crazy happens," I say. My days are wrapped around my fall schedule, so I only come in on Monday, Tuesday, and Friday.

If I time it right, I can make the 1:20 p.m. train home from Penn Station.

I pull into the garage, and there's no sign of Jillian's car. "Shit," I mutter. When I walk into the kitchen through the garage door, everything looks exactly as I left it this morning. I take some chicken out of the freezer and throw it on the counter to defrost. At least I'll get an early start on dinner.

Where the hell could she be? I wonder.

I check my phone for the hundredth time. Nothing. I send her another text.

Jillian, I'm home. Will you be home soon? Love, R

I toss the phone onto the granite island and wait. Five minutes pass. Nothing. Ten minutes. Still nothing. I let out an exasperated breath and head to her office.

My eyes sweep over her desk. Her laptop is missing, but

that's not unusual. She routinely goes to Starbucks for a change of scenery when she writes. She also tends to ignore her phone if she's in the middle of a tough scene, and I know she's scrambling to finish Becca and Drew's revisions by Friday. I sigh and feel only marginally better.

Still, I don't like it. If she'd only kept her promise and called me, I wouldn't be trashing my day trying to find her and worrying like an insane lunatic.

I trudge back to the kitchen and pick up my cell. No Jillian. I dial Kitty.

"Hi, sweetie, is everything okay?" she asks.

"Not sure, Kitty. Jillian went to see the doctor this morning, and I haven't heard from her. She sent a short text hours ago saying she'd be in touch later. It's just not like her." I drag my hand over my pulled-back hair.

"I'm sorry, Raine. I haven't heard from her. Let me try to reach her, and I'll call you back, okay?"

"Sure," I say, frustrated to think she might pick up for Kitty but not for me. Kitty calls back a couple of minutes later.

"No luck, I'm afraid. If you don't hear from her in an hour, call me back," she says. "And if I hear from her, I'll call you."

"Okay, will do. Thanks, Kitty." I hang up, somewhat relieved that I'm not being singled out.

Fuck it. I'll go downstairs and work out. If nothing else, she should show up by dinnertime.

By six-thirty, I've worked out, I've called Kitty three times, and I've made dinner, which is drying out in the oven.

I nearly jump out of my skin when my cell phone rings. I snatch it off the counter. "Where the hell are you, Jillian?" I say, tightening my hand around the phone. "I was about to call John and ask him to put out an APB on you! Kitty and I were so freakin' worried."

"Raine, I'm sorry, please calm down," she says. Her voice sounds weird. An icy finger of fear zips down my spine.

"What's the matter? Why haven't you called or texted me

back?"

She takes a deep breath. "I'm fine. I'm sorry. I'm just working."

"Where are you?" I ask.

"In Spring Lake. I'm going to stay here tonight."

I feel like I've been punched in the gut. We haven't slept apart since the night of our first date. I'm suddenly overcome by a crazy sense of desperation. "I'll come down."

"No, please don't. I'll be home tomorrow night."

"But, Jillian—"

"Raine, I just need some time alone . . . to work," she says. But that's not it, I know it. She's hiding something. She's never needed to be alone to work before.

Oh, my God.

"Jillian, did he tell you have cancer or something?" I ask, terrified, as a lump rises in my throat. Please, God, don't let that be it. I'm holding the phone so tightly it digs painfully into my palm. I feel hysteria rise inside me. I can't lose her to that nasty disease.

"No, Raine. I'll be fine, I'm not dying. Please don't worry, sweetheart," she says. Even though she uses her usual endearment, I don't hear the same love and warmth in her voice.

Tears well in my eyes, making me feel like a whiny child. "Why are you pushing me away? Did I do something wrong?" I hate myself for sounding pathetic, but I can't help it, I need to know what's going on.

Her voice softens then. "No, Raine. I promise, you haven't done anything wrong."

"Then what are you hiding from me, Jillian? Why won't you tell me? I thought we told each other everything." Fear builds inside me. I'm positive now that something is very, very wrong. My hands tremble, like my body is going through some sort of weird drug withdrawal.

"Raine, please, just give me tonight, will you? I promise that I'm not doing this to hurt you. I just need a night alone.

This isn't about you . . . it's all about me."

"Are you breaking up with me?" I blurt as I steel myself for gut-wrenching pain.

She hesitates, and I think my lungs might collapse. "No, Raine," she says evenly. "That's not what this is about. I'm going to go now. I'll see you tomorrow."

"Fine," I snap. "See you tomorrow." I hang up and hurl my phone across the kitchen where it bounces off the nearest wall.

"Fuck!" I scream, cursing the fact that I love her with such abandon that she can get this far under my skin and unwind me to the point of lunacy.

I grit my teeth and pick up my keys. There's no way I'm staying here tonight alone wondering what bad piece of news she's afraid to tell me.

Less than thirty seconds later, I'm out the door, heading south to Spring Lake.

Chapter 40

Jillian

I'M CURLED UP, fully clothed, on the bed with the lights on. I ignore my rumbling stomach even though I feel weak from lack of food and dehydrated from crying. I'm staring into space when the door slams shut downstairs.

Shit! From the sound it, he's taking the stairs two at a time. Within moments, he fills the doorway. I sit up and glance at Raine's half-crazed expression.

"I'm not leaving until you tell me what the fuck is going on." His voice is a mixture of anger and controlled hysteria. He's wearing the look he has when he's been losing his mind with worry and unable to find a satisfactory resolution. His eyes home in on my face and he frowns when he has a chance to process my wet eyes and blotchy face.

His feet pass over the threshold and he comes into the room. "Jillian, what—"

I hold up my hand. "Please, don't." I'm not ready to see him. I'm not ready to talk about this. My anger flares at his intrusion. Couldn't he give me tonight like I'd asked? I glare at him. "Raine, you shouldn't have come."

I know it's unfair for me to shift the blame, but I can't hold myself back. I need tonight to wrestle into words what no words can adequately describe, and to deal with the well of shit that has been dredged up inside of me today. Having this conversation before I'm ready will only guarantee a terrible outcome. How do I tell the man I love that I don't want to be a mother? The thought squeezes the air from my lungs and make me feel like a bear caught in a trap. My first reaction is to lash out, and gnaw off my own leg. How can that even remotely make for a productive conversation between us?

Shock infuses his face, and his head snaps back like I've slapped him. "What could be so awful that you can't tell me?" Then a look of horror passes over his face. "Did I give you a sexually transmitted disease?"

I close my eyes and shake my head. I almost laugh. I wish it were that simple. "No."

His eyes pop wide. "Did you give me one?"

This time, a snide laugh escapes through my lips. "God, no."

A red flush creeps up his neck, and his face creases into an angry mask. He throws his hands heavenward. "Then what the hell on earth could be so fucking horrible that you run away from me, shove me aside, and look like you've been crying your eyes out for hours? What? Just tell me!"

I lunge up off the bed with my hands stiff at my sides. "Can't you just respect my privacy for one night? That's all I asked. Is that so much to give? I've met you halfway whenever you've asked. You can't meet me halfway on this? One goddamn night? Just because we're in a relationship, doesn't mean you have a right to every thought in my head every hour of every day. There are times when I need to be alone . . . without you. Without anyone. It doesn't mean I love you any less. It means that I have things to work out in my head that I'm not ready to talk about. Understand?"

My throat is raw from screaming and I'm breathless. The muscles in his jaw twitch as he grinds his teeth and glares back at me and says coolly, "No, I don't understand. There's nothing I wouldn't tell you now."

I look down and clutch my head in my hands. Walking in circles, I get ready to explode. "God, I keep forgetting how young you are sometimes, how idealistic. Life isn't always so simple or black and white, Raine!"

His hands work at his sides as his blue eyes bore into me and his nostrils flare. "I'm not ashamed to give everything I have to you, Jillian. I told you I wouldn't hold back, and I haven't! Isn't that good enough? Or are you back to thinking I'm some dumb, young kid who you can fuck and throw away?" he shouts.

My head snaps up. How did we land here? "Don't ever accuse me of that again, Raine. I've never thought that, ever. I'd never use you or throw you away! I love you! That doesn't disappear just because we have a fight or I refuse to share my every thought with you."

His face is cherry red. "Then just tell me what's wrong!"

I squeeze my eyes shut and scream, "I'm pregnant!"

His wide blue eyes stare at me in shock, and his mouth hangs open, speechless. For a moment, his blond brows twitch up and his lips form a look of happiness. He walks toward me slowly, and I watch as his expressions turns to confusion and then to something else . . . He grinds to a halt a few feet away from me.

He swallows, and his voice comes out in a harsh whisper. "You don't want it. That's why you didn't want to tell me."

Hot tears fill my ducts, and I cover my face, unable to look him in the eyes. Damn him for coming here. Damn him for forcing me to tell him.

He pulls my hands away from my face. His eyes well and turn glassy. "You don't want our child?"

I squeeze my eyes shut.

"Look at me, Jillian," he says through clenched teeth. "You want to throw away our baby?"

I say nothing. His hands tighten on my wrists as tears spill down his cheeks. "Is it because you don't think I'll marry you?" he whispers. My heart wrenches in two as he struggles to understand if he's the reason for my decision.

I shake my head.

His voice quivers, and he shakes me. "I'll marry you, Jillian. Tomorrow if you want. If that's not the reason, then why? Why don't you want our baby?"

I have no answer.

His face twists in pain. "How can you love me and not love our child? A part of us!"

"It's not that easy!" I scream. I haven't had time to figure that out, and now I probably won't get it. My heart lurches as I realize I was right about him. I knew he'd want to keep this child. There would be no compromise, only my giving in to his wishes and resenting him for it. I recognize his cravings for family, and his obsessive need to feel that he's loved and valued. I get it. What better way to have it than by having a child?

"Yes, it is that easy," he says through his gritted teeth.

I twist away from him. "You'll never understand." How could he ever understand the source of my panic? I can't even explain it. Not to mention the most obvious issues. Even if I wanted this child, the risks at my age can't be ignored. Never before has the gap in our ages felt so acute. How do I explain the angst of being sixty years old when the child graduates high school?

"Make me understand," he says, passing the backs of his hands over his wet eyes and then planting them on his hips.

We're back to where we started, yet I still haven't found the words. How do I distill all my pain, guilt, and fear into a logical explanation? Even if I do, we're both rooted on opposite sides of this decision. Me and my "two kinds of stubborn" Raine.

"I can't," I whisper and wipe my face.

"I'm not letting you have an abortion, Jillian."

"Letting me? You're not *letting* me?" I snarl, as the feral animal inside me rises. The noose around my neck tightens. Regardless of my intentions, I've been wrestling with my choice all day. It's not something I'm taking lightly. But in my mind, it's still more or less my decision. My eyes turn hard. "You need to go back to Chatham tonight, Raine." My heart goes numb as grief prepares to kick my door in. I don't want to lose him, but I know now that I can't keep him. My head is a muddled mess, stuck in an impossible puzzle that I can't solve. We've reached a stalemate, at least for tonight.

"Don't dismiss me, Jillian! I'm the father of this baby. Don't I get a vote?"

Rather than answer, I shake my head.

Raine sways on his feet. "Oh, my God! You already did it, didn't you? You got the abortion today. That's why you didn't call me!"

He misinterprets my answer.

"I—" As I'm about to correct him, my mouth clamps shut and I stay silent. A light bulb goes off in my head, waking me from my stupor, and I see the answer with crystal clarity. My breath hitches. I know why this all happened. I killed Drew, and I never paid. Maybe this is the only way the universe can think of to exact the price, by taking my happiness and forcing me to let go of Raine.

Whether it's today, tomorrow, or next week, we can argue until we're hoarse, but it won't change the fact that we're sitting on opposite sides of an impossible situation. No one will win that way. I love him more than I love myself, but I have to stand up for what I believe in. I'd rather he hate me than compromise his position and resent me for it later. He has a rare sense of honor that I don't want him to abandon. It's better to rip off the bandage and save us days of fighting and an ugly good-bye. He can win this way—he can forget me and start over. He deserves a better life with someone younger who can give him the things he so richly deserves, including a family of his own.

My heart rips in half for hurting him, but it's the best option I can think of in the state I'm in. Maybe I'm wrong. I don't know. But I've always known his warm, generous soul deserves more than I can give him, yet I selfishly took him as mine.

This is his out—he just doesn't know it yet.

"Answer me!" he screams as his face turns a bright shade of red under his wet cheeks.

With whatever air remains in my lungs, I release him. "I'm sorry, Raine," I whisper as a tear slips down my cheek. I let him believe these words mean he's drawn the right conclusion, when, in truth, I'm apologizing for the hurt I'm about to unleash between us. I take solace in knowing that I'm doing this for him. I'm giving him the freedom to go find his best life.

His tears come faster now. "You killed our baby!" He shakes his finger at me. "You're dead to me, Jillian!" He stalks to the door, and turns. "My father told me he wished my mother had aborted me. You're no better than him!" He disappears through the doorway.

His words cut through me, and I clamp my hand over my mouth to keep from screaming in agony. The door slams below, and thirty seconds later, his truck roars out of my driveway.

I drop to my knees, take my hand from my mouth, and scream at the top of my lungs until I pass out on the floor.

Chapter 41

Raine

I THROW BACK my fifth scotch, enjoying the burn as it travels down my throat and hits my gut.

"For fuck's sake, Mac! Slow down, will ya?" Declan glares at me from across the bar with a bottle of Macallan in his hand. A medium-size crowd clusters around the TVs to watch *Monday Night Football*. Lucky for me, Fi is off for the night. I can't imagine exchanging any words with her that would even border on pleasant. The only thing worse would've been if she tried hitting on me. I'd have seriously lost my shit.

I slam my glass on the mahogany bar. "Hit me again," I snarl. My goal is to get tanked enough that I either don't remember, or don't care that Jillian just ripped my heart out and shredded my happiness right before my eyes. Emptiness eats at my insides as I struggle to breathe.

Declan holds out his hand and wiggles his fingers at me. "Give me yer keys."

I frown at him.

"Give me yer feckin' keys!"

Blowing out an exasperated breath, I wrestle my fingers into the pocket of my jeans to retrieve them, and toss them onto the bar. He snatches them up and pours me another scotch.

He rests the bottle on the bar and leans his elbows on the polished mahogany. "Tell me what happened, Mac," he says in a kind voice.

I drain the glass and feel my head roll in a pleasant wave. "I can't talk about it, Declan. Not yet." How do I explain that Jillian went behind my back and killed our child? That she took away our chance to be parents . . . for me to be a father. I knew that being with Jillian meant there might not be kids in our future . . . because she couldn't have them, not because she would do anything in her power not to have them. She betrayed me in a way that I never thought possible.

A lump rises in my throat when I realize, just like my father, she stole my future out from under me. "Pour me another one," I say, sliding my glass across the smooth wood.

"Will I drive you home later?" he asks.

I blink, and pain shoots to my middle. "I don't have a home," I whisper. "I'm staying at the Hyatt around the corner. I can walk." I sway in my seat as the scotch finally catches up with me.

"Ah, Mac. Please tell me you'll go home and try to work this out with Jillian," he says, his eyes filling with concern.

"There's nothing left to say." My tongue feels thick in my mouth.

"There's got to be. Don't do anything rash. You had a fight. Couples have fights all the time without breaking up," he says. "You and Jillian have something special. Don't throw it away on a whim. I'll check back with ye in a few minutes."

Wrong. We *had* something special. I would've never left. But I did. On a whim? Definitely not.

"Hey!" I yell after him and slam my fist on the bar as he walks away. He turns, and I point to my glass.

"Yer cut off, before you get too drunk and do something stupid yer likely to regret in the mornin'."

I screw my face up in a scowl and curse at him under my breath.

Thirty minutes later, I stagger to the hotel, numb and

barely able to get the electronic key in the room door. I may have actually achieved my goal, because I feel nothing. No pain. Nothing.

Fully clothed, I drop onto the bed face down. It doesn't take long for the alcohol in my gut to rebel. A wave of nausea rolls through me, and I propel myself toward the bathroom. I get there in time to stick my head in the bowl and lose the contents of my stomach. I flush, and wipe my mouth with the back of my hand.

The cool tile feels good through my jeans as I rest, sitting against the bathroom wall. Not easy given the small size of the bathroom and the length of my outstretched legs. My lungs heave as pain returns to the hole inside my chest that used to contain my heart. I hoist myself up, lean on the sink, and brush my teeth. Then I use the walls to keep me up as I stumble back into the bedroom and collapse into bed.

When the phone rings, I ignore it and I wait for Jillian to answer it. I keep my eyes pressed shut against the light filling the room. How could it be morning? It feels like I just went to sleep. The phone keeps ringing.

"Dammit," I mumble into the pillow, knock the receiver out of the cradle, and then hang it back up. And it all comes flooding back . . . Jillian's not here. Pain assaults me in an unceasing wave. I curl into a fetal position, and hug my knees. I want it all to be different. For my life to be the way it was before yesterday happened, enjoying the ignorant and blissful existence that I had.

Anguish hollows out my insides, and I have trouble breathing because of it.

I stay motionless for a full hour before I inhale deeply and drag myself into the shower. I stick with the plan to go to the city, hoping I can lose myself inside my project and find some relief.

I'm not exactly sure how I make it to work. My body seems to know where to take me. I sit down at my desk and plug in my phone. The drained battery flashes to life through the cracked screen, and the phone chimes with unheard voicemails.

"Hey, Raine," Karen says. When she looks up from her computer, she does a double take. "Holy crap, are you okay? You look sick."

I know how I look, and it's frightening. I scared myself when I looked in the mirror this morning. The nonstop throbbing in my skull from all that scotch is definitely contributing to the sunken look around my eyes.

When I glance at my phone and see Jillian's name—three times—agony rips through me. Like a masochist, I listen to the first one.

"I just wanted to make sure you're okay. I'm sorry ... I love you."

I grind my teeth together and delete the message. Without listening to the other two, I delete them. I slam my phone down, cradle my head in my hands, and force myself to take in one deep breath after another.

I feel Karen's hand on my shoulder and look up. She hunches down next to my desk, so that we're at eye level. "Did something happen with your girlfriend yesterday?" she asks. I'm touched by her concern. My emotions are so raw right now that any kindness shoots straight to my soul.

I nod, and say the words. "We broke up."

Her eyes are warm. "I'm sorry. Is there anything I can do to help?"

"Can you get me a new life?" I ask, and let out a sarcastic laugh. I feel bad for being an ass and shake my head. "Just kidding."

In truth, I'm only half joking. My words hit me hard. I can't go back to my life before Jillian, and I can't live with the constant reminder of what I lost. I'm sick of loss, I've had enough. I need a new life. I need to cut myself off from Jillian and the massive vortex of pain that threatens to pull me under and drown me.

Karen stands, and gives me a sad smile. "Maybe not, but I know what it's like to want to disappear after a bad breakup. Let me know if you think of anything."

I size her up and blow out a breath. "I'm looking for a place to live. You wouldn't happen to know of any place, would you?"

Her lips turn up in a smile. "Ironic, but I think I can help you there. How do you feel about Brooklyn?"

My eyebrows rise, and I give her a pained smile. "Sounds like as good of a place as any."

"My brother is a doctor, and he's looking for a roommate. Want me to set up a meeting?"

"Can I see it today? I'm kind of in desperate need of someplace to live," I say, feeling my spirits lift.

Her face brightens. "I have a key. I'll give him a call and see if he minds my showing it."

My face darkens. "One favor?"

"Sure, what is it?"

"No one can know," I say. "If I move in with him, you can't tell anyone. Agreed?"

Her smile transforms into understanding. "Agreed."

"Shake on it?" I say, holding out my hand.

Hers is soft and warm in mine, but it's not Jillian's. It will be a while before I'm able to touch another woman without it feeling foreign and unnatural. I ache with loneliness at the thought.

I release a breath and start my laptop.

"Raine, how badly do want to start over?" Karen asks from her desk.

Badly enough that I want to hide and lick my wounds in peace. "Real bad."

"If you're serious, I can show you a few things right now," she says.

"Like what?"

"Do you have a Facebook account?" she asks.

"Yeah."

"Delete it," she says.

My eyes widen. "Seriously?"

She arches her brow and gives me a pointed look. "Seriously, and don't stop there. Delete everything."

"Wow. I'll think about it. Thanks."

The rest of the day carries me along in a painful blur.

When I get back to Morristown to pick up my packed truck, my intention is to leave and to not come back until the ache in my chest dies, which could be never. Before I go, I walk up to the Green in the center of town. Decorated and lit for Christmas, it taunts me now with loneliness rather than filling me with joy. I give the town one last look. My gaze falls on the church across the street. There's one more thing I have to do.

Silently, I enter the chapel and head for the candles flickering along the side wall. I light one and kneel in front of the dancing flames. I offer my prayer in Swedish over the hard lump in my throat.

"Mamma, please take care of my child until I can join you both. I love you."

By midnight, I have a new place to live and I've virtually dropped off the grid. For better or for worse, I have a chance to reinvent myself without Jillian. And I'll do that . . . right after I learn how to breathe again.

Chapter 42

Jillian

I PULL INTO THE empty garage in Chatham. Almost twenty-four hours has passed since Raine stormed out of the beach house. He hasn't returned any of my phone calls or my texts, and I don't blame him. I launched a live grenade into our relationship and blew it up.

When I walk into the kitchen and see the garage door opener and the credit card used for our groceries lying on the island, I know I won't find any evidence of him left in the house. Robotically, I walk toward Robert's office. The portrait is gone. I continue on to the front door. His keys are lying on the floor where they fell when he shoved them through the mail slot before he left, knowing he wasn't coming back.

I hug myself and sink down onto the floor, unable to stop the emptiness from engulfing me. Sobs rise from my lungs and break free, echoing off the walls. The house is hollow without Raine.

I'm not sure how long I stay on the floor in the foyer, only that daylight has fled and I'm enveloped in darkness when I finally decide to move.

After a trip to the kitchen for some crackers and seltzer, I settle into my office and return to the world of Becca and Drew. There's no comfort there. Once I became a protagonist in my own life, my creative energy gravitated to Raine, leaving my imaginary world lifeless. I sense Becca and Drew's resentment. They've barely spoken to me in two months. I've been left to force their movements on the page—one painful word at a time. Even my diaries no longer give me comfort.

I stare at the laptop screen with my fingers hovering motionless over the keyboard, unsure where to start. My final-pass revisions need to be done for Brigitte by Friday, if I don't self-combust before then. I can clearly distinguish the chapters written pre-Raine, and those written after. More accurately, I can distinguish when I stopped seeing Drew inside of Raine. The day he became his own person in my eyes and I fell in love with him.

My cell phone trills next to me and I flinch.

"Hi, B," I say, suppressing a sniffle.

"I have great news!" she says.

"Really?" I say flatly. She could tell me I've won the Pulitzer Prize for Literature right now and I wouldn't care.

"It's a done deal! The publisher approved one of Raine's covers for *Twisted Up in Drew*. As a matter of fact, they all tested well, and they'd like to add him to their list of freelancers."

"That's great," I squeak out, and burst into tears.

"Oh, my God, what's the matter?"

I can't speak, instead I sob into the phone.

"I'm coming over," she says with alarm.

"No! Really, that's not necessary," I say through my tears, still wanting to be alone with this. The last thing I need is to rehash the last day and a half. I'm not ready. I might never be.

"Then start talking or I'm grabbing my car keys," she says.

"Raine left. We broke up." That should be enough to start. "I just need some more time to process it all before I'm ready to talk about it without melting into hysteria. Can you give me a few days?"

"Oh, Jillian. I'm so sorry, honey. Please tell me if there's anything I can do."

I hear the sympathy in her voice. I've been her shoulder to cry on for almost twenty-five years, and she's been mine. But I can't go there yet without spilling the rest of the story. That's the part I can't share with her right now.

"I can still come on Saturday . . . without Richard," she says. We had plans for the four of us to finally get together after all the craziness of the last few months—my first time meeting Richard, and hers meeting Raine.

"Maybe. Let's play it by ear," I say after regaining some control. "Thanks for everything, B. I mean it."

"Call me tomorrow?"

"I'll try." That's all I can promise.

A day of non-stop revisions interwoven with non-stop grief has left me ragged. I crawl into bed. After a moment, I slide over onto Raine's side. When I reach under his pillow to hug it closer, my fingers touch a swath of cotton and my heart skips a beat. I pull it out. It's the T-shirt he kept there in case he got cold during the night. He's a thrasher when he sleeps, routinely waking up without any covers on his side of the bed. I close my eyes, press it to my nose, and inhale. The heady scent from the base of his neck fills my senses, and for a moment I imagine him next to me.

I lay the shirt next to my face and drift off into an exhausted and fitful sleep.

"Wanted, Dead or Alive . . ." Drew sings Bon Jovi in perfect tenor. I join in with my less than perfect alto. My hand taps on the steering wheel in time with the music as we sit at the red light. The light turns green. My foot presses the accelerator. The sun glare makes me squint, and for a moment I drive blinded by the sun.

My body is thrown sideways before the seat belt locks and sinks painfully into my side. My world spins with the speed of the Tilt-a-Whirl ride on the boardwalk. A deafening crash. The sound of twisted metal and squealing tires tears through the air. My scream is lost somewhere inside my burning lungs. The airbag deploys in my face and pins me to the seat.

I think I black out. Then there's nothing but silence. My eyes flutter open, and I cover them to protect them from the bright whiteness.

"Uncover your eyes, Jillian," whispers a familiar voice.

I take my hand away and let my eyes adjust. I'm sitting in the wreck with my seat belt on and the deflated air bag in front of me. The hood of the car is hissing with steam, but the seat next to me is empty. I stare at it in confusion. The other car is wrapped around mine. I take in the scene. There's silence and a lack of movement.

The driver's door cracks open next to me. Drew stands on the other side, backlit by a radiant light with his tawny hair loose at his shoulders. It's so bright that I have to narrow my eyes to slits. He reaches in. "Give me your hand, Jillian."

"What happened?" I'm relieved that he got out unharmed. I unbuckle my seatbelt, and take his hand.

He shrugs and smiles. "Exactly what was supposed to."

I let him pull me to my feet. Pain shoots through my ribs as he leads me to the curb and my eyes adjust. "I'm sorry, Drew. I didn't see the other car. I never meant to . . ." Then I remember he's dead, and I gasp. Tears spring to my eyes.

"Shh." He tips my chin up so that I can stare into his bright blue eyes. "Can you do something for me?"

I choke back a sob and nod. He brushes a lock of my hair behind my ear. "Forgive yourself," he whispers, and pulls me into his arms – strong, sure, and familiar – yet different from Raine's. My shoulders shake against him as I weep into the soft cotton of his shirt.

"I've missed you so much," I say.

"I know, baby," he says softly, and his voice sounds like Raine's. "But this wasn't your fault. Stop punishing yourself."

"What – what?" I sputter.

"Don't be afraid to let go," he whispers into my hair.

I clutch him tighter. "Am I keeping you here?"

"No, baby. You're keeping yourself here."

I think about what he says, and wonder if he's right. "But I was driving," I say.

Pulling away, he takes my hand, places it on my heart, and shakes his head. "It would have happened anyway."

I stare at him, stunned, and absorb the weight of his words.

"Can you do something else for me?" he asks.

"Anything."

He takes my hand from his heart and places it on my stomach, covering it with his. "Don't be afraid to accept the gift you've been given."

As if to prove the point, there's a premature flutter inside of me . . . my baby . . . Raine's baby.

My eyes connect with his, and I nod, fighting back another sob.

He smiles and kisses me on the nose. "Live your best life, Jillian. The one I couldn't give you . . . promise me."

"I promise," I whisper, and he takes me into his arms one last time.

I wake up with Raine's T-shirt underneath my cheek, soaked with tears, and my hand clutching my abdomen. I'm not sure what to make of the dream, but I believe in God and Heaven so I accept the possibility of divine intervention. If nothing else, I have a sense of closure I never expected, and with it, a sense of peace.

"Thank you, Drew," I whisper as the memory of his touch fades.

All I know is that I have a lot to think about, and I may finally understand what I've been struggling with all of these years.

I never left the car.

Denying myself true happiness, and the things I could've had with Drew, was the payment I exacted from myself to ease the guilt.

I think about Raine's baby inside me, and the sense of panic is gone. A smile works its way onto my lips. Maybe I can do this after all. But there's only one way to find out. I need to call Raine and try to work this out. I dial his cell phone with shaky fingers. It picks up on the second ring.

"The number you have dialed is no longer in service."

Chapter 43

Jillian

"HI, DECLAN," I say, and take a seat at the bar. I hope my makeup effectively hides my puffy eyes.

"Ah, Jillian. How're ya keeping, darlin'?" he asks warmly with sympathy in his green eyes. I take it as a sign that he has a hint of what's happened. "What can I get fer ya today?"

"A club soda."

He takes a glass, presses a button on the tap to fill it, and then perches a lime on the rim before handing it to me.

"Have you seen Raine?" I ask, trying to keep the desperation from my voice.

Declan releases a breath, and leans across the bar. "I'm guessing yer question has to do with yer tiff on Monday evening?"

Nodding, I fight to control my rising panic and blurt, "He disconnected his phone, shut down his email address, quit his internship. He even deleted his Facebook account. He's disappeared, and I really need to find him." I squeeze my hands around the cool, wet glass to center myself.

"I wish I had some better news, Jillian. But I don't. All I can tell you is he walked in last night to pick up the keys to his truck, and then he quit. Said he was going away. That he needed to start over. He refused to tell me anything else because he knew I'd tell ya. If it matters, I encouraged him to go home and fix whatever it is that's broken. Yer the best thing that's ever happened to Mac. I mean that sincerely."

My lips turn up into a pained smile. "Thanks, Declan. I guess I'm too late." My voice comes out breathless and shallow.

He shakes his head. "I don't know what happened between the pair of ye, but I know he loves you more than himself. He's off licking his wounds. Give him some time, and he'll see the error of his ways."

Tears well in my eyes for the hundredth time in forty-eight hours. "I'm not sure, Declan. He thinks I did something unforgivable, and I let him think he was right."

He gives me a quizzical look. "But I'm takin' it that you didn't really do it?"

A hot drop rolls down my cheek. "No, I didn't. I was afraid, so I let him believe something that wasn't true."

He shakes his head and takes my hand. "I'm terribly sorry, darlin'. If I see him again, I'll gladly deliver yer message."

"Thanks." I pull out a five dollar bill and lay it on the bar.

Declan pushes it away. "Yer money's no good here, Jillian. Yer family. It's on the house."

I blink away more tears as he walks away.

I head home after I pick up my prenatal vitamins and some take-out from Taco Truck. I'm craving Mexican today. Probably a lousy idea I'll pay for later. My stomach is still empty from this morning's daily purge. Over the past few days, I've noticed I'm better by lunchtime.

I turn on my phone and it chimes with Kitty's fifth voicemail. I can no longer avoid her, so I send her a text.

K, Raine and I had a small disagreement. Please don't worry. Frantically working toward my deadline. Call you this weekend when I'm done?

I breathe a sigh of relief when she replies.

Okay, I understand. Love you. K

By three o'clock, I'm frantic. I don't know what else I can do to find Raine, short of asking John to use his contacts to hunt him down. Raine's words haunt me: "You're dead to me, Jillian." Still, I didn't expect him to do something this extreme to hide from me.

I pace in my office with my hand glued to my belly, going over the last few days in a continuous loop. Drew's words come back to me, and I wonder if my best life actually includes Raine. Maybe it doesn't. Maybe it only includes our baby. The only piece of him that I'll ever be allowed to keep. But the fact that he's out in the world thinking that I betrayed him and killed our child is unfair to him. Needless hurt he doesn't deserve. Even if he no longer loves me or wants to be with me, he needs to know our child lives.

I drop down onto the couch, rest my head in my hands, and pray for inspiration. I wait, and nothing comes. Empty of ideas, I move to my desk. I still have a job to do. Commitments to uphold. I power up my laptop and resume the edits on my manuscript, jumping to the section where I left off. It's the love scene that Raine thought set "unrealistic expectations for women." Our first night at the beach house comes rushing back: the residual traces of bruising on Raine's face as he studies my pages with focused concentration, and my horrified reaction when he bursts out laughing, followed by his copious note taking.

So much has happened since that night. Little did I know then that Raine's "skills" would surpass Drew's in my imagined love scenes.

Rummaging through my files, I find the pages with his handwriting. I smile in spite of myself as I pull them out and reread his comments. My eyes home in on one line:

This would be soooooooo much hotter with an older woman and a younger guy. Don't you think?

I freeze. Oh, my God . . . could it be that simple?

Excitement wells up inside me. "Thank you, sweetheart," I mumble. I hit SAVE on *Twisted Up in Drew,* and open a new file.

I write. My heart and soul pours through my fingers and onto the page.

I cry, and I keep writing.

Darkness fell hours ago.

I take a bathroom break.

I resume writing, continuing to empty my well.

My eyes grow bleary, and I push ahead.

The sun rises.

I take another bathroom break and throw up. I settle back down, and my fingers fly frantically across the keyboard.

Once the nausea passes, my stomach growls. I take my prenatal vitamins, eat, and resume writing.

At midday, I curl up on the sofa and sleep for three hours.

When I wake, I shower and then write some more.

I "rinse and repeat" this schedule for the next few days with a heavy emphasis on writing and crying, punctuated by throwing up and eating, but lacking, for the most part, an adequate amount of sleeping and showering.

By Saturday afternoon—I think it's Saturday—or maybe it's Sunday? Whatever day it is, I'm done. I've syphoned every thought, feeling, and regret into a new manuscript. I hit SAVE for the last time, print a hard copy to edit, and make a backup copy on my external hard drive.

I drag myself upstairs, take a quick shower without washing my hair, and fall into a deep, dreamless sleep the moment my head hits the pillow.

Chapter 44

Jillian

DING DONG! Ding Dong! Thud! Thud! Thud!

My eyes cracks open in the darkness. My cheek is wet where drool collected on the pillow. I wipe my face and snap on the light next to the bed.

"Jillian! Are you in there?" Brigitte is screaming through the front door.

I stagger downstairs, turning on lights as I go. I click open the lock.

"Come in," I say, still groggy and half-asleep. I step aside for her to enter.

"I've been calling you for days! I thought you were dead!" she screams at me. Her face is ruby red.

"I'm sorry, B. I was working," My voice comes out in a hoarse whisper from not using it for however many days it's been.

"You look like shit," she says, and strides past me into the hallway. Dressed casually in high boots, jeans, and a turtleneck under her Burberry cashmere pea coat, she looks great—as usual. "Don't lie to me and tell me you couldn't take my calls because you were finishing the *Twisted* manuscript. Damn you, Jillian. I was picturing you with slit wrists on the goddamn bathroom floor!"

"Come on, B. Don't be so dramatic. You know me well enough to know I'm not the suicidal type."

She frowns deeply. "Well, what was I supposed to think when you missed your deadline and didn't return any of my calls? Besides, you've never been this much in love, and depression can be deadly."

I wipe my hand over my face. "I'm not depressed, B. I'm emotionally distraught. There's a difference."

She paces to and fro and then stops and plants her hands on her hips. "Fine. I really don't mean to push you, but what the *hell*, Jillian? I even waited an extra day before I barged in here."

I take a deep breath. "How about I offer you a glass of wine, and show you?"

She narrows her eyes and gives me a sideways stare. "Show me?"

I nod. "Yes. Show you."

Interest sparks in her eyes. "I'm intrigued," she says begrudgingly and follows me to the kitchen.

I make some hot water for a cup of tea in the electric teapot Raine bought for us after he moved in and then open a Cabernet for Brigitte.

"Aren't you joining me?"

"Long story," I say.

When she takes the glass, I notice the sparkling diamond on her ring finger.

"B, you got engaged!" I gush.

Her face softens, and she smiles. "Richard proposed on Friday over dinner. If you had called me back, you would've already known."

I ignore her barb. "I'm so happy for you." My heart floods with warmth. She sets down the glass, and I give her a hug. "I want to hear all about it."

"Um . . . yeah. Right after you show me what you've been doing," she says, wearing a determined frown.

I sigh, and pour hot water over a teabag. "Take your wine

and let's go to my office." After picking up my mug, I lead the way.

"Have a seat." I motion toward the sofa and retrieve the hard copy of the manuscript from inside my desk.

Her eyes light up and she holds out her hands. "What's this?" Her question dies when she sees the title, and her eyes go wide. She rapidly flips the page, and I watch her eyes dart over the opening paragraphs. Her gaze meets mine, and her lips part. Without a word, she takes a sip of wine and sinks back into the couch to read.

"I'm going to take a shower and wash my hair. Will you be okay here?" I ask.

Her head bobs absently as she dives into the manuscript.

Two hours later, Brigitte's glass is empty, and she's midway through the pages.

"B, do you—"

She holds up her hand to silence me, and shakes her head.

. . . want another glass of wine? I guess not.

Smiling, I fire up my laptop and open *Twisted up in Drew*. An hour and a half later, my final revisions are complete. I email the file to Brigitte's account, and take a moment to bask in relief.

I look up when I hear a tissue being removed from the box next to the sofa. Brigitte is on the last few pages of the story. Tears cascade down her face in tiny streams. Her lips move as she reads.

"Holy Mother of God, what a story," she says and closes the manuscript. She mops up her cheeks and then dabs at the black mascara smudges under her eyes. "I can't believe you're pregnant. Oh, my God. Congratulations." She comes over, pulls me into her arms, and squeezes me tight. "We have to find Raine. He has to know!"

"I don't know, B. Maybe it's for the best he doesn't know right now," I say, after having given it some serious thought over the last few days.

She jerks away. "What? Why? How can you say that? After the story you just wrote?"

I touch my abdomen. "Maybe this is his chance to find the life he really deserves. You know what I mean, with someone . . . younger. At least the baby will never leave me."

"What? You're not making any sense, Jillian," she says with a wild look in her eye. "What are you saying?"

Anger wells up inside me. "I'm saying that if he could leave me this easily, what's going to stop him from doing it again? From hurting me all over again? Don't you understand? He ripped my heart and lungs out by leaving me, and the only thing keeping me sane is this baby inside me—the one piece of him that I'll always have. The only piece of him I'll ever be guaranteed to have!" I sound insane, and I know it. I may have gotten over the hurdle to keep the baby, but I underestimated the lengths Raine would go to disappear from my life.

Her fingers graze my shoulder. "That's not fair, Jillian. Not to cast stones, but you made this bed. He loves you. You owe him a chance," she says softly. "Don't throw it all away on a misunderstanding."

"Brigitte, he dropped off the face of the planet so that I couldn't find him. Who does that?" I scream as my grief turns to anger.

"Someone who's hurting as much as you are, Jillian," she says softly.

"You're right." I expel a breath and clasp a hand to my forehead. "It's my fault. I did this. But I need some time, B. I just need some time to figure it out."

"Fine. But I want to publish this as soon as possible. Jillian, this is the best novel you've ever written, and I want to get it out there before *Twisted*."

I eye her suspiciously. "Why?"

She paces and draws her hand to rest on her chin. I recognize that look. Oh, boy. Brigitte's on a roll. "Because it's better, and it will help the sales of *Twisted* when it comes out. I'd like to see this in print in the spring. It will be tight, but I can pull some favors to get accelerated reviews and a book tour scheduled. I already have a smaller press in mind that can get us the distribution we're looking for, while allowing us to retain a better percentage on ebook sales. You're never going to hear me say this again, but this draft can go to proofread after a minor line edit."

I stand and look at her with my mouth hanging open. "It's that good?"

She stares me down. "Yes. It's that fucking good."

Chapter 45

4 months later . . .

Raine

OUR ADMIN SHELLY pops her head in the room where I'm working. "Raine, there's someone here to see you."

I look up from my computer, unhappy at the interruption. I'm working on designing a campaign for a client and I'm on a deadline.

"Who is it?" I ask.

She shrugs. "Her name is Brigitte Young. Mid-forties, if that helps."

The name sounds vaguely familiar, but I can't seem to place it. I get up and follow Shelley through the busy hallway, past the marquee with our company name, Conrad Designs, and into the quiet waiting area off the lobby. A slender, dark-haired woman stands, wearing a nice suit and heels and carrying a courier-size manila envelope with thick contents.

I don't recognize her. I thought I would, but I don't.

She gives me a smile filled with trepidation and extends her hand as I walk toward her. "Raine? I'm Brigitte Young."

I shake her hand, struggling to place her. "I'm sorry. Do we know each other?"

Her smile turns hopeful, and she motions toward the cushioned seats. "Sit and I'll explain."

My eyes are drawn to the envelope she clutches on her lap, and I get an uneasy feeling in my gut.

"I feel like I know you well, but it doesn't surprise me that you haven't made the connection. I believe we were supposed to meet in early December. I'm Jillian's agent . . . and also her friend."

It takes a second for her words to sink in before my heart kicks in my chest. Despite my anger at Jillian, and having endured the hardest four months of my life because of her, next to my mom's death, I can't help but think the worst. I shift to the edge of the seat and push down the bile rising in my throat. "Is Jillian okay? Has something happened to her?" I ask in a rush.

Brigitte's shoulders droop in relief, and she places her hand on my shoulder. "She's fine, but she'd kill me if she knew I was here. That said, it took me some time to find you."

"How did you . . . find me?"

She gives me a tight smile. "Private detective."

My fingers dig into the arms of the chair. "Why were you looking for me?" I feel like my life has just taken a turn onto a surreal highway. It's taken me months to get over the agony in my heart and replace it with numbness. Something stirs and then awakens in my chest.

Brigitte lowers her head and shakes it while her hands grip the envelope as if her life depends on it. "Forgive her, Raine. She made a mistake. She loves you. You're truly the love of her life."

My stomach jumps. Brigitte's words make no sense, and my anger bubbles to the surface.

"How could you say that?" I grit out through my clenched teeth. "She aborted my baby and pushed me out of her life." My heart hammers and I suddenly have trouble breathing.

Brigitte shakes her head. "No, she didn't. She didn't abort the baby," she says softly, and when she looks up, her eyes glisten.

The air leaves my lungs entirely and I feel faint. "What?" The reserve I painstakingly built around my heart begins to crack.

She offers me the package. "It's all here, Raine. The whole story — Jillian's love letter to you."

I hear what she's saying, but I don't really comprehend it. I take the package.

"Open it," she whispers earnestly.

My fingers move without my direction. I slide the book out of the envelope and freeze. My hands tremble. I bite my quivering bottom lip to contain the emotion welling deep in my chest.

I stare at the cover. It's a picture of me looking at the camera with my hair blowing. I'm surrounded in multicolor rain. At first, I think there's no mark of Jillian anywhere on the cover until I notice the lacy scrollwork under the title. It's the design of the tattoo she has at the base of her spine. My vision blurs as I read the title of the book right before I feel hot tears roll down my cheeks.

Caught Up in Raine.

I wipe them away with the back of my hand and try to swallow past the lump in my throat.

"Give her a chance, Raine. You both deserve it. Here, take this." Brigitte places an event card in my shaking hand. "It's in two weeks."

"She's keeping the baby?" I manage to whisper.

Brigitte nods. "It's the only part of you she thought she'd be able to keep."

I cover my eyes and try not to release the sob dying to burst from my lungs. She could have had all of me. I've never given myself to someone the way I gave myself to her. She threw it all away. She threw me away.

My anger flares again and I force myself to suppress my

emotional reaction. I stubbornly wipe my eyes and try to pull myself together.

Brigitte stands. "It's an amazing story, Raine. I think it'll be a best seller."

I stand, feeling shell-shocked and not knowing what else to say. "Thanks."

She walks toward the elevator, and then looks back one more time. "You still have a chance to write the ending." She adds, "I like your haircut. It suits you."

I follow and watch in a state of shock as the elevator doors close, and run my fingers through my spiky hair. I cut it all off when I lost Jillian. A mental fog envelops me in a protective layer, and I stuff the book back into the envelope. I return to the waiting area and sit immobile in a chair for another five minutes, and then I do the best I can to erase any evidence of my breakdown. I clear my throat and head back to my work space.

It's two o'clock, and I'm mentally shot for the day. I'd planned on working late and chilling for the weekend. So much for peace and tranquility. I pack my laptop and all my paperwork into my backpack and then head to my boss's office.

"Jen, I need to leave. Personal emergency," I say, a heavy frown carved into my brow.

She looks up and flinches when she sees my face. I must look worse than I thought. "Uh, sure. Let me know if you need any help on the campaign. Will you be in on Monday?"

I nod. "Yeah, I'm planning on it. I'll call you if anything changes. Thanks."

She gives me a weak smile. "See you then."

I'm back in my Brooklyn apartment in thirty minutes. It will be hours before my roommate, George, returns. After changing into sweats, I set a glass of water next to me on the nightstand and open a new box of tissues. I have a feeling I'll need them as I rip the bandage off my emotional wound. Part of me wants to burn the fucking book, and the other is so eager to read it that I'm having trouble breathing. I'm still trying to wrap my head around the fact that I'm going to be a father. That's the part of me who's sitting here on my bed, eager to read the story with my name and image on the cover.

I take a deep breath and slip the book out of the envelope. The cover design touches me, and I wonder if the publisher gave Jillian final approval to use the one we chose for Becca and Drew's story. A pang of sadness tears through me as I remember those days . . . the happiest of my life. The book shakes in my hand, and I put it down, wondering if I have the strength to re-live it without shredding my heart all over again.

I'm going to be a father, I think, and pick it back up. Inevitably, I'll see Jillian again if that's true. Even if she won't let me be part of her life, she can't deny me the right to see my child.

Another deep breath and I open the book. It doesn't take me long to need the first tissue, and I'm only on the dedication page.

> *To Raine, the father of my child.*
> *Thank you for sharing your heart.*
> *I will love you . . . always.*

The lump rises hard and fast in my throat, and the pain I've kept buried rips through me. Tears trickle down my cheeks and along the side of my nose, dripping onto the page and raising wet patches on the paper. I make no move to brush them away. The words blur until I can no longer read them.

Why hasn't she tried to find me? Why hasn't she told me any of this? My heart beats painfully next to my rib cage. I don't understand why it's only here on this page and not something I already know. If she loves me this much, why hasn't she come for me?

My emotions consume me as the book lies frozen in my hands until the tears slow and finally stop. My breathing comes back under control, and the wetness dries in tight salty trails down my cheeks. I wipe my face with my hand and blow my nose as I wait for rational thought to return.

It's true. I didn't make it easy for her to find me ... afterward. I admit it, I hid from her, leaving my old life behind and running to Brooklyn. I quit my internship and found the job I have now. My freelance work experience and my portfolio were enough to secure me a part-time spot while I finish school. From the extra money I saved while living with Jillian and the insurance money, I had the means to accelerate my curriculum and take more classes this semester. At this pace, I'll finish by the end of the summer. Conrad Designs has already offered me a full-time position when I graduate.

For a brief moment after the breakup, I toyed with the idea of reapplying to Princeton. Then I realized ... I'd changed. More accurately, being with Jillian changed me. I'd moved on and let go of that dream, trading it for the dream held within these pages.

After I blow my nose one more time, I'm ready to turn the page.

Chapter 46

Raine

IT TAKES ME UNTIL three in the morning to finish the book, and half a box of tissues, which now lie in wet, crumpled balls on the floor next to my bed. My roommate came home with his girlfriend two hours ago, and they finished having sex thirty minutes after that. I really wish this place had thicker walls.

All is quiet in the apartment.

My eyes are puffy and sore. I close the book and wonder how something so right could go so wrong. How two people could love each other so much and fuck it up so badly.

I sigh and slump back into my pillow. Brigitte was right; the ending has yet to be written, and I'm the one who has been given the task to write it. The God's honest truth is that I want to go home. I want a life that includes Jillian and my unborn child.

I want to be a father, and have a family. I want to have everything that was only an illusion for me growing up. I don't care that I'm young. In my bones I feel ancient.

I roll off my bed and walk to the closet. I shove aside all the crap and take out my duffel. I root through all my precious items until I find what I'm looking for—a small, black velvet bag.

Taking a deep breath, I bury my fingers inside and hook my pinky through the shank. I pull out the five-carat diamond and lay it in my palm. My mother's engagement ring. The ring she gave me on her deathbed. Staring at it, I remember . . .

She pulls the ring from her finger. Her weak hands crush it into my palm and close my fingers around it. "Take this, Raine. Hide it. Keep it safe. Don't tell anyone you have it. When you find the woman you cannot live without for fear that your heart will cease, put it on her finger. Tell her how much you love her and spend every day of your life showing her how much. Do you understand?"

Tears stream down my cheeks as I nod and answer her in Swedish. "Yes, I promise that I will."

She closes her eyes and winces in pain as her face grows paler. "Love is everything. Find it for yourself and treasure it always. You are my heart." Her cool, dry hand brushes my cheek. "I love you. Be strong, and take care of yourself, since I cannot."

I draw her into my arms and rock her.

"Mamma," I say in Swedish, "I love you."

. . . And her last breath leaves her body.

I wipe my eyes with the back of my hand, stare at the brilliant blue diamond, and think about the one point two million dollars stored in its value. Dad had serious wealth back then.

It could have changed my life long ago and put me back on the path I originally intended to take. But that would have meant breaking my promise to my mother. I'd rather live an impoverished existence than one that's morally corrupt like my father's was.

I drop the ring back into its pouch for safekeeping.

Chapter 47

Jillian

"WHAT'S YOUR NAME?" I smile as I look up at the chubby young woman. I'm surprised at the incredible turnout so far on the book tour, and we haven't even made it out of Manhattan yet. The bookstore is filled to capacity. Brigitte insisted we stay at a hotel the next two nights, since I have five book events across the city over the next three days. "Our last girls' hoorah," she'd said. She's probably right. At almost seven months pregnant, I feel like a freaking elephant. Luckily, I don't look as big as I feel, but still, I'm planning on sitting around with my feet up after this leg of the tour ends in two weeks.

"Adrienne," she says and giggles.

> *To Adrienne,*
> *Good luck in life and love. May you get caught up in someone, and never look back.*
> *Best,*
> *Jillian Grant*

I hand her back the signed book, and she moves aside to let the next customer in the line move up. The place is packed. I have a feeling I may be here well beyond the store closing if they allow people to stay.

Rachel kicks me in the abdomen, and I flinch. I'm wearing

a floor-length, cranberry velvet maternity dress that Brigitte gave me yesterday as a gift. I rub my belly over the soft fabric to calm Rachel. It feels like she's hosting a rugby tournament inside me tonight.

"Keep it down in there, sweetheart," I mumble, loving her so much already. Like her father, she's impossible not to love.

Brigitte comes over for the tenth time tonight, looking as nervous as a cat in a hen house. "B, what the heck is the matter with you tonight?" I whisper. "You're making me crazy."

"Nothing," she says, and looks at her cell phone. "How are you feeling? Do you need anything?"

I glance at the water bottle on the table in front of me. "Nope, I'm fine." Then I look at the crowd in front of me and sigh. "Who's next?"

I sign the next book for a young African American woman named Nia, and when I look up, the air rushes from my lungs. My mouth opens and then shuts without a word as I stare.

He looks different: his tawny hair is short and spiky, and he's wearing a suit. His blue eyes connect with mine as he clutches the book to his chest. Still gorgeous as ever, he looks different, older.

My hands grasp the edge of the table, and my heart lurches a moment before Rachel kicks me again.

"Raine?" I whisper. I think I say his name aloud, but I can't be sure. I can't even be sure that if I reach out to touch him he won't just disappear. Melt away back into my dreams. "Is it really you?" I ask, and fight back my welling tears.

His blond brows knit together with the same look of concentration he wore when I first opened my front door and found him on my doorstep the day of the photo shoot.

He presses his lips together to stop them from quivering, and nods.

The heavy mantle of anguish I've carried for months over whether I'd ever see him again falls away. I've ached for him, body and soul. After the book was published, I made a promise to myself that I'd find him after the baby was born . . . and I'd do what I couldn't do the night we parted — I'd give him a choice.

I rise to my feet, and my belly clears the table.

Taking a step back, his eyes widen and focus on my abdomen. I step around the table and reach for his hand. A rush of electricity travels through me on contact, and I feel like I've found the other part of me that I've been missing.

I place his hand on my belly. "Meet your daughter," I say as my eyes overflow until I can no longer see him clearly.

He pulls me into him, but my belly prevents me from getting as close as I used to. "God, I've missed you," he says, and crushes me to his chest. "I'm sorry for what I said."

My heart leaps. "Come home, Raine," I say, unable to hold back. My fingers dig into his back, and I release my well of love and pain. "I'm sorry, too . . . I love you. Please come home."

He squeezes me tighter, and his shoulders shake next to me as the crowd looks on. One person claps, and then another, until the bookstore erupts with thunderous applause and whistles.

He tips my chin up with his finger, and our wet eyes connect. "I love you, Jillian. Marry me?" His gaze holds mine.

"Yes," I whisper, and our lips touch and remain there until the world recedes around us, and once again, I'm caught up in Raine.

Epilogue

Two years later . . .

Jillian

I SQUINT IN THE SUNLIGHT at Raine and Rachel playing at the water's edge from where I sit on my beach chair under an umbrella. I clutch the first pages of my next book in my hands. Rather than bring my laptop, I printed a copy since it's easier to spot editing errors. Brigitte will skewer me if I don't have my changes back tomorrow. It's the last book in my contract.

Much to my current publisher's chagrin, *Caught Up in Raine* was, by far, my best-selling novel. Going viral, the book spent a respectable number of weeks on the *New York Times* best-seller list, and caught some attention in Hollywood. The movie comes out next spring. I stare at the pages in my hand. After this book is finished, I plan to take a year off to focus solely on my family, and to fill my inspirational well.

My eyes shift to the large diamond on my ring finger. Even in the shade covered by the umbrella, light refracts off of my engagement ring in a Technicolor rainbow. I promised Raine the day he proposed that I'd never take it off.

Raine leans over from where he's sitting to place another bucket of sand onto the sandcastle he's building with Rachel.

His tanned chest glistens in the sun. I catch a glimpse of the tattoo he has over his heart. He designed it himself and had it done the day Rachel was born. Three intersecting rings, each containing one of our initials inside: R, R, and J. I was breast-feeding Rachel after the C-section when he came back and first showed it to me. He said he'd finally found something that meant enough to him to permanently engrave in his skin.

I smile as I look at him, and my heart brims with love. His tawny hair finally touches his shoulders again. After he came home, I told him how much I loved it when he wore it long, but I let it be his decision what to do.

"Rachie, help Daddy put sand in the bucket," he coos, and then glances over at me and winks. Rachel's silky brown hair is up in a high ponytail, and she stares back at him with the same big, blue, marble-like eyes. Her chubby legs carry nothing more than regular baby fat, but they are long. The pediatrician says she's in the top percentile for height and thinks she'll be tall when she grows up.

"Dada, shubel," she says and tries to dig next to him in the sand.

"That's it." He loosens some sand where she's digging and puts it on her plastic shovel. He holds the bucket, and she dumps it inside and squeals with delight.

"More," she says. He repeats the process. The sun reflects off of his wedding band as he gathers more sand.

I drink in Raine and Rachel with my eyes. I consider myself the luckiest woman in the world. I've never been this happy in my entire life, and I'm committed to living the rest of my life without fear. I'm no longer afraid that Raine will leave me someday, or believe that I don't deserve happiness. I've kept my promise to Drew, and I'm living my best life. Most of all, I think I've finally forgiven myself for his death.

I glance at my newly acquired washboard abs. I couldn't stop laughing when Raine actually did manage to bounce a quarter off of them. We're training for our first triathlon together, and I'm the healthiest I've ever been. No more muffin top for me. Raine still does all the cooking — frankly, he can't eat mine, and neither can I — and is my personal trainer. Still the best trade I've ever made for a room.

Next month, Raine, Rachel, and I are going to Stockholm to see his mother's family before we head to Paris to celebrate our second wedding anniversary. Neither of us has traveled much, and it's something we're committed to doing together.

This fall, we're moving into our new, custom-built house in Morris Township. In his spare time, Raine managed the project from start to finish, working with the architect and design firm to build the house of our dreams. He was hired full time at Conrad Designs when he graduated, and is now their client operations director. Even with all that is on his plate, he still manages to be my exclusive research partner for all the love scenes in my novels. His one stipulation is that I alter them enough so that I don't set unrealistic expectations for women.

Raine

Rachel squeals with delight as we make our sand castle, and it fills my heart with joy. When I look at her, I see Jillian with my eyes, and shades of my mother. Together, they are the three people I love the most in my life.

I glance at Jillian under the umbrella, and she smiles at me. It lights up her face, and I smile back. I once thought the happiest days of my life were when I first met Jillian, before our breakup. But now I realize I was wrong. The best days of my life have been since we got back together and every day since then. I'm living my best life now with my wife and my daughter — my family — and nothing could ever take me away from them again.

I'll even go out on a limb and safely say my dreams have come true . . . all because Jillian asked me to be her cover model.

I found out that Drew is buried in the same cemetery as my mom. After Jillian and I were married, I stopped by to leave flowers on my mom's grave for her birthday. But before I left, I swung by to see Drew for a *mano a mano* chat.

I thanked him for coming before me and giving me this chance. I promised him that I would do what he had wanted to but couldn't. I would take care of Jillian and give her the love she deserved and never leave her.

I'm not sure if I reached him, but I left with a sense of peace.

Want more? If you enjoyed *Caught Up in RAINE*, get caught up again with Jillian and Raine in these two new digital novelettes coming soon:

Rediscovering RAINE: Experience Jillian and Raine's magical night after their kiss at the bookstore.

Caught Up in RACHEL: Be there as Jillian and Raine welcome Rachel into the world.

Sign up for release news, special contests, and giveaways at www.caughtupinraine.com and www.lgoconnor.com

PRE-ORDER for *Rediscovering RAINE* now available on Amazon, B&N, iTunes, and Kobo!

One more thing before you go: Don't forget to write a review for *Caught Up in RAINE* and leave it on your favorite retail and /or social media outlet of choice. If you really liked CUIR, please help me spread the word! Recommend it to your friends, book clubs, libraries, and anyone else who will listen. Thank you from the bottom of my heart, times a thousand!

About the Author

LG O'Connor is a member of the Romance Writers of America. A corporate marketing and strategy executive for a Fortune 250 company, she writes adult paranormal and contemporary romance. *Caught Up in RAINE* is her first romantic women's fiction novel. She is also the author of the four-book urban fantasy/paranormal romance series, *The Angelorum Twelve Chronicles*, which is available where all fine books are sold. A native 'Jersey Girl,' she lives a life of adventure, navigating her way through dog toys and soccer balls in Morris County, New Jersey. When she's feeling particularly brave—she enters the kitchen.

CONTACT:
   Website / Blog: www.lgoconnor.com
   Facebook: www.Facebook.com/lgoconnor1
   Twitter: twitter.com/lgoconnor1
   Goodreads:
   www.goodreads.com/author/show/7690970.L_G_O_C
   onnor
   Book Site: www.caughtupinraine.com
   Email: lg@lgoconnor.com

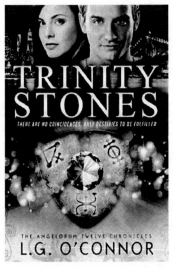

TRINITY STONES, Book One in the *Angelorum Twelve Chronicles* series is available now where all fine books are sold.

"O'Connor tackles important world building, while also kicking off the story with a bang." ~**Publisher's Weekly**

On her 27th birthday, Cara Collins, a single New York investment banker with an anxiety disorder receives a stunning inheritance and is taken under the wing of angels. When Dr. Kai Solomon, Cara's longtime friend and first love, is kidnapped by dark forces, Cara must choose: accept her place in a 2,000 prophecy foretold in the Trinity Stones as the First of the Holy Twelve who will lead the final battle between good and evil...or risk losing everything she holds dear.

Genre: Paranormal: Angels / Urban Fantasy / Romance
Audience: Ages 18+ / adult language and content
Publisher: She Writes Press
ISBN-13: 978-1-938314-84-1 (Trade Paperback)
ISBN-13: 978-1-938314-85-8 (eBook)

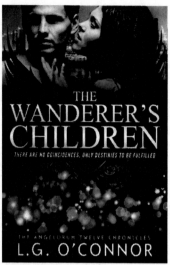

WANDERER'S CHILDREN, Book Two in the *Angelorum Twelve Chronicles* series is available where all fine books are sold.

"Combining a marvelous talent for emotional resonance with a naturally light, playful attitude towards sex and romance, L.G. O'Connor creates a rich, complex world that realistically explores joy, pain, fame, child abuse, and the insanely complex and frightening realities of pre-established hierarchies. Although set in a supernatural milieu, the emotions and situations these characters find themselves in ring with a clarity that is unforgettable. **THE WANDERER'S CHILDREN** *(4.5 stars) is a satisfying and nuanced read for fans of the series and newbies alike."* **~IndieReader**

Cara's second chance encounter with rock star Brett King is no coincidence. One of the Wanderer's Children, he and the blood of his secret siblings are the key to gathering the rest of the Twelve…if betrayal and Lucifer don't rip them apart first.

Genre: Paranormal: Angels / Urban Fantasy / Romance
Audience: Ages 18+ / adult language and content
Publisher: Collins-Young Publishing
ISBN-13: 978-0-990738-10-7 (Trade Paperback)
ISBN-13: 978-0-990738-14-5 (eBook)

HOPE'S PRELUDE, Book 2.5 in the *Angelorum Twelve Chronicles* series is available where all fine books are sold. See where it all begins... For fans of the series or those tipping their toe into the World of Angelorum for the first time, this prequel novella gives us a glimpse into what happens to shape destiny before *Trinity Stones* begins and hints at what will happen next in the series.

"A unique twist of the angels vs. demons mythology that blends science with religion and includes characters that grab you by the heart!" - **Maria V. Snyder, New York Times Bestselling Author**

While dealing with visions of her death, Dr. Sandra Wilson races against the clock to develop a genetic vaccine that will, in the future, save the life of the one who will lead the final battle between angels and demons.

Enter the world of the Angelorum, and get a view into the genetics project that started it all as destinies entwine to deliver us one step closer to battle. There are no coincidences...

Genre: Paranormal: Angels / Urban Fantasy / Romance
Audience: Appropriate for readers of both the adult and young adult versions of the series
Publisher: Collins-Young Publishing
ISBN-13: 978-0-990738-17-6 (Trade Paperback)
ISBN-13: 978-0-990738-16-9 (eBook)

COMING NEXT in *The Angelorum Twelve Chronicles:*
BOOK of FOUR RINGS, Book 3, May 2016
Series conclusion, **WELL of SOULS,** Book 4, February 2017

CPSIA information can be obtained
at www.ICGtesting.com
Printed in the USA
FFOW03n0233110416
23153FF